RUNA

FRENCH
THE SECRET

BY
TRIPLE F

All rights reserved.

Front-Cover designed using *Canva.*

https://www.tripleferotica.com[1]

All rights reserved.

This is a work of fiction. Similarities to real people, places, or events are entirely coincidental.

RUNAWAY BOY TO FRENCH ASSASSIN 2: THE SECRET SERVICE YEARS

First edition. May 16, 2023.

Copyright © 2023 Triple F.

ISBN: 979-8223139140

Written by Triple F.

Table of Contents

About the author:

Hi everyone! My name is Triple F, which is not my real name but that's what I use as my pen-name. This is the 2nd of the Runway Boy to French Assassin series and in this particular story the main character Commandant Guillaume Moreau goes on three separate missions. I have written many fictional stories already and my main genre is Erotic-Comedy (i.e. funny erotica) and this particular story is in the non-erotica genre. If you are interested in purchasing my Erotic-Comedies please go to my website which is: https://www.tripleferotica.com[2]. Enjoy!

PROLOGUE

Commandant Guillaume Moreau is fast asleep on the Amtrak train route from Portland, Maine to Houston, Texas. He is wearing a wig, cap and sunglasses to disguise himself more so no-one would recognize him. Guillaume needed all of his strength to rescue Valeria González and her son Mateo Perez to take them to Quebec on his return. Whilst Guillaume was sleeping there were two uniformed Police-Officers looking at him in a weird way; they were both very suspicious about him. "Hey Frank! I am very suspicious about that guy sleeping over there. Look at the way he's dressed." said Officer No.1, "Yeah me too, James....lets be very discrete about this so we don't cause a scene." responded Frank; the two Police-Officers continued to observe Guillaume.

Guillaume was still sleeping like a baby he then begins to go more into a deep-sleep. As he does his Daemon begins to speak to him whilst he's dreaming! His Daemon then says: "Guillaume! I need to first tell you that you need to be extra vigilant on your mission but, you have the power to do this! Also, before you see this particular dream I need to tell you to rescue Mateo first as he is a child and then his mother, Valeria. Secondly, I am going to show you how Valeria and Mateo got separated....watch carefully!"

All of a sudden Guillaume's Daemon begins to show him what occurred that day; Guillaume was going to be in for a shocker! The dream begins with Valeria and Mateo making the long arduous walk to the Mexican-US Border. It was an extremely painful journey for them and to make things worse the two of them don't have good clothes to wear. They had been on the road for many days trying to get away from Valeria's estranged husband and the criminal organization he works for! Guillaume was feeling very tensed at seeing all of this; it reminded him of when he was 12 years old when he first ran away from his old school in England and made the long route to Scotland.

Still dreaming Guillaume sees Valeria and Mateo with other Mexicans who are equally as desperate to reach for the Mexican-US Border to enter the USA for a better chance at life. Next, Guillaume sees all of the Mexicans including Valeria and Mateo sneaking across the border into Brownsville, Texas. However, when all of the Mexicans cross the border into the US all of a sudden there are gun-shots and cannons shooting away! People are screaming there are many explosions everywhere; many are getting killed! Guillaume then sees Valeria and Mateo get unexpectedly separated amidst all of the chaos. Most of the Mexicans get killed but, a number of them survive and managed to escape. However, as Valeria and Mateo had got separated the two of them get lost; Guillaume then sees a picture of an American Man with brown hair wearing sunglasses. He had a mean & nasty look on his face; Guillaume wonders who he is! Guillaume then briefly sees Canadian Intelligence Agents aborting their mission making their way back to Canada. Next, Guillaume sees Valeria alone in Brownsville desperately looking for her son, Mateo. He then sees Mateo

all alone frightened looking for his mother frantically!
Guillaume still sleeping begins to get very agitated at seeing
the whole incident; the two Police-Officers on the train had
noticed this and get more suspicious about him!

It was towards the end of his dream Guillaume's
Daemon speaks to him again. He says: "Now you've seen
what happened; you know now what you've got to do! The
CIA are mainly behind all of this; they are onto Valeria
and Mateo and the Police there have been ordered to kill
them both. They are all in on it; plus the man with the
brown hair and sunglasses is CIA! You must kill him at
all costs...he is extremely dangerous! Oh by the way a few
seats away on the train there are two Police-Officers who are
looking at you weirdly...use whatever means necessary but,
don't kill them!" Guillaume then suddenly wakes up huffing
& panting breathing very heavily. It was already morning in
Texas and the train was about 1 hour away from Houston.
Guillaume decided to take a few deep relaxing breaths to
calm down so he could get ready for his mission...he was
feeling dehydrated and very hungry. His Daemon then says
to him: "Guillaume, get some breakfast before you go on
your mission...you need it! Don't worry about Mateo he will
be fine for now!" Guillaume then gets up from his seat and
goes to buy a big bottle of water; he purchased a 2-litre bottle
and when he paid for it he went back to his seat. Guillaume
then opened the bottle-top and drank all of the water in one
go; he drank every drop. The passengers on the train were
all in complete shock at how Guillaume drank that amount
of water in one go. The two Police-Officers looked at each
other with surprised looks!

The train was 20 minutes from Houston Station Guillaume's Daemon then warns him that the two Police-Officers are going to talk to him. Guillaume then decided to immediately get his rucksack down from the luggage-compartment; when he did Guillaume just sat down quietly minding his own business. Officer James then looked at his colleague Frank....he was ready! "Frank shall we go and talk to him?" whispered Officer James, "Yes we should!" replied Officer Frank; the two Police-Officers got out of their seats and made their way towards Guillaume. When the two Officers approached Guillaume they then began to question him. "Excuse me, I need to ask you something; where are you going?" asked Officer James; Guillaume just ignored James so as not to blow his own cover. The two Police-Officers looked at each other with bewilderment; the other passengers on the train were all very bewildered as well. "Hey! My colleague asked you a question...WHERE ARE YOU GOING? Boy!" asked Officer Frank; again Guillaume refused to respond. The two Officers just stood there looking at each other not knowing what to do! Guillaume's Daemon then warns him: "Guillaume, it's time to make a move and take action. You have no choice!" Then Guillaume begins to get up from his seat! "Hey! Where do you think you're going?" questioned Officer James; Guillaume then looked at the two Officers without saying a word! Then all of a sudden Guillaume begins to use his Martial Arts on the two Officers. The two Officers tried to attack Guillaume but, they were no match for him! Guillaume was able to knock both Police-Officers down and weaken them a lot; the passengers on the train were all horrified! Next, Guillaume got both of their handcuffs and cuffed both Officers to the legs of the seats. The passengers were all too scared to approach Guillaume....the train-staff were also in shock. Guillaume then put his rucksack on his back and made his way calmly to the train-doors. When the train reached its final destination of Houston Guillaume then got off and made his way out to look for somewhere to eat.

Chapter 1:

Breakfast Bust-Up!

It was a little later in the morning that Police-Officers arrived at the scene on the train where Guillaume assaulted the two Police-Officers earlier. The assaulted Officers explained what happened from beginning to end. "Why were you two suspicious of him?" asked one of the Police-Detectives; the two Police-Officers just looked at each other completely dumb-founded! They didn't know what to say. "Well he was kind of acting weird!" said Officer James, "You know you can't go on that. At this moment I can't go on anything. You two need to be more careful!" explained the Police-Detective. The Police decided to put out a search warrant for Guillaume; but, they decided that they only want to question him. The Police then disbanded to look for Guillaume.

Guillaume had managed to find a café-diner to have breakfast; he was feeling extremely hungry. His Daemon then says to him: "Go there and eat; by the way the Police are looking for you for the train incident!" Guillaume then enters the café-diner and looks up at the breakfast menu board. He then sees one there which was: 2 eggs, bacon, sausages, beans, hash-browns & mushrooms plus coffee. Guillaume then decided that would be best for him even though he doesn't eat those kinds of foods...he was more of a

7

healthy person. However, Guillaume then realized he had to build his strength as much as he can for his difficult mission. Guillaume waited in the queue with other customers at the counter until he is ready to be served. Towards the back-end of the queue were four uniformed Police-Officers who were there to have their breakfasts before they commenced their shifts. The names of the Police-Officers are: Mike, Nigel, Peter & Steven.

When it was time for Guillaume to be served as the breakfast he wanted was a no.5 he indicated to the waitress by holding up four fingers and one thumb. The waitress acknowledged Guillaume and gave him a ticket number after he paid for his breakfast. Guillaume then went to look for a table to sit at and there was one right in the corner of the café-diner. It was a table for one but, Guillaume wanted to be away from everyone as he needed to be discrete as he can! When Guillaume's breakfast arrived he immediately tucked in straight away; everyone was so surprised at how fast Guillaume was eating his breakfast including the waitresses. "Wow he's hungry!" said Mike, "Yeah tell me about it!" said Nigel; the four Police-Officers continued to observe Guillaume whilst they were waiting in the queue. The four Police-Officers were now getting very suspicious about Guillaume; what are they thinking? "I'm wondering, why is he wearing a cap & sunglasses?" pondered Peter, "I had the same thought too!" responded Steven. The Police-Officers ordered their breakfasts then they all went to sit at a table for four. As they all sat down the Officers continued to observe Guillaume non-stop. Guillaume's Daemon then warns him about the four Police-Officers observing him! Guillaume realized this and just carried on eating his breakfast.

It was a little later on that Guillaume had finished eating his breakfast; he only had his coffee to drink left. Before Guillaume went to drink his coffee he went into his rucksack and pulled out a packet of hygienic wipes. He took one wipe from the packet and cleaned his plate thoroughly; Guillaume had to do this so as not to leave any trace of his own DNA. The four Police-Officers all looked at each other with puzzled looks! "Why did he do that?" asked Peter, "Beats me! Now I'm really getting worried!" said Steven, "Let's not do anything yet, he's still hasn't finished yet. Wait for him to make a move and then we'll make our move!" suggested Mike; the other three Officers agreed with Mike.

Guillaume had managed to finish his coffee and like he did with his plate he used a hygienic-wipe to clean the coffee-cup to wipe out his entire DNA. The waitress who served Guillaume had noticed that he was finished and decided to collect the crockery for washing. "Did you enjoy your breakfast, Sir?" asked the waitress; Guillaume didn't say anything and nodded a 'yes' response to the waitress. Guillaume then gave her a $20 tip as a sense of gratitude! "Wow, thank you Sir! You have a nice day!" said the waitress gleefully as she went. Guillaume was then ready to leave and collected his rucksack to make his way out. When the four Police-Officers saw this they all got up and went to approach Guillaume; the four Police-Officers then stood right in front of him! "Where do you think you're going boy?" asked Nigel; Guillaume stood there saying nothing. The Police-Officers, the staff and customers all froze looking at

Guillaume. "Hey! I asked you a question! Where do you think you're going, boy?" asked Nigel a second time; still Guillaume refused to answer. Then Guillaume dropped his rucksack on the floor and put his hands on top of his pelvis in a Martial Arts stance. The Police-Officers all looked at each other completely bewildered! "Man, you're fucking weird!" said Mike; Guillaume then looked at Mike with a stern look on his face! Mike then started to get a little worried and so did the other Officers. All of a sudden Guillaume did a Martial Arts punch on Mike and knocked him down to the floor. The other three Officers then attempted to apprehend Guillaume but, with Guillaume's huge Martial Arts background the Officers were thwarted! Then Peter and Steven both went for Guillaume but, he did a somersault over the two Officers and then using punches & kicks Guillaume then knocks them out cold. Nigel then went for Guillaume but, he was no match for him! Guillaume did so many Martial Arts on Nigel he managed to knock Nigel completely out! Mike then got up feeling a little dazed; when Guillaume saw this he then did a spinning Martial Arts kick on Mike. Next, Guillaume then dragged each Police-Officer and using their hand-cuffs he cuffed each one of them to a metal-railing attached to the counter. The customers and staff all froze there in shock! They all didn't know what to do; Guillaume then collected his rucksack and made his way out! As Guillaume was outside one of the staff saw another Police-Officer on duty and went to approach him in a rush. "Hey Officer that man over there just assaulted four of your colleagues in our café-diner!" explained the staff-member pointing to Guillaume. "Hey you guy in the cap, I want a word with you!" shouted the Police-Officer; Guillaume then turned around and saw the Police-Officer! He decided to make a run for it and went into a place with a lot of bushes. The Police-Officer went after him but, Guillaume then teleported straight to Brownsville. When the Police-Officer got to the bushes Guillaume was nowhere to be seen!

Later on the four Police-Officers who were assaulted in the café-diner gave their statements to their colleagues. They couldn't give much description of Guillaume as he was well-disguised! But, when the other Officers heard about this they realized that it was the same person who assaulted the two Police-Officers on the train. "It's the same guy as earlier on the train!" said one of the Officers, "Yeah I had the same thought! Who the hell is that guy?" pondered another Officer. The Police-Officers decided that Guillaume had to be apprehended as soon as possible realizing that he could be very dangerous!

Chapter 2:
Mateo alone

It is winter in the State of Texas and even though it is one of the hottest States in America it is unusually extremely cold. Winter is really bad in Texas with very blistery cold winds which is making the extreme weather there much worse! There is Mateo Perez at 8 years old all alone in Texas looking for his mother. Mateo is cold, hungry and very scared; he doesn't know what to do! He can't find anyone to help him; he so badly wants his mother! Unfortunately for Mateo the clothes he is wearing has many holes and are not suitable for the harsh weather he's in.

In Texas the people there ignore Mateo as he's Mexican and most of the population in Texas are prejudice towards Mexicans. At 8 years old Mateo is very smart and quick-witted so he's aware of what is going on. But, for Mateo he is getting more & more anxious considering he has yet to find his mother. However, in his heart he knows that she is still alive but, doesn't know where to look. What is worse for Mateo is that he hasn't eaten anything in the last few days since the explosion at the Mexican-US Border. Mateo is getting weaker & weaker; what he does is go everywhere around the town of Brownsville and then when it is night-time he goes into the park bushes to sleep to get away from everything.

Meanwhile Guillaume was able to teleport to the outskirts of Brownsville after the fracas he had with the Police at the café-diner that morning. Luckily for Guillaume no-one saw him appear out of nowhere! All of a sudden Guillaume had a flashback and saw Mateo; he could see how cold & frightened he is. Guillaume was now starting to get worried about Mateo considering he is a young child and that he's vulnerable! Guillaume's Daemon then spoke to him again: "Guillaume, don't keep worrying about Mateo he'll be fine for now. What you need to do first is to steal a car and get proper winter clothes for both Mateo and his mother, Valeria. They will not survive the winter with the clothes they are wearing right now!" Guillaume acknowledged his Daemon and immediately did a remote-view on where he could find the nearest car-dealership to steal a car. Guillaume managed to find one and teleported away immediately! In his mind he was thinking there's no time to lose...Guillaume really wanted to rescue Valeria and her son Mateo!

Chapter 3:

Stealing a car

Guillaume was able to teleport somewhere in the town of Brownsville and noticed the car-dealership he remote-viewed earlier. Immediately Guillaume went invisible so no one could see him; then casually Guillaume walks towards the car-dealership. As Guillaume got closer to the car-dealership a customer opened the door and he managed to sneak in without anyone noticing.

Whilst invisible Guillaume looked around to see what car he could steal as his getaway vehicle. He had to be extra careful as there were a lot of customers around inside the dealership. Suddenly Guillaume sees a red Honda Civic Coupe 3-door car and thought that would be perfect as the getaway vehicle. His Daemon then says to him: "That car would be perfect! The keys are round the back, you need to teleport there!" Straight away Guillaume teleports to the car-keys room and when he does he begins to look for the key. Using his super-sonic eyes within seconds he finds the matching keys for that particular car. Guillaume then takes the keys and teleports to the car straight inside of it. When Guillaume got inside the car he then carefully puts the key into the ignition. He then waits inside for the right moment; suddenly his Daemon says: "Do it! Now's the time!" Immediately Guillaume turns on the ignition; everyone inside the dealership all turn around when the engine was switched on. "Hey which car is it?" asks one of the staff; suddenly Guillaume put his foot on the accelerator and drove through smashing the windows. He went straight onto the road and sped off! "Somebody call the Police!" shouted a staff member; immediately someone telephoned the Police!

Later on in the day the Police arrived at the car-dealership to investigate the theft of the car by Guillaume. The staff and customers who were there all gave their statements. The Manager of the car-dealership told Police that no one could give any description of who the assailant was. The Manager and the Police looked at the camera-footage to the point where Guillaume stole the car. When they all saw this they all went into shock; they all could not see who went into the car. Even from the side they didn't see anyone in the car unaware that Guillaume was invisible. "Well this is very baffling! There's no one in the car; how did someone steal a car like that?" asked one of the Police-Officers with a puzzled look on his face; the Manager himself couldn't deduct on how the car was stolen! "How much was the car worth?" asked another Police-Officer, "It was worth $10,000!" replied the Manager; the Police-Officers couldn't do anything further so they decided to leave the incident as that and return to the station.

The car that Guillaume stole was reported on the media with the footage shown; many people who watched the footage were all baffled at how the car was stolen. Also, reported on the media were the two incidents that Guillaume was involved in when he assaulted the Police-Officers on the train and the café-diner. Guillaume

Moreau was now becoming a marked man; however, for the authorities it would be a nightmare for them as they have no clue what Guillaume looks like!

Chapter 4:

Stealing new clothes

Late evening had appeared in Brownsville and Guillaume is driving around in the stolen Honda Civic Coupe. He was looking for a clothes shop so he could get proper warm clothing and shoes for Valeria & Mateo. His Daemon then speaks to him again: "Guillaume, 3 blocks down the road there's a massive clothes-shop with everything you need for all weathers. Just park the car out of sight so you don't get caught!" As Guillaume drove down he sees the clothes-shop so then he finds a secluded place to park the car. After Guillaume parked the car he then went into his rucksack and pulled out his hand-gun to take with him just in case! Next, Guillaume did some remote-viewing on the clothes-shop to check it out; luckily as he remote-viewed there was not a soul in sight! Guillaume then decided it was time to teleport into the clothes-shop!

As Guillaume teleported into the clothes-shop he did this by going invisible. Guillaume then looked around to see if there were any security cameras inside...there was! So what Guillaume did next was to close his eyes and using the power of his mind he broke the camera system and switched them off in the process! After Guillaume did this he was able to appear in physical form. Guillaume then went to look around the clothes-shop to see what clothes he could get for Valeria & Mateo; by chance Guillaume saw an empty cardboard box and then thought as he has a lot of shopping to do he took the box! As Guillaume went around looking for the right clothes he first saw a big rucksack and took it and put it inside the box...it was going to be for Valeria. Guillaume then saw a smaller rucksack and thought it would be good for Mateo; he then decides to take it. Whilst still going around the store Guillaume then took some toiletries such as bath-towels, shower gels, hand soap, toothbrushes, toothpaste and shampoo. Guillaume realized that both Valeria & Mateo are going to need a good wash before they make the long journey to Quebec. Especially being out in the extreme cold would have made it worse for both Valeria & Mateo. In the same store Guillaume saw a section which sells homeopathic remedies and so he took some.

Guillaume had spent some considerable time in the shop looking for the correct clothing but, he did find what he needed and took them. Also, Guillaume saw a section where they sell sleeping-bags; Guillaume then followed his intuition and took two of them! One of the sleeping-bags was a double one and the other was a singular sleeping-bag. Guillaume looked at the box and realized that it was all he needed and teleported out of the clothes-store back to his stolen car. When he teleported to the car his Daemon then warns him: "Guillaume, there are 2 cops patrolling around. Don't let them see you!" Guillaume then puts the box underneath the car and immediately goes invisible! Luckily, the patrolling cops didn't see Guillaume and just went by; when the patrolling Police were far into the distance Guillaume then went to get the box of items and put them into the car-boot. Guillaume then quickly went inside the car and drove off to somewhere more secluded!

Guillaume was able to find a very secluded area in Brownsville and so he parked the car. He was feeling a little tired and decided to go into the back-seat to lie down and get some sleep before morning; Guillaume realized he needed it. Before Guillaume went to sleep he immediately went invisible again and as he did he went to sleep; Guillaume realized it is NOW OR NEVER!

Chapter 5:
Valeria lost

Valeria González is walking around Brownsville in the early hours of the morning desperately looking for her son, Mateo. Valeria didn't get much sleep the previous night due to sleeping outside in the extreme cold plus the fact she was frantically worrying about where her son is! What is worse for Valeria is that even though she & Mateo are both in Brownsville they are both far apart from each other.

It was late morning that Valeria was going around many parts of Brownsville still looking for her son Mateo; she just didn't know where he is located. In her heart Valeria knows that Mateo is still alive but, the big question for her is where's Mateo? Valeria just didn't know where to look!

In a small shop down in Brownsville there was an owner named Carlos who received a message about Valeria. Carlos secretly works for the Mexican Criminal Organization that Valeria's estranged husband also works for. "Hey Miguel I have a message from the Big Boss!" explained Carlos, "Oh really, what is it?" asked Miguel, "That woman Valeria González; she's been spotted somewhere in Brownsville. Tell the guys to find her and then kill her!" ordered Carlos, "Will do boss! She's the one that's trying to stop us and the Americans from invading Canada?" asked Miguel, "Yes that's the one! Unfortunately we don't know where her son is and whether he's dead or alive!" explained Carlos; Miguel immediately went to contact the men to order Valeria's killing!

Back at DGSE (Q) Générale Lévesque was in her office wondering how Guillaume is doing on his mission; she even wondered if he is still alive! Générale Lévesque then sent an e-mail to one of the DGSE (Q) staff named René; the e-mail said: "Can you come to my office now!" A few minutes later René arrived in Générale Lévesque's office; he was wondering what she wanted! "Madame, you wanted to see me." said René, "Yes René I did! Have you heard anything from Commandant Moreau?" asked Générale Lévesque, "Well to be honest I haven't, Générale. But, I was watching the US News and there were reports that two Police-Officers were assaulted on a train and four Police-Officers were assaulted at a café-diner in Houston." explained René; Générale Lévesque then looked at René with a puzzled look on her face. "Oh! And why are you telling me this?" pondered Générale Lévesque; René then took a deep breath! "Well Madame on both occasions they described that it was a dark-skinned man who did Martial Arts on all of those Officers. Also, when Commandant Moreau went by train he took the Amtrak train from Portland, Maine to Houston, Texas. Madame, I think it's definitely Moreau! But, on a good note they are more or less very unsure what Moreau looks like...he is well-disguised, Madame!" explained René; Générale Lévesque had a slight relieved look on her face! "Well René I did instruct Moreau to use extreme measures when necessary. Besides I know how resilient he is. All of the Martial Arts he studied in China, Japan & Korea have

helped him big time! That's why I put him on the mission!"
explained Générale Lévesque; all DGSE (Q) had to do was
sit & wait!

Chapter 6:

Mateo rescued

It is 08:30 hours and Guillaume was still asleep in the car. Whilst sleeping he receives another message from his Daemon: "Guillaume, Mateo is heading towards the Highrose Mall. You can get him there but, be warned the Police are on to him and they are going to kill him!" Guillaume suddenly wakes up with a big jolt! He looked at the time and realized that he slept for quite a long while; Guillaume was still invisible! Guillaume got up and took a few deep breaths; then he went to the driver's side and switched on the ignition to turn on the engine. Guillaume then looked around and suddenly appeared visibly; he then drove off to the Highrose Mall to rescue Mateo Perez.

Mateo was walking towards the Highrose Mall; he wanted to get somewhere warm and dry. He was still feeling anxious and confused; he began to get even more frightened every time. Just outside the Highrose Mall were two Police-Officers one was called Tom and the other Jim. The two Police-Officers are also colluding with the Mexican Criminal Organization who are attempting to take over Canada. "Hey Jim, I just had word that Mateo Perez has been seen near the Highrose Mall. We need to get him, find where his mother is and then kill them!" explained Tom, "Yeah! Let's go into the Highrose Mall...he's probably inside there. Bearing in mind that he has been sleeping on the cold streets of Brownsville he will need to get somewhere warm quickly!" explained Jim; Tom nodded at Jim and the two Police-Officers got out of their Police-Cars making their way to look for Mateo. Inside the Highrose Mall Mateo was walking around minding his own business; the people in the mall looked at Mateo in a weird way giving him nasty looks! Mateo was getting even more worried; he didn't know who to turn to. Also, in the Highrose Mall are the two Police-Officers looking for Mateo; as there were so many people in the mall and as Mateo is a small boy it was going to be difficult to find him. Both Officers Tom & Jim were having a nightmare trying to look for Mateo; they went everywhere!

Guillaume had just entered the Highrose Mall still wearing his wig, cap & sunglasses so as to be discrete. He went straight into remote-viewing mode to look for Mateo; he couldn't do it properly as he was a little dazed. Then all of a sudden he felt Mateo's presence from far away; Guillaume realized that Mateo is in the mall. Officer Jim then overhears a member of the public discussing about a scruffy & smelly Mexican boy...Jim realized that it is Mateo! "Hey Tom, I just overheard people talking about a dirty looking Mexican boy...it has to be Mateo!" explained Jim, "Brilliant! Let's split up; he must be close by!" ordered Tom; the two Officers then split up to look for Mateo! About 15 minutes later as Jim was going around looking for Mateo he suddenly sees a little boy at a distance. Then Mateo locks eyes on Jim and realized immediately that Jim is going to kill him! Mateo then makes a run for it and Jim immediately radios

Tom whilst chasing Mateo! "Hey Tom, I've got him but, he's getting away!" radioed Jim, "Keep on him Jim. I'll go the other way!" responded Tom as he went a different route.

Meanwhile Guillaume was in the middle of the shopping-mall frantically looking for Mateo; he just couldn't think straight. All of a sudden Guillaume's Daemon speaks to him again: "Guillaume, listen now! The Police are chasing Mateo you need to get to him quickly! Don't worry I'll direct you!" Suddenly Guillaume then says to himself "SHIT!" Some members of the public had noticed what he just said. Guillaume then made a run for it! Mateo was still running from Jim he then sees a door which leads into the back way and goes straight through it! Jim had noticed this and went through the same door as well. Mateo was running down the corridor as fast as he can; he then suddenly turns left at the end to another corridor. However, at the other end of the corridor Tom suddenly appears around the corner; Mateo was now trapped! Guillaume was still running around until he sees the same back-door which Mateo went through; he realized that Mateo is around the back. Guillaume then goes through the back-door in a big haste!

There was Mateo caught by the two Police-Officers Tom & Jim; the two of them manhandled Mateo. As Mateo is a little boy he had no chance against the two Police-Officers! "Well, well Mateo. Look what we have here! So where's your mommy? We want her right now!" demanded Tom; Mateo was too scared to talk...he felt very trapped! All of a sudden Guillaume came around and saw the two Officers manhandling Mateo! "Hey you two, let the boy go!" demanded Guillaume, "Hey this don't concern you!"

responded Tom, "I'm not going to ask you again...let the boy go!" shouted Guillaume, "Who the hell you do think you are?" asked Jim aggressively, "I am the boy's Guardian Angel!" replied Guillaume; all of a sudden Guillaume did Martial Arts kicks, punches and throws! He managed to get both Police-Officers to the ground and when he did he snapped both of their necks. Both Police-Officers were now dead; Mateo was on the floor with shock on his face! Guillaume looked down at Mateo and then gave him a wry smile. "It's OK Mateo, I know who you are. I'm here to help you and your mother." explained Guillaume; he then extended his hand to Mateo. Then Mateo grabbed Guillaume's hand and was pulled to his feet...he felt relaxed being with Guillaume. "Are you OK?" asked Guillaume; Mateo then looked up at Guillaume for a bit. "Yes!" replied Mateo, "Good! I know you're probably feeling tired & hungry. Don't worry I'll take you somewhere safe and then you can have a good wash. I have some new clothes & shoes for you; I'll sort you out first and then we'll go and rescue your mother. For now, let's get out of here quickly!" said Guillaume; Mateo went with Guillaume to make their way out of the Highrose shopping mall.

A little earlier someone had called the Police in regards to the other Police-Officers chasing Mateo and so the Police disbanded to the Highrose Mall. When Guillaume & Mateo returned to the shop-floor there were many Police-Officers everywhere looking for Mateo; Guillaume had realized this and so had to tread carefully. The two of them made their way towards the entrance and suddenly a Police-Officer sees Mateo. "Hey you little boy, I want a word with you!"

shouted the Police-Officer as he went towards Guillaume &
Mateo. As soon as the Police-Officer approached the two
of them Guillaume immediately put the Police-Officer into
a Martial Arts grip and threw him to the ground. Next,
Guillaume did a spinning Karate kick on the Police-Officer
and when he was dazed Guillaume then snapped his
neck...the Officer died instantly! People in the mall were
horrified at what Guillaume just did and one of the Officer's
colleagues saw this as well. "Hey you!" shouted another
Police-Officer as he went for Guillaume; again he did
Martial Arts moves on the other Officer. The Police-Officer
was no match for Guillaume and like the previous one he
had his neck snapped off! "Come on Mateo, let's get out
of here quickly Monsieur!" said Guillaume; there were some
other Police-Officers who saw what happened and they all
chased Guillaume & Mateo in the mall. As Guillaume &
Mateo were running from the Police Guillaume's Daemon
then says to him: "Use your hand-gun on the Police. Yes
you have to kill them!" Immediately, Guillaume stops with
Mateo beside him and gets out his hand-gun, turns around
and shoots the chasing Police one-by-one. People in the
shopping-mall all screamed; they couldn't believe what
Guillaume had just done. Guillaume & Mateo began to run
again to escape but, more & more Police kept on going
towards them! "Mateo move to one side, Monsieur!"
ordered Guillaume; straight away Mateo moved to the side!
Then what Guillaume did next was to somersault over the
Police...everyone including the Police were stunned at this!
When Guillaume leapt over the Police he immediately
attacked them using all of his Martial Arts from the three

countries he trained in. Even though there were a number of Police on Guillaume they all couldn't cope with his Martial Arts abilities. Using his bare hands Guillaume killed each Police-Officer by snapping all of their necks; again the public were all shocked at Guillaume's physical abilities. Guillaume then grabbed Mateo and ran again. Two more Police-Officers then went after them and called out to them as well. Then using his super-vision Guillaume sees two sharp knives on a table at a mini-café; Guillaume went to the table and grabbed both knives one in each hand. Next, at the same time Guillaume then throws the knives at the two chasing Police-Officers and they went through both of their faces. The two Police-Officers immediately died from the impact; people were again shocked at not only the two deaths but, also how Guillaume was able to do this! Guillaume & Mateo were able to get outside and they went to the stolen car. "Monsieur, get in the back-seat and strap yourself in!" instructed Guillaume; Mateo got in the back-seat and put on his seat-belt. Guillaume then switched on the engine and drove off at high-speed nowhere to be seen!

Later on in the day Police-Detectives were investigating the chaos at the Highrose Mall; they were all in shock over the killings of the Police-Officers! The Police-Detectives all took statements from different witnesses; the big problem was that members of the public could not give an accurate description of Guillaume as he was well disguised! "Detective, there's been no accurate description of the perpetrator." explained a Police-Officer, "How can one man do all of this?" asked the Police-Detective with a shocked look on his face. The Police went to look at the security cameras but, could not see clearly that it was Commandant Guillaume Moreau. "My God this guy is some kind of Martial Arts expert!" said one of the Police-Officers; everyone looking at the camera footage could see this. However, they were all completely stunned at Guillaume's Martial Arts abilities! "There's something I've just realized. In Houston there were attacks of some Police-Officers at Houston Train Station and at a café-diner too. The description is the same as that guy too!" explained one of the other Police-Officers. The Police then realized that something big is going down and they all decided to return to the Police Station to investigate it further.

In an abandoned warehouse in a secluded area of Texas were a group of people. They are all CIA Agents; at a desk was a man with brown hair & sunglasses sitting there. It was the same man whom Guillaume saw when he was sleeping on the Amtrak train. The man with the brown hair was only known as 'Zack'; he is the one in charge of the whole operation. As Zack was sitting at his desk reading some documents a man by the name of Bob suddenly approached him in a state of panic! "Sir, sorry to bother you but, we've had some new developments!" explained Bob, "OK tell me, what is it?" asked Zack; Bob then hesitated for a second and took a deep breath! "Well what has happened the boy Mateo Perez, Valeria González's son. He was suddenly taken by a mysterious man; we don't know who he is!" replied Bob; Zack suddenly looked up at Bob with a very stern look on his face. The CIA Agents were also starting to get worried! "Which man, what happened?" asked Zack; Bob then went on to explain about the incident at the Highrose

Mall in Brownsville. Then Bob showed Zack the footage
of the whole fracas. When Zack and the rest of the CIA
watched the footage they all went into complete shock. They
were stunned at Guillaume's Martial Arts skills; however,
they could not clearly see what he looks like as he was well
disguised. "Who is that man?" asked Zack angrily; everyone
in the warehouse froze in fear! "Sir, I think he's Canadian
Intelligence." explained Bob, "What makes you think this?"
questioned Zack, "Well sir, witnesses said he had a French
accent...he kept on using the word Monsieur to Mateo. He
must be French-Canadian; I think Canadian Intelligence are
on to us and our Mexican friends!" explained Bob; Zack
then realized that Bob was on to something! "Is there any
news on Valeria?" asked Zack, "No sir. Not much there but,
our Mexican friends are working on it! I have been informed
that they might have a lead on Valeria!" replied Bob; Zack
just sat there mulling over a few things. "Mateo is not
important right now, only his mother is. She has all the
details of our plans to conquer and take over Canada; we'll
hold back for a bit but, warn our Mexican friends about this
so they are aware!" ordered Zack; Bob nodded in agreement
and immediately left to warn their collaborators. Zack was
now beginning to worry about Commandant Guillaume
Moreau!

Driving the car Guillaume had managed to find an
abandoned small house far away from Brownsville on the
outskirts. Guillaume's Daemon told him to go there as there
are no occupants. Very near the house were many bushes
so Guillaume decided to park the car there to keep it out
of sight. "OK Mateo we can get off here." said Guillaume;

he then got out of the car and helped Mateo get out as well. Guillaume then went to the car-boot and opened it to collect the box of stolen clothes the other night. Beforehand, Guillaume had already bought a lot of food to feed Mateo and Valeria for when he rescues her. When Guillaume made his way to the front-door he opened it and the two of them entered inside; what surprised Guillaume was that the house is in a fairly good condition considering it had been abandoned for some time. "OK Mateo, just take your shoes off here and then we'll go and find the bathroom so you can have a good wash." said Guillaume; straight away Mateo took off his shoes and left them on the inside porch and then went with Guillaume to locate the bathroom. The two of them eventually managed to locate the bathroom and so Guillaume went to check if the water taps are working; luckily they were working! What was even more surprising is that there was hot water as well. Mateo took off his clothes and went into the bath; Guillaume then went to get the shower gel, shampoo and towel. Guillaume gave Mateo a good wash including shampooing his hair; there was so much dirt coming off Mateo as he was being lathered. When Mateo was completely cleaned down Guillaume dried him using a bath-towel. Next, Guillaume then gave Mateo a dressing-gown to put on. Guillaume then collected the box of clothes and the two of them made their way to the living-room. When they arrived in the living-room Guillaume went to switch on the electric-heating so Mateo could get warmed up; then he gave some food for Mateo to eat. "Here you go Monsieur, bon appetit!" said Guillaume; Mateo had a big smile on his face when he saw food considering he hadn't eaten in days. Whilst Mateo was eating & drinking Guillaume went into the box and searched for Mateo's new clothes for him to wear. "Mateo, here are some of your new clothes. As we are going out again later you'll need to wear good strong clothing; hooded-jumper, t-shirts, socks & jeans. Also, I've bought strong walking-shoes for you and your mommy plus waterproof winter-jackets with hats & gloves!" explained Guillaume as he showed Mateo; his face lit up with joy when he saw his new clothes. "With your old clothes they will need to get burned so we can get rid of the evidence." further explained Guillaume; Mateo nodded in agreement. For now the two of them were going to rest until later to rescue Valeria González.

It was about 3 hours later Guillaume was in the Honda Civic drilling holes at the bottom of the back seat; the car itself has a back seat which can open from the top for extra storage. Whilst Guillaume was doing that he suddenly gets a message from his Daemon again: "Guillaume, I know where exactly Valeria is located. She's on a different side to where Mateo was but, for now she is safe. You will need to rescue her soon as the people who want to kill her are getting closer to her. Don't worry I'll tell you where to go!" Guillaume acknowledged his own Daemon. When he finished in the car he went back inside the house. As Guillaume got back inside he saw Mateo sitting down all quiet minding his own business; so he went up to Mateo. "Hey Mateo, are you OK?" asked Guillaume with a concerned look on his face. "Yes thank you!" replied Mateo, "Oh OK! Anyway there's something I need to tell you and it's important. We're going to leave soon to rescue your mommy. However, when we get there you'll need to stay in the car and go inside the seat compartment to stay out of sight. It will be too dangerous for you to come with me, do you understand?" asked Guillaume; Mateo nodded a 'yes' to Guillaume. As Mateo was still wearing his dressing-gown Guillaume then went to get his new clothes and helped Mateo to put them on. Guillaume first got a fresh new pair of underwear and then a t-shirt for Mateo to put on; next, Guillaume helped Mateo to put on the leg-thermals as it was extremely cold outside. Mateo then put on a pair of jeans and then he put on the hooded-jumper; he felt so comfortable & happy in his new clothes! Guillaume then gave Mateo a pair of thick woolly socks to put on and then the new walking shoes. As Mateo was still getting ready Guillaume then took the box of items to the car and put them in the boot with Mateo's old clothes & shoes. Guillaume went back inside to get Mateo; he was all dressed up ready to go! When they got to the car Guillaume showed Mateo the seat which can lift up to go inside; he explained to Mateo that he had to make holes so he could breathe inside. Mateo understood this and when they got inside the car Guillaume turned on the engine...they were now off to rescue Valeria González!

Chapter 7:
Valeria located

Guillaume was driving down with Mateo sitting in the back-seat; Mateo was feeling a little anxious at the whole thing and Guillaume could feel this. Guillaume's Daemon was giving him directions so he could get to Valeria faster; however, at this present time Guillaume was still far away. It was about 5 pm in Texas and as it was winter it was pitch-black outside but, it was darker than usual. Guillaume's Daemon then says to him: "There's a night-club called 'The Rat' Valeria is going in there to keep out of sight as they are getting close to killing her!" Guillaume realized he had to put his foot more firmly on the accelerator and so he did! He was very determined to rescue Valeria González and get her to safety!

Valeria González is all alone at night on the cold streets of Brownsville; she is feeling very numb & weak. It has gotten much colder there and considering the clothes she's wearing it is making it difficult for her to cope. Valeria also has to contend with that she has a very old and worn out rucksack to carry on her back! In the far distance Valeria notices a strange-looking man following her and he looked Hispanic. She then realizes that it is one of the Mexicans who are out to kill her and so she then begins to walk a little faster to get away from him. On the other side of the street

was another Hispanic man out to kill Valeria as well; Valeria
was now getting more nervous! She ran as fast as she could
to get to anywhere safe! Valeria then sees a night-club called
'The Rat' she uses her intuition and makes her way there. It
was as predicted by Guillaume's Daemon that Valeria would
make her way to that particular night-club. When Valeria
got there she notices a fracas going on between the bouncers
and some people who want to get in. Valeria then realizes
that this is her big chance and manages to sneak into the
night-club without paying. The two Mexican Assassins had
got a quick glimpse of what Valeria just did but, they
couldn't get in just yet as the bouncers managed to calm the
situation down; they had to wait before they could enter.
A few other Mexican Assassins came by and the main man
explained what had happened. The Mexican Assassins
decided that some of them will go inside to find Valeria
and some will stay outside just in case Valeria leaves the
night-club. Unfortunately, for the ones who are going into
the night-club had a long wait in the queue!

Guillaume had managed to arrive to the part of
Brownsville to where Valeria is located but, he couldn't see
where she is. However, he drove by 'The Rat' night-club and
so decided to find a parking space somewhere else. There
was a street on the left about five minutes walk from the
night-club and so Guillaume thought he should park on the
side there. When he parked the car Guillaume looked to see
if anyone was around; luckily there wasn't a soul in sight!
"Mateo, I'm going to get your mommy now, you have to
go under the seat. Here's my torch just in case you need
it." said Guillaume as he handed Mateo his torch. Mateo

quickly lifted the back-seat to go inside and then closed it. Next, Guillaume then went into his rucksack and took out an extra hand-gun plus extra bullets. Then he got out some hand grenades to take with him; Guillaume then got out of the car and locked it then made his way to 'The Rat' night-club. As Guillaume was walking down his Daemon tells him that Valeria is already inside the night-club and some of the Mexican Assassins are in there too looking for her. Guillaume was also informed that some of the Mexican Assassins are outside waiting for Valeria. Guillaume goes to the bottom of the street and turns right to make his way to the night-club; as he turns right he sees a strange man with a dark-green jacket near a small alleyway. Guillaume's Daemon then says to him: "That's one of the Mexican Assassins, kill him now there's no time to lose!" Guillaume then goes up to the assassin from behind and pulls him into the small alleyway and immediately kills him by snapping his neck! Guillaume stays in the alleyway out of sight and immediately goes into remote-viewing mode; he went to see where Valeria exactly is sited. Whilst remote-viewing he sees where Valeria is in the night-club plus in a big flash he sees two of the Mexican Assassins in the men's toilets; they are having a discussion. One of them is called 'Max' and the other is called 'Vaz'. "Hey Vaz do you know where this Valeria is?" asks Max, "Not really amigo; I cannot see her there are so many people!" replied Vaz, "Well let's keep looking and then we'll kill her and get our money!" said Max; Guillaume could see the conversation they are having. He realized it was time to make a move and so he teleported to 'The Rat' men's toilets!

Valeria was sitting at a table alone in the night-club fearing for her life; she kept on looking to see if any of the Mexican Assassins are around. There were some night-clubbers who were looking at her with dirty looks which made Valeria more nervous. In the men's toilets Guillaume suddenly appeared to Max & Vaz; they were in complete surprise to see what he had done. "Hey! How did you do that?" asked Vaz, "Well Vaz, let's just say I possess magical powers!" replied Guillaume, "Hey! How did you know his name?" asked Max with a puzzled look on his face. Guillaume didn't reply and immediately using his Martial Arts skills he knocks both Max & Vaz down! Guillaume then went over and snapped both of their necks to kill them. Luckily, as there were no witnesses in the toilets Guillaume then dragged the two dead men and put them into a toilet-cubicle each. Using his powers of telekinesis Guillaume locked the two toilet-cubicles; as he left the men's toilets he deliberately broke the handle to lock the men's toilets door permanently. Guillaume then went around looking for Valeria as quickly as he can. However, the problem was that there are three Mexican Assassins who are also looking for Valeria; Guillaume had to be extremely diligent! As Valeria was still sitting down unable to do anything one of the Mexican Assassins spots her and begins to get his gun ready; Guillaume's Daemon immediately warns him of the impending danger to Valeria! All of a sudden the Mexican Assassin goes up to Valeria and begins to point his gun to her head; Valeria then begins to panic! Guillaume suddenly sees the Mexican Assassin pointing his gun to Valeria; he then sees a sharp cocktail-knife on the counter and rushes to get it and throws it towards the Mexican Assassin. The knife itself goes through his hand which was holding the gun. The Mexican Assassin screams in agony and some of the night-clubbers had noticed this and they became stunned; Valeria then wonders what is going on! All of a sudden Guillaume comes out and immediately with his hand-gun he shoots the assassin straight in his head killing him in the process! Everyone in the night-club screamed and ran out in a state of panic; the other two Mexican Assassins noticed what occurred and they went straight for Guillaume. Immediately, Guillaume does Martial Arts moves on them and then kills both of them by snapping both of their necks. A bouncer suddenly sees what is happening! "Hey! What are you doing?" shouts the bouncer; Guillaume says nothing and immediately does a spinning flying Kung-Fu kick knocking out the bouncer in the process. Valeria was shocked to see what Guillaume had just done! "Don't worry Valeria I'm here to help you!" said Guillaume, "What?" asked Valeria with a surprised look on her face! "I have your son, Mateo...don't worry he's safe. Do you have yours & Mateo's passports?" asked Guillaume, "Yes I do! They're in my bag here!" replied Valeria; all of a sudden Guillaume's Daemon warns him that the other Mexican Assassins are entering the night-club! "Stay here under the table!" ordered Guillaume; immediately he sees the other assassins enter and straight away shoots many of them! "Give me your bag quickly. Let's go out the back way!" ordered Guillaume; immediately both he & Valeria run to the back-door to escape! They ran all the way down the corridor to the outside of the back-end of the night-club. Upon escaping they ran down the back alley of the night-club and immediately some of the Mexican Assassins that were left begin to chase after them. However, Guillaume then got out a hand-grenade and threw it at the remaining Mexican Assassins; the grenade then explodes killing all of them! When Guillaume & Valeria exited the alleyway into the street Guillaume then orders Valeria to turn left immediately into the other street and so she complied. "Go to the red Honda Civic car Madame!" orders Guillaume; when they got to the car the doors are opened and they both get inside. "OK Mateo, you can come out!" shouts Guillaume; immediately Mateo comes out of the seat and sees his mother. "My son I'm so happy to see you!" said Valeria with elation as she hugged Mateo! "Strap yourselves in you two; this is going to be a bumpy ride!" said Guillaume; when all three of them put their seat belts on Guillaume immediately turned on the car ignition. The engine was switched on and then Guillaume drove off speedily!

Chapter 8:
Reunited!

Guillaume was driving at high speed down the road with Valeria and her son Mateo in the car too. So far from his perspective one-half of the mission has been completed...Valeria & Mateo have finally been reunited! "My name is Commandant Guillaume Moreau. I'm in the French Secret Service DGSE Quebec; I have been ordered by the Canadian, Quebec & French Governments to get you two to Quebec safely!" explained Guillaume; all of a sudden Valeria had a puzzled look on her face! "What! You're a French Secret Agent in Quebec?" asked Valeria, "Yes that's right; you've hit the nail on the head!" replied Guillaume, "I didn't realize that there are French Secret Agents based in Quebec!" said Valeria, "Well now you know!" said Guillaume; as he was still driving he could hear loud Police sirens. It was Police-Cars after Guillaume, Valeria & Mateo. Guillaume's Daemon then warns him about the oncoming Police! "The Police are here chasing us; but, don't worry they won't get us!" said Guillaume; Valeria then looked behind her and could see the chasing Police-Cars! "Oh my God, there's five of them and a Police-Helicopter too!" explained Valeria; all of a sudden one of the chasing Police-Cars gets close to the three of them and Guillaume had noticed this. "Valeria, go into my glove-compartment and give me a hand-grenade!" ordered Guillaume; immediately Valeria goes into the glove-compartment and when she sees the hand-grenades she gets one and then gives it to Guillaume. "OK, next when that Police-Car gets closer I'll tell you to open your window!" further instructed Guillaume; the Police-Car eventually got closer & closer to them and then they got right next to the left-side of Guillaume's car. "Valeria, open your window now!" ordered Guillaume; Valeria immediately winds the passenger-side window down. Then all of a sudden Guillaume threw the grenade through the Police-Cars window and then he sped off in the car. The Police-Car suddenly exploded due to the grenade; there were now four Police-Cars left chasing them! "Sorry I had no choice...it was the only way!" explained Guillaume, "No I do understand!" said Valeria; behind them nearby was another Police-Car. Guillaume had noticed this and asked Valeria to give him another grenade and so she did! "Open the sun-roof!" ordered Guillaume; Valeria immediately opened the sun-roof and straight away Guillaume threw the grenade and when it hit the chasing Police-Car it exploded straight away!

About 15 minutes later Guillaume had managed to get to the freeway and drove at an even higher speed. However, he still had three remaining Police-Cars and the Police-Helicopter chasing him! The Police didn't want to get too close to Guillaume just in case he had more grenades. In the right-view mirror Guillaume could see another Police-Car approaching his right-side. Immediately, Guillaume winds his window down and when he did he then gets out his hand-gun and pointed it at an angle behind him and shoots the two Police-Officers in their foreheads killing them instantly. The Police-Car swerved to the right uncontrollably and then flips over several times and then it exploded. The two other chasing Police-Cars were both in complete shock at what they had just witnessed! The other chasing Police-Cars immediately put their foot on the pedal and went straight for Guillaume! However, Guillaume could sense the two remaining Police-Cars chasing him and so he demanded another grenade straight away and Valeria give him one. Guillaume then threw the grenade through the sun-roof and it hit one of the Police-Cars; it then exploded and the other chasing Police-Car crashed into it exploded too! Guillaume had managed to kill all of the Officers in the Police-Cars and all there was left is the Police-Helicopter. As all of the Police-Officers are dead the Police-Helicopter decided to go after Guillaume in the car. One of the Police-Officers in the helicopter then went to get out a rifle! Guillaume's Daemon then warns him: "Guillaume, I need to warn you there's a Police-Officer in the helicopter who's going to shoot you. Take action now!" Guillaume acknowledged his Daemon and immediately followed his intuition to get his hand-gun again. Then Guillaume winds down his window again and keeps his hand-gun in his right-hand. Suddenly, the helicopter is above him but, at a distance to his right; the Officer then gets his rifle ready! But, Guillaume immediately points his gun towards the helicopter and still looking straight ahead he immediately without looking shoots the Armed Officer dead. Then Guillaume shoots at the helicopter several times and when he hits the rotor-engine the helicopter then explodes. "How did you do that without looking?" asked Valeria with shock on her face! "Something I learned when I was in China!" replied Guillaume; all three of them were now safe for the time being. Guillaume then drove off hastily to find a safe place to crash for the night!

It was a long drive but, about two hours from Houston Guillaume had found an abandoned former Church and so decided to stop there. "It's best if we crash at that Church for the night. There's no-one there so it's perfect for us." explained Guillaume, "Oh good; I'm so tired, cold & hungry!" said Valeria; Guillaume then looked at Valeria with concern. He then realized Valeria was physically & emotionally exhausted considering what she had gone through the past few days. It was then starting to rain heavily and Guillaume drove the car right next to the abandoned Church to make it easier for Valeria & Mateo. "Wait in the car for a bit. I need to check out the Church and find the entrance door." explained Guillaume; Valeria nodded at him in agreement. Guillaume then got out of his car and went to look for the Church entrance-door and he did manage to. Luckily the door was unlocked and when Guillaume opened it he immediately went into remote-viewing mode to check it out; it was completely empty! Guillaume's Daemon then says to him: "The Church is fine all of you are going to be safe here. No-one will know you're there!" Guillaume then made his way back to the car. "Valeria, Mateo the coast is clear. We can stay here for the night." explained Guillaume, "Good! At least I'll have a roof over my head!" responded Valeria, "Let's get all of the stuff out of the car and get them inside the Church. I've got some food and new clothes for you, Valeria!" explained Guillaume; Valeria & Mateo got out of the car and Guillaume instructed Mateo to go straight into the Church in which he complied. Guillaume then gave Valeria the box of food and she took it straight into the Church; next Guillaume went to get the box of new clothes and the two new rucksacks then put them all inside the Church near the entrance-door. Afterwards Guillaume went back to the car to get his rucksack and the two hand-guns; he closed the boot & doors and then made his way into the Church. When Guillaume got inside the Church with the remaining items he closed the Church doors and placed a chair up against the doors to block it.

Inside the Church Guillaume noticed Valeria sitting on one of the pews shaking a lot; her son Mateo looked on with great concern. This reminded Guillaume when he first ran away and reached the Outer Hebrides in Scotland; at the time when he first entered Martha's house he was shaking a lot all over. "Hey Valeria; I'll see where the washroom is so you can have a good shower. It looks like you really need one." said Guillaume, "Yes I really do; thank you!" responded Valeria; Guillaume immediately went to look for the washroom. When he located the washroom Guillaume went to take a look at it inside. In the washroom was a bath, sink & toilet; Guillaume went to turn on the taps in both the sink & bath. Surprisingly, the taps were running well considering the Church had been abandoned for such a long time. What was even better is that the water was hot as well; there was both hot & cold running water. When Guillaume exited out of the washroom he saw the heating system; again he went to check if it was working and it still is. The Church itself had electric-heating all around the place and so all of it was switched on; Guillaume then went to see Valeria! "Good news Valeria. I found the washroom and there's plenty of hot water. It's all working plus the heating is working too; I've just switched it all on!" explained Guillaume; Valeria had a surprised look on her face! "Wow! That is a surprise! At least I can have a good shower...I've really wanted one for a long time!" said Valeria; Guillaume then got out a dressing-gown with the shampoo & shower-gel and gave them to Valeria. Next, Guillaume got out a bath-towel & flip-flops and then gave them also to Valeria. "There you go all there. When you finish your shower food will be ready and then we'll sort out your new clothes." explained Guillaume; Valeria nodded at Guillaume and then went to have her shower. Guillaume & Mateo went to the kitchen so Guillaume could get food ready for all of them.

Chapter 9:
Valeria reveals all

After Valeria finished her shower she dried herself and then put on her dressing-gown; she then made her way to the kitchen to eat with her son & Guillaume. When Valeria arrived in the kitchen she noticed that the food was ready. "Hey Valeria! Good timing; your food is ready!" said Guillaume gleefully; Valeria had a big smile on her face. "Oh thank you so much! And by the way thank you very much for saving my son & for looking after him. I don't know what I'll do without him, he means the world to me!" said Valeria gratefully; Guillaume had a smile on his face! "No problem, I'm glad I can help you & your son." said Guillaume; immediately the three of them tucked into their food especially Valeria as she hadn't eaten in days. Whilst they were eating Valeria decided to strike a conversation with Guillaume. "So what made you decide to become a French Secret Agent in Quebec?" asked Valeria, "Well when I first arrived in France from China I did Army National Service for two years and then I fully joined the French Army. I was a Helicopter-Pilot for the French Army and then I transferred to the French Air Force where I was a Fighter-Pilot for 4 years. The French Secret Service wanted to recruit me there due to my exemplary military record plus the fact that I have studied many Martial Arts in China,

Japan & Korea. When I was accepted they put me in Quebec
with the French Military to make Canada stronger against
the Americans. The Americans have gotten too far and more
dangerous!" explained Guillaume; Valeria's eyes flew wide
open in surprise at what Guillaume had just said. "Wow!
That's quite a military career you've had. It's a big step going
from China to France; it has certainly paid-off for you big
time!" said Valeria, "Well what happened I was born in
England and when I was 12 years old I ran away from home.
I was very unhappy at home & school in England and I felt
I was getting nowhere staying there hence, why I ran away.
I went to Scotland and a woman called Martha wanted to
help me and let me stay at her house. She and a friend of
hers made contacts with some Chinese people and managed
to smuggle me all the way to China. I wanted to go there
and train as a Shaolin Monk that's why they helped me. I
spent most of the time in China but, once a week I trained
in Japan & Korea as well. I really wanted to learn as much
as I can." explained Guillaume, "And why did you wanted to
go to France?" asked Valeria, "Well my parents come from
Mauritius which is French-speaking and my main heritage is
French. That's why I chose France....it was an easy choice for
me." replied Guillaume, "Ah I see! I know how you feel; I
ran away from home when I was 14 years old." said Valeria,
"Really! What happened?" asked Guillaume, "Well like you
I was so unhappy at home & school and so I decided that
enough was enough and eventually ran away. I lived on the
streets with other street kids in little shacks. At the time even
though we were living in little shacks we had a roof over
our heads and we were all happy and lived liked a family."

explained Valeria; the three of them carried on eating their food.

When they had finished eating Valeria had a great sense of relief on her face; for one she had managed to have her first shower in a few days and also she had managed to eat her first proper food in days! "I can see that you enjoyed all of that food. Certainly looked like you really needed it." said Guillaume; Valeria then took a deep breath! "Yeah you're right! I'm also equally as glad that I have a roof over my head...it is so cold outside all over Texas." responded Valeria, "That's why I have got a lot of new clothes for you & Mateo....especially for this type of weather. I'll show you later what I've got for the two of you." said Guillaume; all three of them went to the box full of the new clothes. Guillaume showed Valeria all of the clothing he stole from the clothes-shop including showing her the proper winter-jacket plus the hats & gloves. "At least when we make our way to Houston Train Station you'll be properly wrapped up warm." explained Guillaume, "Yes I can see that! Wow! Look at these amazing clothes!" said Valeria gleefully; Guillaume then showed Valeria the different types of wigs for both her & Mateo. Guillaume explained to Valeria that they will all need to be disguised so they won't get recognized. Both Valeria & Mateo understood what Guillaume had meant. "Oh Valeria before you put on your night-gear rub some of this tea-tree oil all over your body and your feet too. Mateo you do the same too before you put on your night-gear. What it is as you've been on the streets for so long it will rejuvenate your physical body." explained Guillaume, "Oh I didn't realize this! How do you know of this?" asked Valeria, "I learnt a lot of Chinese Medicine when I was in China and also Japanese Medicine! Oh I've just realised when you finished putting tea-tree oil all over your body wash your hands afterwards. What happens if you rub your eyes it will sting!" said Guillaume; Valeria was given her night-gear and tea-tree oil and made her way to the washroom to put on her night-gear. Whilst Valeria was changing her clothes Guillaume went into his rucksack to take out a paper-pad & pen; he then sat down and waited for Valeria.

A few minutes later Valeria returned with her new night-gear on; she felt very comfortable in them. "Wow! This is so comfy...I love it!" said Valeria with a big smile on her face; Guillaume also had a big smile on his face! "Glad you like it! By the way before we go to sleep would it be possible if you could give details of that gang who want to take over Canada?" asked Guillaume, "Of course I can if it will help a lot." replied Valeria; she then went to sit with Guillaume so she could give all of the important details. The two of them were now both ready! "Well to begin this gang are called the 'Lobos de Fuego'. They were committing all kinds of crimes such as drug-trafficking, money-laundering, selling illegal arms...there are so many that you could write a whole book! When I started working at the factory at first I didn't know what kind of place it really was. I mean I thought it was a normal work-place but, they used it to hide all of their criminal activities. My husband at the time, he knew all along who they are and was working with them just to get a big promotion." explained Valeria; Guillaume had managed to note it all down! Then Valeria went on:

"I then found out by accident that my husband and the Lobos de Fuego did a deal with the US Government about invading Canada and taking over it. Then they are going to use Canada to commit more crimes all over the world. When my husband found out that I overheard the plans he told the Big-Boss and he then gave them permission to kill Mateo & me. That's when I had to escape him with Mateo. I think the CIA are involved as well!" Guillaume then realized that he is onto something big! But, he knew all along that the CIA are heavily involved in this. "I know the CIA are involved in this. My Higher-Self told me!" explained Guillaume; Valeria had a puzzled look on her face! "Higher-Self! What is a Higher-Self?" asked Valeria, "It means your higher version of yourself. Sometimes they call it a Daemon; that's who God really is. When I was in China as a Shaolin Monk we do both meditation and Martial Arts. Meditation is a very important part of the training; so many times I was meditating in the cave there was this one incident where I suddenly connected with my Daemon. Since then I have been able to communicate with my Daemon on a regular basis. If it wasn't for my Daemon I wouldn't have been able to find you & Mateo." explained Guillaume; Valeria's eyes suddenly flew wide open! "Wow! That is extraordinary! Oh by the way, I have documents in my bag, I need to show you something really important." explained Valeria; immediately she went to her old rucksack and pulled out the documents. "These documents are plans on how to commence the invasion of Canada. Also, this is the actual location of the Lobos de Fuego headquarters." said Valeria as she showed Guillaume. "This is brilliant! When we get to Quebec I will pass this on to both the Quebec & Canadian Governments. Very likely the French Military & Government will deal with this." said Guillaume, "Good! I'm worried that my husband may come after me & my son." explained Valeria, "You don't have to worry about this; once they get in we will have to kill all of them including your husband!" explained Guillaume; Valeria then breathed a big sigh of relief! "I'll be glad when he's dead! My husband was very nasty towards me & Mateo. He didn't care about us at all. My husband was a really evil man...all I wanted was a descent life for me and my son!" explained Valeria; Guillaume looked straight into Valeria's eyes with concern. "Yes I can see why you want your husband dead. Oh what other items do you have in your rucksack so we can see what to take with us. The unwanted items we will have to burn them somewhere." said Guillaume, "Yes I can show you now." responded Valeria; the two of them then went to look at Valeria's other items in her bag.

Guillaume & Valeria had spent about 20 minutes looking at all of Valeria's possessions; she had in her bag some old & worn out clothes which had many, many holes all over. Guillaume then realized why he had to get new clothes for Valeria & Mateo as instructed by his Daemon. The other items Valeria took out of her bag were toiletries, the two passports and surprisingly two gold-bars. Guillaume stood there bewildered at seeing the two gold-bars. "Hey Valeria, where did you get these gold bars from?" questioned Guillaume, "Oh yes, that! At my former work-place they had a few gold bars stored away in a cupboard. I didn't know where they got it from. When I decided that I was going to take Mateo and leave I took the two gold bars just in case. I was going to use them as a bargaining tool for the US Border-Guards if required. I had no choice." explained Valeria; Guillaume then realized why Valeria had done this! "OK I understand why you did this. What you have to do when we reach the French Embassy on the Quebec-US Border you will need to declare it to them. At least it will cover you for the time being and depending where it came from if it is not stolen gold they'll return the gold bars to you." explained Guillaume, "Oh OK! As I had stated I have no idea where it came from." said Valeria, "No worries! Also, what we need to do before bed-time is to get all of your new clothes into your new rucksack and Mateo's too. Just leave the clothes that you're going to wear for tomorrow out. With the old toiletries and old clothes we can discard them as you have new ones. Oh and there are new comfy slippers for you and Mateo in addition to the flip-flops. Hopefully your rucksack won't be too heavy." explained Guillaume. What both Guillaume & Valeria did was to get all of the new clothes into Valeria's new rucksack and then as Mateo was quite young and small they only put some of the new clothing into his new rucksack. Guillaume decided to put most of Mateo's new clothes into his rucksack. With Valeria's & Mateo's old worn out clothing and toiletries Guillaume put them all into the cardboard-box. They were all more or less ready for the next day to make their way to Houston Train Station. Guillaume then went to get the two sleeping-bags and all three of them made their way to a small room at the back of the Church. "We can sleep here tonight. The double sleeping-bag is for you & Mateo and the single one is for me." said Guillaume; Mateo then went to get ready to put on his night-gear and tea-tree oil was rubbed all over his body beforehand. When Mateo put his pyjamas on Guillaume then went to take his shower.

A little later on when Guillaume had finished his shower and put on his night-gear he went to get his hand-gun to take with him to sleep with just in case. However, he knew in his mind that they will not get any trouble during the night; the rain outside began get heavier! Guillaume then made has way to the small room behind the Church so he could go to sleep; when he arrived there he saw Valeria looking a little subdued! "Valeria, are you OK?" asked Guillaume with a concerned look on his face; Valeria then looked at him directly. "Well to be honest no. I keep on wondering whether we'll get through all of this; the CIA and everyone else are after us. It's just the three of us verses all of them!" replied Valeria; Guillaume then went to sit right next to Valeria and then he gave her a little smile. "Hey Valeria we will get through this. I know it and I can feel it too. For me failure is not an option, I have a mission to save Canada & Quebec!" responded Guillaume; Valeria again looked at Guillaume directly and realized that he is determined & serious about the mission. "Yes I can see that you are very determined to do this." said Valeria, "Yes I am!" said Guillaume; Valeria then decided to change the subject to get her mind off things! "I suppose being French you like the sport Soccer? My son loves it...he supports Real Madrid in Spain." said Valeria, "Well to be honest I've played knock-about Soccer but, since I went to China I kind of lost interest in it. My sport now is Martial Arts." responded Guillaume, "Yes I can see that. Here in the whole of the

Americas we have our own version of football called Gridiron. It is quite popular but I admit I find it very barbaric and Mateo has the same opinion. However, my ex-husband loves it!" explained Valeria; the two of them went silent for a bit! "Are you able to get any sleep?" asked Guillaume; Valeria nodded a yes to him in response with a smile on her face. She was more relaxed! All three of them had decided that it was time to get a lot of sleep as they are going to have a very long & hectic day ahead of them. Guillaume then took his hand-gun and went to sleep with it in his sleeping-bag! He knew in his mind that he is going to have quite a fight the next day!

Chapter 10:
Night-Club investigation

Later on in the evening at the night-club where Guillaume caused the massive fracas earlier, there were Police-Officers investigating the whole incident. They interviewed a lot of witnesses who were there but, the Police didn't get anywhere! No-one could identify Guillaume as the perpetrator as he was well disguised. Observing from a distance was the CIA Agent Bob; he kept looking on at all of the Police and then decided to approach them. "Who's in charge of all this?" asked Bob; one of the Officers put his hand up...his name was Officer James. "Why are you asking for me?" asked Officer James with a confused look on his face. "I'm from the CIA and the perpetrator you're looking for is of interest to us." replied Bob as he showed his CIA badge; Officer James then went into a slight shock! "Oh! Do you know who he is?" asked Officer James, "Not exactly but, we think he's French-Canadian working for Canadian Intelligence." replied Bob, "Canadian Intelligence! What the hell is going on?" asked Officer James frantically; Bob stood there in silence for a bit. "At this present time I cannot reveal anything as this is secret Government issues." replied Bob; Officer James stood there with a puzzled look on his face! "Oh OK! I'll leave it at that!" said Officer James; Bob left the crime scene immediately in a rush! All of the Police-Officers looked at each other all wondering what is going on!

Bob returned to the warehouse where the CIA has their secret base; he went immediately straight to Zack. "Sir, there's something I need to tell you!" said Bob; Zack then looked up at Bob. "Go on, tell me!" said Zack, "Well Sir, I went to the crime scene at the night-club where Valeria González was. She was taken by that French-Canadian; he has both the mother and the son!" explained Bob, "Did you find anything else about the night-club incident, Bob?" asked Zack, "Unfortunately we haven't much to go on, Sir. No-one could ID the perpetrator!" replied Bob; Zack got off his chair and stood up! "Right get the camera footage of the whole incident at the Highrose shopping-mall. Get that man's face and run it through the systems, tell me who he is!" ordered Zack; immediately most of the CIA operatives went to get the footage of when Guillaume went to rescue Mateo Perez. One of the agents managed to get a video-clip of Guillaume's face of him wearing a cap, wig & sunglasses. However, the agents are unaware that Guillaume is wearing a wig! The agents ran Guillaume's face through the computer systems and waited. However, they hit a very big brick-wall; the systems returned a result saying: NOT RECOGNIZED. The agent showed Zack what happened...his mouth dropped wide open! "How can it return a result of not recognized? I mean who the fuck is this guy?" shouted Zack; all of the CIA Agents looked at each other with confusing looks. Zack kept on pacing back & forth wondering what to do next! About 10 minutes later Zack decided to stop pacing; he then turned around to look at everyone. "Right as we don't know who & where this guy is right now; he really has eluded all of us! My guess is that he's hiding somewhere for the night and then tomorrow he'll move on. So what we'll do is we have to go on by foot & car and capture him. Then we will kill all 3 of them! We haven't lost just yet!" instructed Zack; all of the operatives immediately stopped working and went to get some shut-eye. Zack himself was fuming inside but, determined to capture Guillaume, Valeria & Mateo!

Chapter 11:
Getaway!

It was about 04:30 hours early in the morning; all three of them woke up with ease. In her mind Valeria was thinking that she & Mateo are finally going to be free once and for all. "Well this is it....the final step is soon to begin!" said Guillaume; he was referring to the fact that all there was left to do is to get to Houston Train Station and take the Amtrak train from there back to Portland, Maine. They all went to get themselves quickly washed and then have their breakfast.

A little later on after breakfast Guillaume's Daemon began to speak to him again: "Guillaume, I need to warn you that the CIA are getting ready to seek you out, Valeria & Mateo too. But, don't worry I'll keep tabs on them!" Guillaume then had the thought that he will have to be extra vigilant as much as he can. "Valeria, what we'll need to do is by car we will drive to somewhere and then I will need to get rid of it so we can throw the scent off the CIA!" explained Guillaume; Valeria nodded in agreement. "How long will it take to get to Houston Train Station?" asked Valeria, "Well from here to Houston Train Station it is about a 2-hour drive but, I will have to ditch the car somewhere not too near Houston or someone will be on to us." replied Guillaume, "Oh OK! I understand what you mean." said Valeria, "I'll make sure that I will ditch the car within walking distance of Houston. Oh by the way the box with yours & Mateo's old clothes & shoes we will need to take it with us. There is an area where there are homeless people who warm themselves up on those gigantic fire-cans. We can burn it all there. It will wipe off all of yours & Mateo's DNA." explained Guillaume; Valeria understood the logic behind Guillaume's suggestion. They all changed their clothes and put their night-gears into their rucksacks. When Valeria put on her new clothes she had a feeling of elation; she loved her new clothes it made her feel so comfortable. Once they were all ready it was time to make their way to Houston.

Meanwhile back in the secret CIA hide-out, Zack was pondering on what he should do first and how to seek out and kill Guillaume, Valeria & Mateo. All of a sudden Bob appeared slightly nervous! "Sir, is there anything else we need to do before we move out?" asked Bob; Zack turned around and looked at Bob. "No Bob! Let's all move out now...we have no time to lose." replied Zack; Bob nodded at Zack in agreement and went straight away to inform the other CIA Agents. The CIA went to gather all of their equipment and put them into their vehicles. Zack just stood there observing still wearing his sunglasses; in Zack's mind he really wanted to capture Guillaume Moreau!

Guillaume was driving along with Valeria sitting in the front passenger seat and Mateo sitting in the back. "Guillaume, do you think we'll get through this? There are so many people after all of us!" explained Valeria, "Yes we will. We just need to be a little more cautious; I'll make sure that you and Mateo will get to Quebec safely. Besides with all of the Martial Arts training I have done it will prepare me for situations like this." replied Guillaume as he gave Valeria a little smile; Valeria then smiled back at Guillaume! About 15 minutes later Guillaume then sees a huge river to his right; he then checks the time on the dashboard...it was about 06:30 hours. "Valeria, we can ditch the car here and push it into that river." explained Guillaume as he showed Valeria. Guillaume then turned the car off-road to the right onto the green-grass; he then stopped the car and switched off the engine. When all three of them got out of the car Guillaume then looked all around to see if the coast is clear; luckily there was no-one around. Next, what they all did was to colour their faces differently and then put on wigs to disguise themselves more! Guillaume then went to see in his rucksack how much hand-grenades he had left...he still had plenty! Guillaume & Valeria together went to get out all of the other important belongings from the car including the box of Valeria's & Mateo's old, worn-out clothes & shoes. When the car was cleared out Guillaume next released the hand-brake then both he and Valeria pushed the car into the river. Very quickly Guillaume took out two hand-grenades and released the catch on both of them and threw the two grenades through the rear-window whilst the car was still afloat halfway. "Quickly, move behind those trees!" ordered Guillaume; Valeria & Mateo both moved behind one tree and Guillaume moved behind another! All of a sudden there was a huge explosion; the car exploded into several little pieces! "Now they won't be able to trace us." said Guillaume; next all three of them then went on foot towards Houston....it was going to be about a 40-minute walk for them. The box which contained the old clothes & shoes was carried by both Guillaume & Valeria in one hand each. Luckily all three of them were well-clothed with a strong winter-jackets & walking shoes; it was literally getting colder in Texas.

At about 07:20 hours Guillaume, Valeria & Mateo had managed to arrive at the town of Houston. There was hardly any people in sight in the town only a very few. Guillaume then notices an alleyway in the distance and his intuition tells him to go there. "Hey! Let's go through that alleyway. We can burn your old clothes there." said Guillaume; all three of them then went down the alleyway. Like the town itself the alleyway hardly had anyone in sight; there were so many empty metal-cans. As they all walked on Guillaume then notices an African-American homeless man trying to light a match. He was having great difficulty in trying to light the match....his hands were completely frozen! Guillaume then went up to him! "Hey! Let me do that for you." said Guillaume as he took the box of matches from homeless man. Guillaume then lit the match for the homeless man and made a fire in the metal-can. When the fire was well lit Guillaume and Valeria then went to burn the old clothes, shoes and the cardboard-box. The homeless man had a big smile with a great sense of relief on his face! "Oh thank you kind Sir! I am eternally grateful! I haven't had this much heat in ages!" explained the homeless man; Guillaume had a slight smile on his face. All of a sudden an African-American woman came out of a door with three young children. There was one boy and two girls; Guillaume then wondered who they were! "Daddy is it warm enough?" asked one of the girls; Guillaume then realised that it was his wife and children! "Yes it is my dear. That nice man there helped me lit the fire." said homeless man; his wife and children looked at Guillaume and all smiled at him. "If you don't mind me asking, how long have you all been homeless for?" asked Guillaume with a concerned look on his face! "Just over a year...no-one wants to help us!" explained the homeless man; Guillaume's mouth suddenly dropped with shock! "What the hell! How did this all happen?" asked Guillaume, "Well our previous job my wife & I got laid off and we couldn't pay the rent anymore! Plus the big problem is that in Texas the people here are so prejudice towards us Afro-Americans. We just don't know what to do...I feel so helpless!" explained the homeless man; Guillaume all of a sudden felt so sorry for him and his family! "Hey what's your name?" asked Guillaume; the man then looked up at Guillaume with sadness on his face. "My name is Terrence. This is my wife Denise and my 3 children. My eldest child, my son is called Michael, 9, my daughter Sarah, 7 and my youngest Georgina, 5." replied the homeless man; Guillaume and Valeria suddenly looked at each other with complete shock on their faces! They couldn't believe what had happened to that family; Guillaume said hello to Denise and the children and they said hello to them in return. "Oh my God Terrence I'm so sorry to hear of your misfortune!" said Guillaume, "Hey thanks for your concern. This is where my family & I been living in for the past year." explained Terrence; he then showed Guillaume through a door and the place itself is a small box-size room. Guillaume was horrified when he noticed what they were living in! He really wanted to help

Terrence and his family but, he didn't know how. "Hey Terrence wait here let me get some food for you and your family. You two stay with them I won't be too long." said Guillaume; Valeria & Mateo stayed with Terrence and his family whilst Guillaume went to the shops to buy some food for them.

Guillaume was in a mini-supermarket buying food for Terrence, Denise and their kids; his Daemon suddenly spoke to him again: "Guillaume, I had to make you use your intuition to go down the alleyway on purpose. You need to help that family; I'm going to give you the winning lottery numbers for the next draw. They are 09-15-22-30-52 and the star-ball will be number 1. Give Terrence some money and the lottery numbers and tell him to buy the ticket immediately!" Guillaume immediately took out his small note-book & pen and wrote down the lottery numbers. When Guillaume finished purchasing & paying for the items he left in a haste to meet up with Terrence and his family. Guillaume returned to the small room down the alleyway and saw Terrence and his family sitting down feeling unhappy & scared. Valeria & Mateo looked at the homeless family with grave concern. "Hey Terrence, here's the food I've bought for all of you." said Guillaume as he gave them the bag of food. "Oh thank you so much we haven't eaten very much in so many days. You're very kind!" said Terrence gleefully; Guillaume stood there with a smile on his face. He then had a big thought in his mind! "Hey Terrence, there's a couple of things I need to tell you. I am in disguise and so are these two. I am a French Secret Agent in Quebec, Canada; I'm on a mission to get this lady and her son safely to Quebec!" explained Guillaume; Terrence and his wife had shock on their faces! "What! You're a Secret Agent?" asked Terry as his mouth dropped! "Yes; the US Government are after these two and they want to kill them. The US Government & Mexico are trying to take over Canada and this woman has all of the details." explained Guillaume; Terrence and Denise looked at each other completely stunned! "Canada is such a nice place compared to the US. I can't believe that the US & Mexico are trying to take over Canada; I hope the US & Mexico don't win. I have always dreamt of living in Canada and so does my wife. So what's the other thing you want to tell me?" queried Terrence; Guillaume then pulled out the piece of paper with the winning lottery numbers and gave it to Terrence. "I can listen to invisible voices. It told me that these are going to be the winning lottery numbers and to give them to you." explained Guillaume, "What! Are you serious?" asked Terrence with shock! "Yes I am. I'm going to give you some money; go now to that mini-supermarket and buy yourself a lottery ticket with those numbers. Get the receipt and also buy yourself a small envelope to put your ticket & receipt in. I'll stay here with your family whilst you get your ticket." explained Guillaume; immediately Terrence went on his way to buy his lottery ticket. Guillaume, Valeria & Mateo stayed with Denise and the three children.

About ten minutes later Terrence returned from the mini-supermarket; he then went straight up to Guillaume. "I've bought the lottery ticket and I got the receipt too." said Terrence as he showed the envelope to Guillaume. Terrence then opened the envelope to show Guillaume the lottery

ticket & the receipt. "Good! Just keep it safe with you. And
don't worry you are going to win the jackpot; then you'll
be able to immigrate to Canada. There's enough money to
keep you going for a few more days." explained Guillaume, "I
don't know what to say. I am so grateful for the kindness you
have shown me and my family." said Terrence, "No worries!
I just want you and your family to have a decent &
comfortable life." responded Guillaume, "Thank you for
caring and looking after us." said Denise, "Oh! Can we keep
this all a secret as you're aware that I am on a secret mission."
requested Guillaume, "Of course we will; we completely
understand. I want to wish you well on your mission." said
Terrence; Guillaume, Valeria & Mateo said their goodbyes to
Terrence, Denise and their children. Then when they did say
their goodbyes the three of them went on their way.

At about 08:00 hours Guillaume, Valeria & Mateo
arrived at a big shopping-mall near Houston Train Station.
"What we need to do is to buy train-tickets here at the mall
for the Amtrak train from Houston to Portland, Maine."
explained Guillaume, "Oh I see! Where is Houston Train
Station?" asked Valeria, "It's only 5 minutes walk from the
mall." replied Guillaume; all 3 of them then entered the
shopping-mall. The mall itself was so huge it was the size of
a sports arena. Very near the entrance was the section where
they sell train-tickets for Amtrak trains only; they noticed
that the queue was quite long. They immediately went to
wait in the queue; when the three of them got in the queue
Guillaume looked around the mall and using his senses he
checked to see if there's anything suspicious nearby. For the

time-being there was no danger in sight much to Guillaume's relief.

On the road Zack and the rest of the CIA were driving along towards Houston and they all noticed Police-Cars on the side of the road. The CIA had trouble getting through and had to stop their vehicles. Zack & Bob got out and went to find a Police-Officer to talk to. When they found one both Zack & Bob showed their CIA badges. "Oh you're with the CIA!" said the Police-Officer with a bemused look on his face! "Yes, we're on an assignment and your cars are blocking us!" said Zack, "No worries. I'll get my colleagues to move them so you can go on your way." said the Police-Officer as he went to alert his colleagues. As Zack & Bob were waiting they noticed that a car was being hoisted from the river. It was the car stolen by Guillaume in Brownsville earlier, the red Honda Civic! "Hey Sir I recognize the number-plate; I ran it through the systems and it is a stolen car. It was stolen from a garage in Brownsville; it was also the same car that was linked to a shooting at a night-club in the same town!" explained another Police-Officer; Zack & Bob looked at each other completely stunned! They realized that it was Guillaume who dumped the car in the river. "It's that fucking French-Canadian Agent!" said Bob angrily, "Yes it has to be him!" said Zack; the two of them then went to look for the Police-Officer in charge. When Zack & Bob found the Officer in charge they approached him and showed their badges...the Police-Officer in charge was a man named Officer Matthews. "Hi there myself & Bob here are with the CIA. We overheard about the stolen car; it is of great interest

to us." explained Zack, "What! You're with the CIA?" said
Officer Matthews, "Yes that's right! The person who stole
that car is with Canadian Intelligence and he's
French-Canadian." explained Bob, "Canadian Intelligence!
What is going on here?" asked Officer Matthews with shock
on his face! "Well we have been wanting to apprehend him
for a serious crime." explained Bob, "Sir, I think there's a
shopping-mall not far from here...about 30 minutes drive."
said one of the Police-Officers; Zack, Bob and Officer
Matthews then realized that Guillaume, Valeria & Mateo
could be in the shopping-mall. "Sir, they must be in the
shopping mall!" said Bob; Zack nodded in agreement to
Bob. Zack, Bob and the Police then went into their vehicles
and immediately made their way to the shopping-mall in a
big haste!

Whilst Guillaume, Valeria & Mateo were still waiting
in the queue to buy their train-tickets Guillaume's Daemon
suddenly spoke to him again: "Guillaume, I just need to
warn you that the CIA and the Police are on their way.
They're all coming for you, Valeria & Mateo; you have no
choice you have to kill all of them!" Luckily for the three of
them there was one person in front of them in the queue;
Guillaume then whispers to Valeria: "The CIA are on their
way here. We need to take every caution possible!" Valeria
then looked at Guillaume with a worrying look on her face!
"What are we going to do?" asked Valeria slightly frantic!
"Not to worry. We just make our way to the other side of the
mall and go out of that entrance. The train station is nearer
there." replied Guillaume; it was now their turn to buy the
train-tickets. When they approached the ticket-booth

Guillaume immediately looked at the cashier and did mind-control on her. Guillaume wanted to make sure that the cashier wouldn't remember him, Valeria & Mateo! "I would like to purchase 2 adult tickets and 1 child ticket to Portland, Maine...one-way please!" requested Guillaume; the cashier complied and produced the tickets. Guillaume paid for the tickets and when he received them he gave Valeria her ticket and Mateo's too. Valeria then put both tickets in her jacket-pocket and Guillaume put his ticket into his pocket. They then went on their way.

A few minutes later the CIA and the Police arrived at the mall; all of them then got out of their vehicles. "OK everyone! It is very likely that all 3 of them are wearing disguises. If anyone sees a man, woman and a young boy then we know it is them. Split up everyone and go & get them; we have no time to lose!" ordered Zack; the CIA Agents and the Police all split up and entered inside the mall. Guillaume, Valeria & Mateo were walking along still inside the mall when Guillaume's Daemon suddenly alerts him that the CIA & Police are now inside the shopping-mall. "Valeria they're here but, don't worry just keep going; we'll get out of here." said Guillaume; suddenly all three of them began to walk a little faster! Zack, Bob the CIA and Police were all inside the mall seeking out a man, woman & boy....they couldn't see anything! Bob went further down a bit more and he notices a man, woman & boy at a far distance...it was Guillaume, Valeria & Mateo! Bob then contacts Zack immediately with his cell-phone! "Sir, I have a sighting of the 3 suspects I'm going to follow them just to be sure!" said Bob; when Zack heard the message from Bob he immediately orders two of his agents to go where Bob is! Guillaume's Daemon suddenly speaks to him again: "Guillaume there's a CIA Agent named Bob and he is not far behind you...he knows it's you. You need to split up and entice Bob into the small alleyway which leads to the outside...you have to kill him!" Guillaume then realized that he had to think very quickly! "Valeria, keep walking but, don't stop. There's a guy following me I'm going to entice him to that small alleyway; we need to split up! When I say so you & Mateo go into that bookshop ahead and stay out of sight. I'll come back for you later!" ordered Guillaume; the three of them walked a little casually. Guillaume then took out a grenade from his rucksack and put it into his pocket. "Valeria, go now!" ordered Guillaume; immediately they split up and Valeria & Mateo ran straight into the bookshop! Bob got a little confused and he could only see the back of Guillaume. Again Bob reached for his cell-phone and contacted Zack! "Sir, I can only see the man but, not the woman & her child!" explained Bob, "Stay on the man leave the woman & her boy to us!" ordered Zack; Bob acknowledged the request and went after Guillaume. Two CIA Agents appeared and went to look for Valeria & Mateo whilst Bob kept on Guillaume. Bob was having difficulties keeping up with Guillaume and when he saw Guillaume turn into the small alleyway Bob went there too in a rush. However, as soon as Guillaume got into the alleyway he immediately went invisible and took out the grenade! Guillaume then sees Bob enter the alleyway and he immediately releases the catch and very carefully puts the grenade into Bob's jacket-pocket! Bob was unable to see where Guillaume is and immediately goes outside; Guillaume still invisible teleports away to the men's toilets. Bob stood outside wondering where Guillaume is...he got a little frustrated and took out his cell-phone to call Zack. "Sir, I can't find him...he's disappeared!" explained Bob, "What do you mean he's disappeared?" asked Zack aggressively, "Well Sir...." all of a sudden the grenade exploded! Bob was dead; his organs exploded everywhere on the ground. Zack heard the explosion over his cell-phone! "Bob....Bob! Where are you?" asked Zack angrily...he got no reply.

A few minutes later Guillaume came out of the men's toilets and went to look for Valeria & Mateo. In the bookshop Valeria & Mateo were hiding out of sight behind one of the book-shelves. There were customers in the bookshop wondering why they were acting so weird. Two of the CIA Agents entered the bookshop looking for Valeria & Mateo; they had strong suspicions that they are in the bookshop. One of the CIA Agents had brown-hair and the other had blond-hair; they both looked around but, couldn't see either Valeria or Mateo. "Hey you stay here at the front and I'll go and look for them." said the blond-haired agent; the brown-hair agent nodded in agreement and waited in the front-end of the bookshop. Guillaume got to the outside of the bookshop and his Daemon spoke to him again: "Guillaume, the brown-haired man you see is a CIA Agent. There's a blond man in there too. You know what you've got to do!" Guillaume then realized that he had no time to lose; immediately as soon as he entered the bookshop he went straight for the brown-haired agent. Guillaume then dropped his rucksack and without hesitation he attacked the brown-haired agent using his Martial Arts moves. The brown-haired agent was taken aback from the surprise attack by Guillaume. The customers and staff in the bookshop were in shock at what Guillaume is doing to the CIA Agent; then all of sudden Guillaume went for the kill and snapped the agent's neck...he was now dead! Everyone was horrified at what had just happened! They all couldn't believe their eyes...they all froze in shock! Guillaume then picked up his rucksack and went to find Valeria & Mateo with the help of his Daemon. Valeria & Mateo were still hiding behind the bookshelves feeling trapped & scared; they were both hoping that Guillaume would get to them soon. All of a sudden the blond-haired agent finds the two of them; Valeria then realizes who he is! "Hello Valeria & Mateo. Now your time is up!" said the blond-haired agent. Then from behind Guillaume knocks down the blond-haired agent with a surprise attack. Guillaume then kicks the CIA Agent in his face and then he snapped his neck off! Some of the other customers witnessed what had just occurred and they all went into shock! "Come on let's go and stay right behind me!" ordered Guillaume; Valeria & Mateo nodded in agreement and as Guillaume walked on Valeria & Mateo were right behind him.

As Guillaume was walking along making his way out of the bookshop his Daemon speaks to him again: "Guillaume, get your hand-gun ready; when you get to the front of the bookshop there is going to be a Policeman there. Do what you have to do!" As soon as Guillaume heard the instruction from his Daemon he immediately reached for his hand-gun; Valeria had noticed this and began to get a little worried!

"Guillaume is everything OK?" asked Valeria, "Yeah everything's fine. I just got a strong feeling!" replied Guillaume; all three of them just walked on nervously! When they got to the front-end of the bookshop as expected a Policeman was there. Without any hesitation Guillaume pointed his hand-gun and shot the Policeman in the head; he died instantly. Everyone in the shop were all horrified at what they saw; outside on the shopping-mall floor the Police & the CIA could hear the sound of the gun-shot from a distance. "Hey did you all hear that? It sounds like a gun-shot!" queried one of the CIA Agents; the people in the mall heard the gun-shot too and began to get worried. Immediately, the CIA Agents and the Police went to look to where the source of the gun-shot is; in his mind Zack knew it was Guillaume! As soon as Guillaume, Valeria & Mateo left the bookshop they all saw the CIA Agents and Police approaching nearby; suddenly both Guillaume & Zack locked eyes on each other from a far distance! Guillaume then realized that when he was sleeping on the train his Daemon showed him Zack, the one he had to kill! "Hey! That's the French-Canadian; let's get him! One of you go and look for Bob!" ordered Zack; Guillaume then realized that he had to take immediate action! "Valeria, you & Mateo stay to one side whilst I deal with the CIA & Police!" ordered Guillaume; straight away Valeria & Mateo hid away out of sight. Without hesitation Guillaume gets his hand-gun and starts shooting at the Police and the CIA Agents killing some of them already! Everyone in the shopping-mall screamed at the sounds of the gun-shots running around like crazy! They all feared for their lives!

When some of the CIA Agents got nearer to Guillaume, immediately Guillaume then did Martial Arts kicks & punches on them. He managed to kill a number of them by snapping their necks; then when another CIA Agent tried to apprehend him, Guillaume did a somersault over the agent. The Police and the other CIA Agents were in shock at Guillaume's physical abilities! Then all of a sudden Guillaume killed the CIA Agent instantly by snapping his neck! Guillaume then used his hand-gun and shot more Police & CIA Agents; at a far distance he then sees Zack very clearly! Using his hand-gun Guillaume takes aim at Zack and then shoots him in the head...Zack was now dead! "What the fuck? He's killed Zack!" shouted one of the agents....they all stood still in shock! Their leader was dead! Immediately, Guillaume grabbed his rucksack and made a run for it with Valeria & Mateo; one of the Police-Officers attempted to shoot Guillaume but, he missed by a long way. Guillaume then turned around and shot the Police-Officer dead; Guillaume continued to run making an escape! "Valeria, you & Mateo when you go out of that entrance head straight towards the park; it's virtually next to it!" ordered Guillaume; they all made it out of the other entrance towards the park.

When the three of them got out of the shopping-mall diagonal to the left was an entrance to a small-park. All of a sudden gun-shots were heard...it was more of the Police shooting at them! "Valeria, get into the entrance and wait there!" ordered Guillaume; when Valeria & Mateo got through the park-entrance they stayed to one side. When Guillaume got through he took off his rucksack and went to get some grenades and threw them at the chasing Police-Officers. The grenades exploded killing all of the Police and some of the CIA Agents. Then all of a sudden there were two Police-Cars approaching and immediately Guillaume threw a grenade to each Police-car killing them instantly! All of the Police-Officers had now died there were only five CIA Agents left! Guillaume picked up his rucksack and with Valeria & Mateo they ran a little further down the small park. "Valeria, take my jacket & rucksack then you & Mateo go and hide in those bushes over there. I have to get rid of the 5 remaining CIA Agents!" explained Guillaume; before he gave his jacket & rucksack to Valeria, Guillaume took out another hand-gun. Valeria & Mateo then ran into the bushes and just waited there until Guillaume was finished with the CIA. Both hand-guns had a lot of bullets in them so there was plenty of security for Guillaume! What Guillaume then did next was to crawl under one of the bushes and waited for the remaining CIA Agents to appear. About five minutes later the remaining CIA Agents had entered the small park...they all knew that Guillaume, Valeria & Mateo were there! "Hey we know you're Canadian Intelligence; we don't want to hurt you. We just want the woman and her son, that's all!" called out one of the agents; Guillaume could hear every word but, he didn't respond! Next, what Guillaume did next was to go into invisible mode....he realized that he has to kill all of them now! So what he did was to teleport right behind the CIA Agents but, stayed invisible! The CIA Agents were treading slowly & carefully looking around for their three suspects! They didn't realize that Guillaume was behind them getting ready for the kill! All of a sudden Guillaume got out both hand-guns and shot two of the CIA Agents at the same time....there were now three left! The remaining three agents turned around looking to see where the two gun-shots came from...they were now starting to panic! Guillaume then teleported somewhere else and stayed invisible. The three agents were still looking around with Guillaume behind them; Guillaume was waiting for the right moment! Closely behind one of the CIA Agents Guillaume was getting ready to make his next kill; then all of a sudden using his bare-hands Guillaume snaps another CIA Agents neck. The other two agents suddenly turned around to see their colleague dead! "What the fuck is going on! Where is this guy?" asked one of the agents; the other agent stood there frozen with fear! Then Guillaume suddenly appeared visible and the two CIA Agents couldn't believe what they had just seen! "Hey! How did you do that?" asked the agent frantically. Guillaume didn't respond and immediately did Martial Arts kicks & punches on the two agents. Even though it was a 2-on-1 situation the two CIA Agents had no chance against Guillaume. When the two CIA Agents were completely worn-out Guillaume then killed them instantly by snapping both of their necks; Guillaume had achieved his objectives! Guillaume then went to look for Valeria & Mateo; and when he found them Valeria breathed a big sigh of relief! "It's all OK now Valeria, they're all dead!" said Guillaume; Valeria had a slight smile on her face. "Good! I feel a lot safer now!" responded Valeria; Guillaume nodded a little at Valeria in agreement. "Let's just go & get the train back to Maine." said Guillaume; Valeria then returned

Guillaume his jacket & rucksack. Guillaume then put on his jacket and his rucksack over his back. "When we get out on the other side of the park we're only 5 minutes away from the train station." explained Guillaume; the three of them then made their way to Houston Train Station.

When Guillaume, Valeria & Mateo arrived at Houston Train Station an Amtrak train was already there waiting to go to Portland, Maine. They showed their tickets to the train-conductor and then boarded the train. Guillaume then went to find a private-cabin for all three of them and he did. When they got into the private-cabin they put their rucksacks into the luggage-compartment and went to sit down. "It's best if we keep our disguises on until we get nearer to the Quebec-US border." explained Guillaume; Valeria understood what he meant and complied. The train-conductor then blew the whistle to signal the train to depart; the train was now in motion...it is now on its way to Portland, Maine. Freedom waits for Valeria & Mateo!

Chapter 12:
Safe & Sound!

There was a huge Police presence in the Houston shopping-mall who were investigating all of the killings caused by Guillaume Moreau. What shocked the Police was how one person was able to kill that many people. Some Police-Detectives were in the park where Guillaume killed the five CIA Agents. The area where Bob was killed, again some of the Police were in complete shock at all of Bob's organs splattered everywhere. The Police-Detectives and forensics just didn't know what to do!

Guillaume, Valeria & Mateo were about 30 minutes from Portland Train Station in Maine. It was a long journey for them but, they all had a comfortable ride in the end. "Well Valeria, Mateo we're nearly there to Portland Station." said Guillaume with a slight smile on his face. Valeria breathed a sigh of relief and then gave a big smile. Mateo was equally as happy & relieved considering what he went through the past few days! What all three of them did was to collect their rucksacks from the luggage-compartment and then put on their winter-jackets, hats & gloves on. They all still had their disguises on.

The train had eventually arrived at Portland Station and the three of them then got off the train and made their way to the US-Quebec Border. They were going to be as discrete as they can so no-one will recognize them. It was going to be quite a journey for them but, it wasn't going to be a difficult one! About after two hours they were still on their journey with about 45 minutes to the French Embassy on the Quebec border. They had walked and taken different modes of public-transport on their long journey. Guillaume then looked around and noticed that the coast was as clear as day! "OK, we can take our disguises off! There's no-one around plus there aren't any security-cameras." said Guillaume; they all took their wigs off and cleaned their faces off too! When that was done they put their woolly-hats & gloves back on and then pulled the jacket-hoods over their heads. They wanted to be a little more discrete just in case; the three of them were now about 30 minutes from the French Embassy.

They arrived at the French Embassy on the Quebec-Border and Guillaume showed his DGSE badge at the entrance. He also explained about Valeria's & Mateo's situation in which was acknowledged. Inside the French Embassy Valeria gave in her passport & Mateo's too; the officials immediately processed the paper-work. Guillaume just stood there observing what is going on; he felt at this time his mission has been accomplished! Straight away Valeria told the Embassy Officials what the USA & Mexico are attempting at planning the invasion of Canada. Valeria even showed the secret documents she stole from her previous work-place; they were all shocked at what the USA & Mexico are planning! "Commandant Moreau; we have all the information we need. We're going to pass these on to both the Canadian & Quebec Governments then a plan of action can be established." explained one of the officials. When they finished with Valeria the officials took her & Mateo immediately into Protective Custody. Guillaume had to wait so he could give his final mission-briefing.

Guillaume spent about 90 minutes giving his final report to the French Embassy; he had to lie a few times so no-one will find out about his paranormal powers especially teleportation! However, the French Embassy Officials were completely satisfied with Guillaume's account of the mission; when that was done it was filed and locked away out of sight. "Thank you Commandant Moreau, that is all we need." said the official, "No problem! By the way I'm really exhausted is it OK if I can stay the night and return to Quebec the next morning?" asked Guillaume, "Of course you can Commandant. I can see how drained you really are." replied the official, "Thank you. Can someone inform Générale Lévesque that I am well." requested Guillaume; the official nodded at Guillaume and immediately went to inform DGSE (Q). All Guillaume wanted to do was to have a big rest!

At DGSE (Q) Générale Lévesque was at her desk doing some paper-work when she got a knock on her door. "Entrée!" replied Générale Lévesque; it was René! "Madame, I have some good news! I have just received a call from the French Embassy and they have informed me that the mission was a success. Commandant Moreau is staying at the Embassy tonight then he'll return to Quebec tomorrow!" explained René; Générale Lévesque had a big relief on her face! "That's brilliant news! Let the Embassy know that I need Moreau to report here as soon as possible."

ordered Générale Lévesque; René nodded in acknowledgment and immediately went to deal with Générale Lévesque's request!

It was well into the evening and Guillaume had a hot shower in which he needed very much; he wanted to go to bed early that night. All of a sudden he gets a knock on his bedroom door; Guillaume went to open the door....it was Valeria! "Sorry to bother you Guillaume I know that you're going back to Quebec tomorrow. I wanted to say thank you for your help and for keeping Mateo & me alive. I will never forget you!" said Valeria; Guillaume then smiled back at Valeria in return. "No problem I'm glad that I was able to help. And yes you're right I'm going back to Quebec the next day; my boss needs me for something else." explained Guillaume, "No rest for the wicked!" joked Valeria; Guillaume nodded! Valeria then hugged Guillaume and gave him a kiss on his cheek! Guillaume felt grateful at this; he knew how important the mission was to Valeria. The two of them said their goodbyes to each other and afterwards Valeria returned to her room. Guillaume immediately went to bed and turned out the lights...he was looking forward to his sleep!

Chapter 13:
Aftermath!

That same evening Guillaume was fast asleep; he was sleeping like a baby! He then goes into a very deep-sleep and begins to have another out-of-body experience. As Guillaume left his physical body he gets contacted by his Daemon again: "Guillaume, at this moment right now you are going to need a very big rest...so keep resting! Anyway, I wanted to tell you that you're going to develop a new power and it is the power of generating electricity out of your physical body. You will know how to do this...you have the power!" Guillaume's Daemon then left him to sleep and Guillaume continued to be in the deep-sleep state! All of a sudden Guillaume woke up in a flash; he then went to check the clock...it was 10:00 hours. Guillaume had been asleep for well over 12 hours! Immediately upon awakening Guillaume did Reiki movements all over his body. After he finished Guillaume went to the bathroom to have a good wash and then eat breakfast. Later on Guillaume went to get dressed and then got ready to leave the French Embassy to return to Quebec.

A few days had passed since the incident involving Guillaume, the CIA and the Police; the US Authorities had kept on investigating it very thoroughly. The CIA with the FBI had to be called in and they were investigating together very closely. However, it had proven to be very difficult for both Government Agencies; they could not identify the perpetrator, Guillaume. They ran his description over the systems and arrived at a dead-end! At the time of the incident Guillaume was so well-disguised the computer-systems just couldn't recognize him! The FBI & CIA all looked at each other in complete bewilderment; they all just didn't know what to do! The whole incident and the aftermath had made them all very nervous; so nervous that they all just wanted to crawl under a rock! In their minds they were all thinking: "What is this all about?"

After Valeria González gave all of the details about the attempted invasion of Canada by the USA & Mexico it was passed onto the Canadian, Quebec & French Governments to determine the next course of action. They all infiltrated the Lobos de Fuego and killed them all...the mission was a complete success! The Canadian media reported on television about the USA & Mexico attempting to invade Canada; the Canadian public were all horrified at the prospect. They all wondered why the two countries wanted to collude and invade Canada. Then the Canadian media went on in detail that the USA & Mexico wanted to use Canada for all kinds of contraband! It horrified the Canadian public even more! The Canadian & Quebec Governments reported this to the International Courts and they were informed that it will be investigated. When the US Government found out that their plans was reported all over the media they realized that they've all got eggs on their faces! They realized that the battle had been lost to Canada as a whole; in light of all that the US Government decided to close the investigation once and for all! The US Government had hit a very big brick-wall!

A few days had passed and Terrence & his family had won the big jackpot on the US lottery. All of his numbers and the star-ball came out; the whole family won $15 Million USD and it was going to change their lives for the better. What surprised Terrence and his family was that Guillaume knew exactly what the winning lottery numbers was going to be for that particular draw. The whole family temporarily moved to the US State of Maine whilst they waited for their Canadian Immigration application to be approved. It was going to look good for them as they have so much money. When Guillaume heard of Terrence's big fortune on TV he had a big smile on his face; he was so pleased that he was able to help the family out once and for all.

PART 1:
LONDON
INFERNO!

Chapter 14:
Return to London

Guillaume had just finished in one of his Martial Arts classes; he went to get dressed to make his way to town. He realized that he needed a new watch for himself and wanted to buy a good one. When Guillaume arrived in downtown Montréal he went to a watch-shop that sells all kinds of watches; Guillaume wanted a Casio watch as he was a big fan of that particular brand. He browsed through all of the Casio watches and there was one that caught his eye...a Casio Analogue-Digital Wave-Ceptor watch! What was particularly good about the watch was that it is radio-controlled and it gives the exact time in any country around the world. Guillaume's Daemon then says to him: "Buy that watch! It will be the last watch you'll ever have. Oh and by the way you won't need to change the batteries you have the power to make it last forever! That watch is very special!" Guillaume's eyes lit up with elation and so he bought the watch!

Générale Lévesque was in her office in the early hours of the morning; she switched on her TV and had her coffee in her hand. She decided to turn on to the BBC News channel; Générale Lévesque wanted to check the latest in London and around the UK in general. However, as Générale

Lévesque was watching the BBC News there was a piece that caught her eye:

"Good morning everyone I am here in Mainland Scotland and the Police are looking for any witnesses to an incident that occurred back in 1997. Here, there was a man who assaulted a Police-Officer; the Police-Officer himself was suspicious of the individual. The only description we can go on is that he had dark-skin nothing more. The assailant wore a baseball cap & sunglasses plus he had extraordinary Martial Arts skills!"

Générale Lévesque then realized something and decided to listen on just in case. The more she listened on the more worried she became. After the news piece had finished Générale Lévesque then said to herself: "It was Moreau!" That was the time when Guillaume went to Mainland Scotland to attend Martha's funeral. Générale Lévesque sat at her desk with her forehead leaning on one of her hands; she wondered how she was going to handle the situation! What Générale Lévesque did when it came on again she recorded that particular news piece!

It was about 10:30 hours in the morning that Guillaume arrived at DGSE (Q) to speak with Générale Lévesque. As soon as Guillaume entered the building he immediately went to take the elevator to the top-floor to Générale Lévesque's office. Upon arrival to the top-floor Guillaume then went to knock on Générale Lévesque's door; "Entrée!"...Guillaume then went straight in!

Guillaume stood at Générale Lévesque's desk waiting to see what she wanted. "Good morning Commandant Moreau; please take a seat." said Générale Lévesque; Guillaume then went to sit down straight away. "You

requested to see me Madame." said Guillaume, "Yes I did!
First things first; we managed to seek out the Lobos de
Fuego in Mexico and terminated all of them including
Valeria's ex-husband." explained Générale Lévesque;
Guillaume's eye-brows raised a little...he was pleased at the
outcome. "That's good to hear. How are Valeria & Mateo?
If it's OK to ask." pondered Guillaume; Générale Lévesque
then looked straight at Guillaume with a slight smile on her
face. "They are going to be well. What happened when we
infiltrated the Lobos de Fuego we seized all of their gold as
Valeria told us about this. Luckily, it wasn't stolen gold so
the Canadian, Quebec & French Governments will keep it
all for themselves. All of the profits will be divided between
the 3 Governments. The 2 gold bars Valeria took with her
before she made her long journey with Mateo; they let her
keep them. She had them valued and received a 7-figure
sum in total; she's going to buy a good house for herself &
Mateo plus Valeria is going to get home-schooling for her
son." explained Générale Lévesque, "Oh that's great to hear;
at least she will have a roof over her head and her son too,
mortgage-free." said Guillaume, "Yes you're right! Excellent
work, Moreau I knew you could do it!" complimented
Générale Lévesque; Guillaume smiled a little. He was
pleased with himself at the success of the mission! "No
problem; it was all worth it in the end." said Guillaume,
"Oh! I need to get something, I'll be a few minutes." said
Générale Lévesque as she got out of her chair. She then
left her office to collect something; whilst Guillaume was
waiting his Daemon then quickly says to him: "BE
PREPARED; THAT'S ALL I'M GOING TO SAY!"

Guillaume then wondered what his Daemon meant...he became slightly bemused!

A few minutes later Générale Lévesque returned to her office with a CD in her hand; she then went to sit back at her desk. "Sorry to keep you waiting Moreau I had to get something important. Anyway, I need to inform you that our Government wants you in London." explained Générale Lévesque; Guillaume's eyes suddenly flew open. He was not looking forward to it! "Why London? Why me?" asked Guillaume in a confused state; Générale Lévesque then gazed at Guillaume with a slightly stern look! "I'll tell you in a minute but, first I need to ask you a couple of questions before your next mission! Are you ready?" asked Générale Lévesque; Guillaume then looked straight at her! "OK, I'm ready!" replied Guillaume, "Good! I need to ask you first, after the incident when you were on your first mission from Manchester to London you assaulted the UK Police & Interpol Agents. I realized the stress that you were under which is very unusual because I know how very good you are under pressure. I'm wondering whether you can hold it together for when I send you to London. That is my great concern!" explained Générale Lévesque; Guillaume then went silent for a bit! "Well do I have a choice in going to London?" pondered Guillaume, "No! There are two reasons why you must be in London for this mission. Before I tell you the other reason I must ask you the second question. Let me play this CD before I ask." replied Générale Lévesque as she inserted the CD into the DVD player. It was the recorded news-piece of the incident where Guillaume assaulted the Police-Officer up in Scotland; Guillaume then realized why his Daemon said to him to be prepared! "Well this is interesting! When I heard the man was dark-skinned and had great Martial Arts skills I thought could it be you? Then the icing on the cake; I remembered it was at the time of Martha's death. You were still in the French Army back then in 1997; I remember getting you permission to leave to attend her funeral. That's when I realized it was definitely you!" explained Générale Lévesque; Guillaume sat there saying nothing! He realized that he has been backed into a corner. "OK it was me that attacked the Police-Officer up in Scotland!" confessed Guillaume, "So do you have any explanations on why you did this?" questioned Générale Lévesque; Guillaume then took a deep breath! "Well Madame a few days after the funeral I had to meet John in a private setting. He was Martha's close friend, the one who helped me get to China back in 1989. What happened the Police found out that I stayed at Martha's home before I went to China and they were all after me for the multiple murders. The day I went to meet John I first went to buy a newspaper at a small shop and there was a Police-Officer in there too. People looked at me weirdly and after I paid for the newspaper I quickly went on my way. The same Police-Officer followed me and called out to me; then he put his hand on my shoulder I put him in a Martial Arts grip and flipped him over. I did a Martial Arts kick on him and then carried on walking to meet John. Générale, I had no choice!" explained Guillaume; as displeased as Générale Lévesque was at Guillaume's actions that day she clearly understood why he did what he did! "OK, let me go and do something. Whilst I'm gone I'll let you cool down for a while; I'll be a little while but, not too long." said Générale Lévesque as she left her office once again.

Générale Lévesque returned to her office 30 minutes later and upon returning she noticed Guillaume was looking a little tensed! "Commandant Moreau, I realize you're a little reluctant to go but, it is of great importance and I have no choice but to send you to London." explained Générale Lévesque; Guillaume was still feeling very reluctant to go to London! "So why do you want to send me there?" asked Guillaume, "Well you know I said there are 2 reasons why I want you to go. The first is that you were born & raised in England for the first 12 years of your life; you would know parts of England well....especially London!" replied Générale Lévesque; Guillaume was now beginning to realize that he can't back out of the mission! "So what's the other reason?" asked Guillaume; Générale Lévesque then took a deep breath! "Well, remember the Yugoslavian-War...it is to do with that! There's a group called the Yugoslavian-6 operating in London." replied Générale Lévesque; Guillaume then had a bemused look on his face! "So what is this all about?" asked Guillaume; Générale Lévesque then handed him an A4-size envelope! "Well this group they were the main guys who orchestrated the Yugoslavian Civil War. But, there is a bigger picture behind all of this. The Yugoslavian-6 wants to take over the whole of Europe and get rid of the EU altogether. They want an authoritarian rule over the whole of Europe!" explained Générale Lévesque; Guillaume then opened the envelope and noticed six names on a piece of paper. "I take it this is the Yugoslavian-6 group?" pondered Guillaume, "Yes it is. The leader is called

Dragan and his other associates are Stojan, Vendran, Novak, Bogdan & Vlatko. We have been ordered to terminate all of them. However, there's a bigger problem." said Générale Lévesque, "OK, tell me!" said Guillaume, "There is a syndicate working with them plus we found out that Police Officers & Detectives are working with them. Plus, there is another reason why you must go to England; there's a group called the Indian-Bandits...they're from Bedford! The town you use to live in before you ran away!" explained Générale Lévesque; Guillaume began to panic a little! "This gets even worse....could it get any better!" said Guillaume sarcastically! Générale Lévesque then looked directly at Guillaume! "I'm sorry Moreau, I know how difficult it is for you but, we have to do this it is a matter of life or death! And please be very vigilant if you get caught by the British Police you've had it! Once they find out who you are i.e. a wanted serial-killer you are well & truly fucked! The UK Police want to hang you to dry especially for the other incidents. That's why I told you to keep it together!" explained Générale Lévesque; Guillaume then realized that he has to keep it together for his next mission! "OK, I will keep it together!" said Guillaume; Générale Lévesque had a slight smile on her face! "Good! What I need to do is wait for the documents on the Indian-Bandits for more information." said Générale Lévesque.

Guillaume and Générale Lévesque had both spent considerable time discussing his upcoming mission; the more it was discussed the more Guillaume became agitated inside his body! "Well Commandant Moreau at this moment in time that's all we've got so far. The further information should arrive any time soon today; so what I want you to do is pack your bags tonight. We're going to fly out to Paris tomorrow morning for a Government briefing and by the way you're going to work with the DGSE Agents based in Paris." explained Générale Lévesque, "Oui Madame!" responded Guillaume; when their one-on-one meeting finished Guillaume immediately left the DGSE (Q) building to return home so he could pack his bags to get ready to go & fly out to Paris. Even though Guillaume still felt reluctant to go he felt it was his duty for the Republic of France!

Chapter 15:
Onward to Paris

Morning had arrived and Guillaume was getting some of his belongings ready to fly out to Paris with Générale Lévesque. A few minutes before he was due to leave home Guillaume had a thought and decided to test his new power, generating electricity out of his body! So Guillaume took three deep breaths and then closed his eyes; he then went deep inside and all of a sudden he could feel electricity inside his body! Guillaume then opened his eyes and with his two hands a ball of electricity was generated. Guillaume couldn't believe his eyes at what he was able to do; when he was ready Guillaume left his residence to make his way to DGSE (Q).

When Guillaume arrived at DGSE (Q) Générale Lévesque was already there waiting inside the building for him. "Bonjour Commandant, are you ready to go?" asked Générale Lévesque, "Oui Madame, I have everything with me ready to go." replied Guillaume; Générale Lévesque nodded at him and the two of them made their way out of the building to get into a car. One of the DGSE (Q) staff members was going to drive them to the airport.

Going through the border-checks at the airport was quick & easy for both Guillaume and Générale Lévesque; once that was completed the two of them boarded the Air

France plane to Paris. Lucky for the two of them the French Government purchased first-class tickets; when they found their seats Guillaume & Générale Lévesque immediately went to sit down. "Wow! I've never been in a first-class before; this is a big surprise!" complimented Guillaume, "Yes, I had to get first-class for us. When we're up in the air we need to discuss the mission in detail." explained Générale Lévesque; the plane was now ready to fly. All of the passengers were strapped in at take-off they were now all on their way to Paris.

Whilst in flight Générale Lévesque was now ready to discuss the mission to Guillaume. She then takes an A4-size envelope out of her bag; the envelope had the words LONDON INFERNO written on it! "Commandant, here's the information I said that I was going to show you. The one about the Indian-Bandits." explained Générale Lévesque as she handed the envelope to Guillaume. He then opens the envelope and there were pages of paper; each one had a photo of every Indian-Bandit member with their names underneath. As Guillaume was going through each of them he nodded his head several times; Générale Lévesque was observing him. "Do you recognize them, Commandant?" asked Générale Lévesque; Guillaume then looked straight at her! "Yes I do, Madame! I recognize their faces but at the time when I lived in Bedford I didn't know their names...until now!" replied Guillaume; Générale Lévesque then smiled at him! "That's why we really needed you for this mission; the Bedford link. By the way the first paper, the really fat Indian man; he is the leader of the Indian-Bandits. Unfortunately, he is only known as

Fhazzaar. No-one has any clue what his full-name is!"
explained Générale Lévesque; Guillaume was taken aback
by this! "Well, this is interesting! I do recognize his face
too from when I was in Bedford! We have to go on the
information we have." said Guillaume; Générale Lévesque
then pulled out another A4-size envelope in reference to
the same mission. "This envelope I have here, there is a
homosexual gang called the 'Bum-Lords' and they are from
Luton. I understand it is near Bedford." said Générale
Lévesque, "Yes it is 30 minutes away by car...I've been there
a few times." responded Guillaume; Générale Lévesque
opened the letter and showed the photos of the Bum-Lords.
"We have photos of all members of the Bum-Lords but,
unsure what their names are. Do you by any chance know
them?" pondered Générale Lévesque; Guillaume looked
closely at the photos of the Bum-Lords. "Unfortunately, I
don't know them at all, Madame. I have never seen them
before in my life." explained Guillaume, "OK no problem.
Hopefully, when we get to Paris they will have more
information. Our people are working on finding out what
their names are! What it is both the Indian-Bandits & the
Bum-Lords are part of the Yugoslavian-6 syndicate and there
are others too!" explained Générale Lévesque, "Looks like
we have a big fish to fry." said Guillaume, "Yes, you're right!
For all our sakes in this case failure is not an option."
explained Générale Lévesque; Guillaume nodded at her in
agreement. Générale Lévesque went on in more detail about
the London Inferno Mission...the more it was explained to
Guillaume the more he realized how important it is to
complete the upcoming mission!

When the plane landed in Paris both Guillaume and Générale Lévesque got off the plane and went immediately to the border-control. It was easy for them to get through the border-checks as they both possess French Passports. After they collected their belongings there was a DGSE staff member waiting for them to drive them to DGSE Paris. Immediately they got inside the car and went straight to DGSE HQ for the mission briefing!

Chapter 16:
Mission briefed

U pon arrival at DGSE HQ in Paris both Guillaume and Générale Lévesque got out of the car and entered the building immediately. At the reception area the two of them showed their DGSE badges and afterwards they went to meet up with the DGSE Chief, Stéphane Bastien. "What is going to happen Moreau is that we are going to meet up with Stéphane Bastien and briefly go over the mission. Then what we are going to do next is to meet the other agents you're working with." explained Générale Lévesque; Guillaume is the only DGSE (Q) Agent on the mission as all the others are French-based! "I understand Madame; let's get this mission over and done with!" responded Guillaume; Générale Lévesque could feel that Guillaume is very uncomfortable at going to London. The two of them got to the elevator and went straight to the top-floor.

They arrived at Stéphane Bastien's office and the three of them had a small briefing about the London-Inferno mission. "Commandant Moreau, it's good to see you again. How's everything in Quebec?" asked Stéphane; Guillaume smiled a little at Stéphane! "It's all good in Quebec I'm enjoying there." replied Guillaume; Stéphane smiled at Guillaume due to his response. "Commandant Moreau was very successful at Operation Brownsville. He managed to avert the hostile take-over of Canada & Quebec!" explained Générale Lévesque, "Yes I am aware of this. Congratulations Commandant Moreau on your mission success." complimented Stéphane, "Merci Monsieur!" responded Guillaume; Stéphane then took out a slim file and handed it over to Guillaume. The file was opened and there was a photo of an attractive blond woman. "The woman you're looking at is named Simone Jane Robinson. Her statistics are behind the photo; she is going to help us eliminate the Yugoslavian-6!" explained Stéphane; Guillaume then looked at Stéphane with a slight confused look on his face! "How is she going to help us? How is she linked to all of this?" asked Guillaume, "Well Commandant, Miss Robinson was forced to work for Dragan & the Yugoslavian-6; her life was at stake. She is the key to helping us; we've done a deal with Miss Robinson to get her out of the UK and to get her to French-Switzerland. It will be safer for her to stay there. The French-Swiss Government are working with us on this mission and they are fully aware. By the way there's more." explained Stéphane; he then looked at Guillaume with a slight concerned look on his face! "OK, tell me!" responded Guillaume, "Well the UK Police are after Simone and they want to arrest her for various crimes involving the Yugoslavian-6. We have to save her and get her out or it's all over! We have all decided that you should be the agent to rescue her!" explained Stéphane, "Oh! OK, I'll do it!" responded Guillaume, "Merci! There will be a briefing with the other agents on this mission. It is going to commence in 20 minutes." explained Stéphane; immediately Guillaume & Générale Lévesque made their way to the briefing-room.

Guillaume and Générale Lévesque were the only ones in the briefing-room; they had to wait for Stéphane and the other DGSE Agents to arrive. To pass the time Guillaume decided to delve more into the file of Simone Jane Robinson; the file was clipped to her photo. As Guillaume was reading the profile of Simone he noticed that she was born in 1979, in other words she is two years younger than Guillaume. He also noticed that Simone is tall for a British Woman at 5'9" that is she is two inches taller than Guillaume; it surprised him a bit! Then there was something that Guillaume read about Simone which gave him a shock! Simone Robinson was a runaway child who has been missing since she was 13 years old; again it reminded Guillaume when he ran away at age 12. Guillaume didn't know what to think; all kinds of thoughts were going through his mind! "Madame this Simone; she ran away at age 13!" explained Guillaume; Générale Lévesque then turned her head and looked straight at Guillaume with a stern look on her face! "Oui I know! What happened when Miss Robinson reported the Yugoslavian-6 to the French Embassy she also explained to them that she was a runaway child many years ago. Simone's parents were extremely nasty to her plus Simone's school-life was really bad. Simone explained that she had no choice and just ran away!" explained Générale Lévesque; Guillaume then realized that even though he was reluctant to go to London that he has to go no matter what! He then became sentimental about Simone Jane Robinson! "Wow! Her story is so similar to mine; I know how she feels." said Guillaume; Générale Lévesque then looked at him again! "Moreau, don't let your emotions cloud your judgement. You have an important mission to complete!" explained Générale Lévesque; Guillaume then nodded in agreement! Stéphane and the five other agents then entered the briefing-room; they all introduce themselves to each other and then all of them sat down for the meeting.

During the meeting Stéphane went on to explain in detail for Operation: London-Inferno; all of them listened carefully with great intent:

"OK everyone! We have realized there's a bigger picture involving the Yugoslavian-6; they all want to take over the whole of Europe and run the whole continent their way. Also, we have found out that there are a lot of members of the UK Police whom are heavily involved. YES it really does get deeper than that! There are rumours that 6 UK Politicians who are also heavily involved with the Yugoslavian-6. But, I would like to stress it is only speculation!"

Hearing this gave the DGSE Agents a great big shock! They pondered whether there are UK Politicians involved and if so, who are the UK Politicians? Stéphane then goes on:

"The Yugoslavian-6 are into all kinds of contraband crime; illegal arms-trading; drug-trafficking & manufacturing too then lastly money-laundering. Now onto Simone Jane Robinson; as she is working with us she is going to be our eyes & ears. We requested that she stay with the Yugoslavian-6 for her own safety as well. That way she won't arouse any suspicion. Commandant Moreau will be the one to rescue Simone Robinson; then we must terminate the Yugoslavian-6 and their syndicate including the UK Police!"

All of the DGSE Agents looked at each other in reference to the orders given to them; the agents realized that they have to be as discrete as they can. But, at the same time they know it had to be done for the sake of the whole of Europe! Stéphane then went on again:

"So on to the next part; we managed to get the other syndicates, the Bum-Lords & the D-Turks. Thankfully we have the names of both syndicates of the Yugoslavian-6. The Bum-Lords are Silas Peale, the leader, Alan Butt, Thomas Whitfield, Albert Faizan, Perry Thornbird, Wilmot Ellis & Parker Hills. The D-Turks are Mustafa Demir, Yusuf Derrish, Serkan Dincher, Burah Doruh, Ozan Dursan, Volkan Durmaz & Ahmet Diyadin. As you can all see all of their surnames begin with the letter 'D' hence, why they are called the D-Turks. So now I have given you all of the information the only thing I need to say is BON CHANCE!"

When the briefing had finished Guillaume and the other DGSE Agents then went to get ready. "Commandant Moreau, I want to wish you well on the mission. I'm going to remain here in France until the mission is completed!" explained Générale Lévesque, "Merci Madame! Don't worry I won't take too long!" said Guillaume as he left the briefing-room to get ready for his mission!

Chapter 17:
Arrival to London

The five French-based DGSE Agents that Guillaume is going to work with all have extensive French-Military experience prior to joining the French Secret Service. The names of the five DGSE Agents are: Capitaine de Corvette Xavier Maurice, Commissaire Capitaine Matthieu Fournier, Commissaire Colonel Christophe Pointu, Commissaire Colonel Raphaëlle Petit and Commissaire Capitaine Thérèse Lavoine. With the exception of Xavier Maurice four of them have served in the French Army for many years; Xavier Maurice was previously in the French Navy.

Guillaume and the other five DGSE Agents took the Eurostar Train from Paris to London Kings Cross International Station. To avoid any suspicions all six DGSE Agents had to sit far away from each other. Also what the DGSE Agents did was to conceal their identity as much as they can so as not to show their faces too much. As Guillaume was sitting on the train minding his own business his Daemon speaks to him again: "Just a reminder that you possess a new power; you will need to use it for your upcoming mission. I know that you're not too happy at going to the UK but, it is of the utmost importance. Don't worry I'll help you along the way for your mission!"

Guillaume then realized that he had to do the mission; he became more determined than ever!

The six DGSE Agents arrived in London Kings Cross International Station; they all got off but, in complete separation. When Guillaume stepped off the train he looked around the station; he was thinking back to 1997 when he was fighting in the Yugoslavian war that he teleported from Yugoslavia to London and murdered both Alice Love & Eliza Murray who were pupils from his old school in the UK! In his mind Guillaume didn't care; he was just glad he did it! Each of the DGSE Agents went to a different border-gate for the passport checks. When Guillaume had his passport checked he used his mind-control to ensure that the Border-Guard wouldn't remember him afterwards. The DGSE Agents got through the border-gate with complete success!

Much later on that same day all six DGSE Agents met at a secret hideaway far away from everything. They were all informed of the secret place beforehand back at DGSE HQ in Paris. "OK everyone where shall we start?" asked Xavier; they all looked at one another. "Well for starters we need to locate some of the Yugoslavian-6's secret bases where they do all of the drug-manufacturing. Remember we have been instructed to blow-up those buildings." explained Matthieu, "Oh by the way, did someone mention about one of the Indian-Bandits being in London?" asked Christophe; Guillaume's Daemon then suddenly says to him: "Volunteer to kill him!" Guillaume then remembers who it was! "Is it Rajak Kumbhare?" asked Guillaume, "Yes that's the one!" responded Christophe, "So where is he located?" asked

Guillaume, "Well he's not far away from here. We need to spy on him and when he leads us to the Indian-Bandits hide-out we need to terminate all of them!" said Christophe; Guillaume then thought this is his opportunity! "Everyone! Let me do this one on my own. Let's not rush into anything just yet; what I suggest you all do is look for the locations of some of the Yugoslavian-6's bases and then we'll meet up later and discuss what we'll do next!" suggested Guillaume; all of the five DGSE Agents looked at one another and all nodded in agreement! Guillaume was going to be the DGSE Agent to deal with the Indian-Bandits; what they all did was to go through the plan and how to get around London. As Guillaume knew London well he discussed with his colleagues in detail on how to get around London with considerable ease.

It was about 17:00 hours and being in the winter-season it was very dark outside. The Agents realized this would be the perfect time to disband and move on with their separate missions. They all left the secret hide-out separately staying well-disguised so they don't get identified; Guillaume then went on his mission to seek out Rajak Kumbhare...he was looking forward to killing him!

Chapter 18:
Déjà Vu

At 18:00 hours Guillaume on his own was able to locate Rajak Kumbhare; he was on his way to a café. Guillaume was observing from a distance; he was wondering whether Rajak is on his own or is he going to meet with someone else? To keep his identity concealed Guillaume was wearing a plain baseball cap, sunglasses and a long wig as a disguise! He then decided to follow Rajak into the café keeping both his distance and a low-profile. There was quite a queue in the café Rajak had a tray in his hands with some food & drink; Guillaume then thought he'll order some food & drink too! When Guillaume looked around he decided to choose carrot-cake and a small carton of almond milk...luckily for him the carrot-cake was 100% free of preservatives & additives. Guillaume wanted something healthy; he was strict about his own health. As Guillaume was queuing up to pay for his items four Police-Officers then entered the café...they were on their break. Two of the Police-Officers were male and the other two were female; they all chose their items and queued up to pay. After Rajak paid for his items he went to take a seat at a small table; Guillaume quickly observed Rajak for a bit. A few minutes later it was Guillaume's turn to pay; he put his tray of items on the counter. "Would you like anything else?" asked the

Barista; Guillaume shook his head a 'No!' answer. "OK! I
take it that you're not that hungry!" joked the Barista;
Guillaume didn't respond at all and paid for his items.
Everyone in the queue and the Police-Officers looked at
Guillaume in a weird way; after Guillaume paid for his items
he went to sit at a small-table in the corner on his own so he
could observe Rajak Kumbhare.

   Guillaume was in the café for about forty minutes; he
had already finished eating his carrot-cake. Rajak was still in
there too minding his own business; Guillaume then took
out a packet of wipes and from it took out one wipe and
cleaned the plate of his own DNA. The four Police-Officers
who were on their break saw what Guillaume had just done
and grew very suspicious of him! As Guillaume was
observing Rajak closely at the same time the four
Police-Officers were observing Guillaume closely!
Guillaume's Daemon then said to him: "Guillaume, I need
to warn you! There are 4 Police-Officers there who are
looking at you suspiciously! Be on your guard!" Guillaume
was aware of what his Daemon told him even though his
eyes were squarely locked on Rajak Kumbhare! Guillaume
then opened the carton of almond-milk; Rajak was
completely unaware that he was being spied on considering
Guillaume is wearing sunglasses. The other customers were
also looking at Guillaume constantly; however even though
Guillaume was aware of this it didn't bother him at all!

   Another 15 minutes later Rajak was finished in the café
and he decided to leave to go somewhere. Guillaume had
finished his almond-drink and put the empty carton into his
jacket-pocket; everyone there grew even more suspicious of

him. As Rajak left the café Guillaume continued to observe
him through the glass-window. Guillaume then got out of
his seat and decided to go and follow Rajak; however, the
four Police-Officers go up to Guillaume and stop him in his
tracks. "Excuse me! May I ask you some questions?" asked
one of the Police-Officers; Guillaume stood there saying
nothing! The four Police-Officers all looked at each other
with bemused looks; everyone in the café were as equally
bemused! "Excuse me! I said can I ask you some questions?"
asked the same Police-Officer angrily; Guillaume then
looked behind himself outside the window! He realized that
Rajak was getting away and needed to act quickly!
Immediately Guillaume did a Martial Arts punch and
knocked the Police-Officer to the ground! Everyone there
went into complete shock at what they had seen; the other
three Police-Officers then attempted to apprehend
Guillaume but they were no match for him! Using all of
his Martial Arts knowledge Guillaume was able to defend
himself and knock all of the Police-Officers down. The
customers & Baristas were completely surprised at
Guillaume's physical attributes; they all wondered where he
got it from! Then Guillaume did spinning-kicks on three of
the Police-Officers knocking them out cold in the process.
The first Police-Officer whom Guillaume punched had
managed to get up but, he was in a completely dazed state;
when Guillaume noticed this immediately he did a Martial
Arts side-kick on him and the Police-Officer went flying
through the glass window! Again everyone in the café froze
in shock! Then all of a sudden a customer went up to
Guillaume and said: "Hey what are you doing?" Guillaume

then pulled out his hand-gun and pointed it at the customer; the customer suddenly backed away from Guillaume! The rest of the customers all cowed down under their tables! They all feared for their lives; however, Guillaume put his hand-gun away and left the café to go after Rajak Kumbhare. One of the Barista's immediately went to call the Police!

On his own Rajak was walking along but, at a distance Guillaume was not far behind him! Rajak suddenly hears something and looks over his shoulder; Guillaume immediately hid out of sight! Rajak couldn't see anything behind him and so walked on; Guillaume continued to follow Rajak. Guillaume decided to get a little closer to Rajak and so he did! Rajak then stopped and went to get out a cigarette to have a smoke; Rajak was about to light up his cigarette when suddenly Guillaume grabs him and pulls him into an alleyway out of sight! In the alleyway Guillaume puts Rajak up against a wall and then gets out his hand-gun and points it directly to his head! "Hands up Monsieur and don't move a muscle!" ordered Guillaume; Rajak complied and raised his hands! "What do you want? I don't have any valuables!" said Rajak; Guillaume looked sternly at him! "I am not after your money...Rajak Kumbhare of the Indian-Bandits!" responded Guillaume; Rajak then went into shock! "What! How do you know who I am?" asked Rajak, "Well Monsieur I am in the French Secret Service. We are after the Yugoslavian-6 in which we are fully aware that the Indian-Bandits being one of their syndicates!" replied Guillaume; Rajak stood there in shock! He didn't know what to say! "So what do you want from me?" further asked Rajak, "Well, firstly I want to know where you are going and I'll spare your life!" demanded Guillaume; Rajak then took a big gulp! "Well I'm going to meet up with some friends of mine down the road!" replied Rajak, "Are they with the Indian-Bandits too?" questioned Guillaume; Rajak then nodded a meekly 'yes' response! Guillaume then stood there in silence for a bit still pointing his hand-gun at Rajak! "OK, tell me their names!" demanded Guillaume; Rajak was hesitant to tell Guillaume. "OK, OK! I'll tell you! My best mate, his name is Paavak Nupur; then there are two more! Their names are Vihaan & Sarthak; that's all!" responded Rajak; Guillaume smirked a little at Rajak and put his hand-gun away. Then all of a sudden he kicks Rajak in his testicles and then snaps his neck; Rajak Kumbhare was now dead! Next for Guillaume was to go after Rajak's associates!

Guillaume was able to locate the place where Rajak was going to meet up with Paavak, Vihaan & Sarthak. He hid away out of sight at first and waited for them to arrive! Suddenly at a distance Guillaume notices three Indian men arrive at that spot; his Daemon then says: "Yes those are the 3 men that Rajak mentioned!" Guillaume then continued to stay out of sight! The three Indian-Bandits men were waiting for Rajak unaware that he has been murdered by Guillaume. "Where the fuck is Rajak....he's always late!" said Vihaan; all three of them looked around...not a soul in sight! "Looks like he's stalling us!" said Sarthak; they still waited! Then all of a sudden Guillaume appeared! "I killed that little fucker!" explained Guillaume; the three Indian men turned around and saw Guillaume! "Who the fuck are you?" asked Paavak, "I am Commandant Guillaume Moreau of the French Secret Service!" replied Guillaume; the three Indian men had shock on their faces! Then Guillaume decided to use his new power for the first time; he generated electricity out of his body and fired directly at the three Indian men. It took them all by surprise; they were all on the ground in a lot of pain! Guillaume then walked up to them! "Right which one of you is going to tell me how to get to Fhazzaar, your leader!" demanded Guillaume, "Honestly we don't know! But, there's a woman called Sahita Hana; she's the wife of Joyab Hana. He has close links to Fhazzaar!" replied Sarthak, "Good, that's all I need!" said Guillaume; then all of a sudden he snapped the necks of the three Indian men and immediately left the scene. Luckily, there was no-one around so he was able to get away easily!

Chapter 19:
Breakthrough!

A couple of hours later Guillaume met up with his colleagues after killing some of the Indian-Bandits. Guillaume also informed his colleagues that he was able to extract information about the Indian-Bandits in some detail. "Everyone, we have a breakthrough. We need to get to Sahita Hana; her husband Joyab has close links to the leader, Fhazzaar." explained Guillaume, "So what shall we do?" asked Xavier, "Well we need to know how we can find Sahita Hana." said Matthieu; all of a sudden Guillaume's Daemon then says to him: "Guillaume, Sahita Hana is a part-time prostitute near Kings Cross Station. She'll be there soon, you can get her there!" Guillaume then wondered how he was going to approach the situation! "Everyone, I found out from the Indian-Bandits that Sahita is a part-time prostitute and that she's at Kings Cross Station!" explained Guillaume, "Oh! Really?" queried Christophe, "Yes! Usually between Kings Cross & Euston Stations there are a lot of prostitutes. I remember from my time there. Looks like nothing has changed there!" replied Guillaume, "What we need to do is apprehend Sahita and take her somewhere secluded and then we'll interrogate her!" suggested Raphaëlle, "That's a good idea! Let me get a van for all of us before we do this!" suggested Thérèse, "We have to be very discrete about this or the UK Authorities will be onto us!" explained Guillaume; all of the DGSE Agents nodded at Guillaume in agreement. When they were ready the Agents disbanded to go and apprehend Sahita Hana!

Earlier Thérèse was able to steal a black Ford van from a car dealership; it was easy for her to do this. Thérèse was driving with Guillaume in the passenger-seat; he had to be in front as he had to give directions around London. The other four DGSE Agents were all in the back; they all had put on their balaclavas on to conceal their identities! When they got near to Kings Cross Station Guillaume & Thérèse could see all of the prostitutes lining up for any potential male-clients. Most of the prostitutes were white British women with some who are oriental and a few of Afro-Caribbean origin. Then all of a sudden they noticed an Indian woman there....it was Sahita Hana! "Everyone, that's her...go around the again and then at the right moment we'll get her!" instructed Guillaume; Thérèse complied and drove around the block. When they reached the prostitution area again they got a little closer and noticed that Sahita was alone; then all of a sudden a car pulled over towards her. "Hey are you looking for a good time?" asked Sahita to the client; the man in the car smiled at Sahita and then nodded! The French Agents had noticed this and wondered on what to do next! "Everyone, let's get her now! We have no time to lose!" ordered Guillaume; immediately Thérèse stopped the van! Guillaume and the other four DGSE Agents got out of the van and then went for Sahita! All of the other prostitutes looked on with horror! Then the agents all grabbed Sahita; she started to kick & scream! "Hey! What the fuck are you doing to me?" screamed Sahita; the Agents said nothing! Then the prospective male-client got out of his car with an angry look on his face! "Hey I got her first; get your own fucking prostitute!" shouted the man; he then pulled out a knife from his pocket! When Guillaume had noticed this he pulled out his hand-gun and shot the man a few times...he was now dead! The other prostitutes and other potential male-clients all screamed with horror; when the DGSE Agents had managed to get Sahita inside the van Guillaume then got out a grenade and threw it at the dead-man's car. Next, Guillaume got into the van and Thérèse drove off...the car then explodes! In the back of the van one of the Agents chloroformed Sahita to knock her out and had managed to achieve this. Next, the DGSE Agents then tied Sahita's arms & legs together; again they had achieved their objectives!

Later on that night the Police arrived at the scene where Sahita Hana was abducted; they were collecting statements from all of the witnesses. However, the Police had reached a dead-end; they had no idea who is behind all of this! They then found out that the van used for the crime was a stolen one but, no-one knows who stole it! The Police were now all pondering is there a bigger picture behind all of this? It had really baffled all of them!

Chapter 20:
Mysterious killings

It was the morning after the incident involving Sahita Hana in the prostitution area of Kings Cross Station; the Police & Detectives were still trying to piece together on what the motive was. Then a Police-Detective named Marcus Williams realized something about Sahita Hana! "Hey everyone, I just realized that Sahita Hana is a member of a group called the Indian-Bandits. They're a criminal gang that is into all kinds of contraband but, mainly drug-trafficking!" explained Detective Williams. The Police were now beginning to wonder if there's a connection with the Indian-Bandits! The Police decided to return to the station to investigate this further.

The BBC News reported the incident that occurred on the previous night at Kings Cross. The News-Reader said:

"Last night at Kings Cross Station a prostitute by the name of Sahita Hana was abducted by a group of masked individuals. Also, at the same time a prospective customer was shot dead by one of the masked individuals who had his car exploded by a grenade. The van used to abduct Sahita Hana was reported stolen earlier that same night. Anyone who has any information about the incident please contact the Police immediately."

Watching the news from his TV was the Indian-Bandits leader Fhazzaar; he was wondering what is going on? Fhazzaar had also found out that the other members of his gang Rajak, Paavak, Vihaan & Sarthak were killed that same night. Fhazzaar was now beginning to wonder is somebody after his gang? "Aarush, can you fetch Joyab for me." ordered Fhazzaar; Aarush Talwar who is one of the main guys of the Indian-Bandits went to get Joyab. When Joyab arrived he noticed a sullen-look on Fhazzaar's face; he was unaware that his wife Sahita had recently been abducted! "Joyab, I don't know how to tell you this but, we've just found out that your wife has been kidnapped!" explained Fhazzaar; Joyab then went into shock! "What! Who the fuck kidnapped her?" screamed Joyab; Fhazzaar stood there feeling helpless! He didn't know what to say! All of a sudden Joyab's brother Nuthan walked in; he heard Joyab panicking! "Hey bro! What's up?" asked Nuthan, "Someone's taken Sahita!" replied Joyab; Fhazzaar went onto explain about the abduction of Sahita and the murders of the four Indian-Bandits. Joyab went into confusion, he was wondering of it is all linked in some way. "Who is doing all of this?" asked Nuthan; Fhazzaar looked at him staying silent for a bit. He had a very worrying look on his face! "It could be Scotland Yard Police but, I think it is more likely MI5!" replied Fhazzaar, "What could MI5 want with us?" asked Nuthan in a startled way; again Fhazzaar paused for a bit! "Well considering all of the stuff we do, it is sufficed to say that is the reason they have vested interests in our group!" replied Fhazzaar; all three men stood there in total silence without saying a word; they felt trapped!

At the Police Station Detectives were still trying to piece together what happened; delving more into the case the Police found out about the murders of the four members of the Indian-Bandits occurred the same night as the abduction of Sahita Hana. The Police were now beginning to realize that the two incidents are linked; at the same time Police looked into the incident where Guillaume attacked the Police-Officers in the café. They realized that Rajak Kumbhare was last seen alive in the café; however, they had great difficulty in identifying Guillaume as he was well-disguised!

Later on that day Fhazzaar went to see the rest of his gang; he had the look as if he had just seen a ghost. All members of the Indian-Bandits looked at Fhazzaar with concerned looks on their faces; they knew something was wrong! "My sources have just told me that it was neither Scotland Yard Police nor MI5 that killed some of our guys the other night!" explained Fhazzaar; all of the Indian-Bandits looked at one another completely stunned! "So if it wasn't the Police or MI5, then who was it?" asked Nuthan; Fhazzaar didn't respond to Nuthan's question as he didn't have any answers. Fhazzaar was now getting scared and he realized all of this will affect his criminal gang; to him it was hurting his business!

Chapter 21:

Sahita interrogated!

There was Sahita Hana sitting on a chair in an unconscious state with her hands cuffed behind her back. Sahita's ankles were also cuffed to the legs of the chair; beside her was a small table with syringes on it. The syringes belonged to Sahita; she was known to be a heroin-addict! Guillaume looked at the syringes; he knew from his time in Bedford, England that Sahita Hana was and still is a drug-addict! Guillaume then asked one of his fellow agents to pass him a glass of water. When Guillaume received the glass of water he immediately threw water towards Sahita's face; immediately Sahita wakes up! "Where am I? What's going on? Who the hell are all of you?" asked Sahita in a shocked state; all of the DGSE Agents including Guillaume stayed silent for a bit! Sahita was now beginning to feel even more scared. "We have been after you for some time!" explained Guillaume, "Hey if you wanted an appointment with me all you had to do was to wait in the fucking line. You're all a bunch of fuckers!" shouted Sahita; all of the agents looked at each other without any emotion. "Shut up you fucking bitch!" shouted Guillaume, "What did you fucking call me? You're so lucky that I'm in hand-cuffs or else I would've smashed your face in!" shouted Sahita; Guillaume stood there with a sarcastic smile on his face.

"Mighty strong words...Sahita Hana of the Indian-Bandits! By the way, you wouldn't have a chance against me as I am heavily trained in the French-Military and in many forms of Martial Arts!" explained Guillaume; Sahita suddenly looked up at Guillaume with a concerned look on her face! "French-Military! Who the hell are you? How do you know my name and that I am a member of the Indian-Bandits?" asked Sahita; Guillaume looked at the other DGSE Agents and then nodded at all of them. "We work for the French Government, we are French Secret-Agents!" replied Guillaume; Sahita's eyes then flew wide open in shock! "What the hell does the French Secret Service want with us?" asked Sahita frantically; Guillaume then looked at her with a stern look. "Well put it this way; we all know that your gang are part of a syndicate controlled by the Yugoslavian-6!" explained Guillaume, "The Yugoslavian-6! What do you want with them?" asked Sahita, "Because they are a very dangerous group who want to take over the whole of Europe which is what none of us want!" replied Guillaume, "So what do you exactly want with me?" demanded Sahita, "Well we need you as a bargaining-tool. We will set you free if you lead us to the Indian-Bandits and once we find them, they will tell us the location of the Yugoslavian-6!" explained Guillaume; Sahita then realized that she has been backed into a very big corner! "I will never tell you; I am loyal to the Indian-Bandits!" shouted Sahita; Guillaume and the other DGSE Agents realized that they have hit a brick-wall! "OK! What we'll do is leave you as you are for a bit whilst we have a little meeting; let me go and get something!" said Guillaume; one of the agents passed Guillaume a hood! Sahita then looked on with fear on her face! "What are you going to do with that?" asked Sahita so meekly; again Guillaume had a little smirk on his face! "Well quite simply I'm going to put this hood over your head!" replied Guillaume, "What? Don't you fucking dare, I order you!" screamed Sahita; Guillaume then showed his gun to her! "If you don't do as I say I'll put a bullet in your head you fucking bitch!" shouted Guillaume; Sahita suddenly stopped talking! Guillaume then puts the hood over Sahita's head and afterwards all of the DGSE Agents went into another room to have a consultation. Sahita was left all alone restrained to a chair with a hood over her head; she was now beginning to feel a lot of fear all over her body!

The DGSE Agents were all discussing on how to approach the situation with Sahita Hana; they were all feeling tensed about it! "Hey everyone, I have an idea!" said Guillaume; all of the agents suddenly looked at Guillaume! "OK, tell us!" said Matthieu; Guillaume then smirked at his colleagues. "Well we could offer Sahita a false deal. Remember we have been ordered to kill all members of the Yugoslavian-6 and their syndicate. What we'll do is tell Sahita that if she helps us we can give her a place to live in i.e. another country. Then when we locate the Indian-Bandits and kill them we will kill her too!" explained Guillaume; all of the DGSE Agents nodded at each other in agreement. "That is a great idea Commandant Moreau, let's do this!" said Thérèse; the agents then made their way to inform Sahita Hana of the deal; they wondered whether she would accept it!

When they got to Sahita, Guillaume then removed the hood; Sahita hyperventilated a little as she gazed at the DGSE Agents! "Well Sahita I hope you're still comfortable, because we want to offer you a deal!" explained Guillaume, "No I am not comfortable considering I've been hand-cuffed for such a long time! By the way, what deal?" queried Sahita; all of the DGSE Agents stood there with stern looks on their faces! "OK listen up and listen good, I will say this only once!" said Guillaume; Sahita then took a deep breath! "OK I'm ready to listen!" responded Sahita; she listened on with intent! "So you are going to tell us where the Indian-Bandits are located; then we need to know where your drug-manufacturing place is. Now bear in mind that we have to kill all of the Indian-Bandits including your husband Joyab. But, you'll be the only one alive and then when we have finished our mission we will take you to another country. However, when you do emigrate you must never return to the UK because once you do you will be arrested!" explained Guillaume; Sahita suddenly had a shock over Guillaume's proposition! "You mean you have to kill my husband?" asked Sahita frantically, "Look Sahita we have no choice...we have been ordered by our Government to do this. Take it or leave it you're getting a good deal!" explained Guillaume, "But, I'm going to be all alone!" said Sahita, "Look you fucking bitch the Yugoslavian-6 started that horrible war in Yugoslavia. My comrades & I fought in that war for the whole of humanity, I am not letting this go all in vain!" shouted Guillaume; Sahita sat there in silence for a bit! She then began to ponder! "OK I'll do it!" said Sahita; all of the DGSE Agents breathed a slight sigh of relief! "Good! But, remember do as I say or I will kill you!" ordered Guillaume; Sahita nodded at Guillaume in agreement! The agents realized now they are getting somewhere; they are now ready to continue the mission. This was a case of now or never!

Chapter 22:
Mission progressing

The DGSE Agents & Sahita Hana spent some considerable time going over the plans of the Indian-Bandits. Sahita informed the agents of where their drug-manufacturing warehouse is located. Sahita also told the agents of the location of Fhazzaar's lair with the main people of the Indian-Bandits; the place itself is situated in the middle of nowhere on the very outskirts of London. "What it is we are all based in a town called Bedford but we meet at the secret lair on a regular basis!" explained Sahita; Guillaume then gave her a slight gaze! "Yes I know Bedford very well. I lived in that fucking shit-hole for 2 years before I left!" said Guillaume; Sahita then had a bemused look on her face! "What! You used to live in Bedford?" pondered Sahita, "Yes I did before I left to go to China and then France." explained Guillaume, "Why France? Are you actually French?" questioned Sahita, "Well my parents are from Mauritius which is French-speaking but, I was born in Crouch End, London. We moved to Bedford in 1987 but, I ran away from home in 1989 and went to Scotland first, then China. Eventually I went to France in early 1993; did my French National Service and after I completed it I joined the French Military!" explained Guillaume, "Oh! How did you get French Nationality that quickly?" asked Sahita,

"Considering my parents come from a French-speaking country & that I mainly have French heritage it was that easy!" replied Guillaume, "I remember back in 1989 that there was a boy who ran away from his school in Bedford. It was headline news!" said Sahita; Guillaume instantly knew it was him that Sahita was referring to! "Yes that boy was me. I got fed up with home & school so I decided to run away. Did me a lot of good!" confessed Guillaume; Sahita gasped in horror! "But, you are a wanted serial killer!" said Sahita; Guillaume then gave Sahita a slightly stern look. "Yes I am fully aware of this! Let's just leave it at that!" demanded Guillaume; Sahita decided not to say anymore on the subject!

Throughout the day the DGSE Agents went to kill other members of the Indian-Bandits one-by-one very discretely. Luckily it was easy for them to avoid detection. Guillaume was also able to eliminate them very discretely but, he couldn't use his paranormal powers or everyone including Sahita would know. However, due to Guillaume's heavy Martial Arts background it was easy for him! At all times Sahita stayed with Guillaume when he was out & about on his missions. The mission was going well for them and the Indian-Bandits were quickly dissipating; the next big task was to go to the drug-manufacturing warehouse to terminate the drug-makers there and then blow up the whole factory afterwards!

Later on in the evening the DGSE Agents with Sahita Hana made their way to the drug-manufacturing warehouse. When they arrived the DGSE Agents hid out of sight behind a lot of bushes. They knew it was in operation as they heard machinery sounds and noticed that the lights were on. "OK everyone, this is it. We go in straight for the kill; there is no turning back!" explained Guillaume; all of the agents nodded in agreement with Guillaume. Sahita stood there motionless; she realized that all those who are close her are all soon going to die. But, she realized that it was the only way for her to stay alive. "Sahita, you stay here out of sight whilst we deal with this." ordered Guillaume; Sahita acknowledged him with a slight nod. The DGSE Agents all got their guns ready and the explosives as well. Very discretely Guillaume and his colleagues crept quickly towards the warehouse; when they got closer they then stopped. Guillaume and the other agents peeped through the window; they noticed all of the Indian-Bandits manufacturing different types of drugs inside. "Everyone, we might as well go in and kill all of them. They will have no chance against us." suggested Guillaume; the other agents all agreed. The DGSE Agents put on their masks and went straight through the entrance-door; immediately they began firing their guns at all of the Indians inside. They all screamed in horror trying to get away but, it was too late for all of them! All of the Indians had been shot & killed instantly; all of the DGSE Agents went to check to see if anyone was still alive. Luckily the coast was clear; all there was left to do was to blow up the whole warehouse! All of the agents then placed plastic explosives around the building; then when that was completed they went back outside. The agents had to get as far away as possible considering that it is going to be a big explosion! When they all got far away enough the detonator was activated and as expected there was a huge explosion! The explosion was so loud it completely rocked some parts of London and it was clearly heard. The DGSE Agents & Sahita immediately left to return to their secret hide-out!

Much later into the night at the exploded drug-manufacturing warehouse the fire-fighters and the Police were there investigating it. There was also Police Forensics on the scene examining the bodies. When they delved deeper into the incident they realized that everyone in that warehouse were all shot and what shocked them even more was that plastic explosives was used to blow up the building itself. They also found drugs all over the place and there were many types of drugs, all classed A, B & C. They all wondered who killed them all and what the motive was. The incident at the warehouse was reported to the UK media and the public were shocked & baffled by what had occurred.

At the Indian-Bandits lair Fhazzaar had been informed that his drug-manufacturing warehouse was destroyed by a deliberate explosion. He also finds out that all of the people who worked there had all been killed! Fhazzaar then begins to realize that his group is fading down fast! "What the fuck is going on? Who is doing all of this?" asked Fhazzaar in an agitated state; the remaining Indian-Bandits all looked at each other bemused as anything! Nuthan Hana who is the brother of Joyab and the brother-in-law of Sahita decided to approach Fhazzaar! "Boss, I wonder if the guys who kidnapped Sahita were the ones who blew up the warehouse. It's just a thought!" explained Nuthan; Fhazzaar then gazed directly at Nuthan! "You know you could be right. The only thing I want to know is who are they?" pondered Fhazzaar, "Maybe it's a rival gang!" suggested Madhu, who is the brother of Aarush Talwar. "It could well be another group like us. They are obviously trying to eliminate the competition!" said Fhazzaar; Joyab then entered with a distressed look on his face! "Any news on the whereabouts of my wife?" asked Joyab; everyone shook their heads a resounding 'No!' "Boss, what shall we do?" asked Nuthan; Fhazzaar stood there in a very confused state! "To be honest I really don't know what to do next. We need to take very drastic action!" replied Fhazzaar; all of the remaining Indian-Bandits stood there like statues without saying a word; they were all trapped into a big corner!

Chapter 23:
Hotel killing

Morning had arrived and all of the DGSE Agents were fully awake; Sahita was also fully awake. Throughout the night Sahita was asleep on the chair with her wrists restrained behind her back and her ankles restrained to the chair legs. The DGSE Agents had to make sure that Sahita wouldn't get away as they needed her for the next part of the mission! Late last night Sahita had informed the agents of an impending huge drugs-deal going down at a hotel in Oxford Circus, Central London. Sahita also told them that three members of the Indian-Bandits Ayush, Kabir & Dev are going to be there with their prospective clients. "OK everyone what I suggest we do is that the five of you go & seek out more about the Yugoslavian-6 and see what plans are going down and find out if there are any other syndicates working alongside them. On a very important note find out which members of the UK Police whom are colluding with the Yugoslavian-6. What will happen Sahita & I will go to the hotel to seek out the three members of the Indian-Bandits and I will terminate them and their clients; it is the only way!" explained Guillaume; his colleagues all nodded in agreement! "Commandant Moreau, are you sure you want to do this on your own?" queried Christophe; Guillaume looked directly at Christophe and gave him a convincing nod. All of the other DGSE Agents looked at each other with bemusement! "Besides my fellow agents it is best that I do this on my own so we can all be discrete. Sahita I need you to freshen up because I need you to be a call-girl for this." explained Guillaume, "What! You want me as a whore? Why?" asked Sahita; Guillaume then gazed directly at Sahita with a stern look! "Just do as I say we have no time to lose. I'll explain everything on the way!" replied Guillaume; Sahita immediately went to the bathroom to freshen up. After breakfast the DGSE Agents and Sahita all went their separate ways for the next part of the London Inferno mission.

On the Central-Line Underground train Guillaume & Sahita sat separately from each other so as not to arouse any suspicions! Sahita sat down but, due to no spare seats Guillaume decided to stand. However, he kept his distance as close to Sahita so he could keep an eye on her. Guillaume wore a long wig & sunglasses plus he colored his face a little darker so people wouldn't recognize him. Whilst Guillaume was standing a man standing opposite looked at him in a peculiar way. He had wondered why Guillaume was dressed up in strange way unaware that Guillaume is a French Secret Agent! The man continued to gaze at Guillaume with strange looks and Guillaume was fully aware. The man then joked: "Hey mate! You're not going to win a fancy-dress contest looking like that!" Some of the other passengers began to laugh at the man's humor. Guillaume then looked squarely at the man; the passenger then began to get a little nervous! He then said to Guillaume: "Hey mate! It was only a joke!" Guillaume didn't say a word and continued to gaze sternly at the man; all of the other passengers had noticed this too! Then all of a sudden Guillaume did Martial Arts on the man and knocked him out with a spinning Karate kick! The passengers all gasped in horror and then they became extremely nervous. "Hey man! What the fuck are you doing?" asked another passenger; Guillaume didn't respond and did a Karate side-kick on the other passenger. The other passenger went flying and was eventually knocked out cold. All of the passengers then all moved well away from Guillaume; they were all feeling scared! Eventually Guillaume & Sahita's stop arrived and the two of them got off and immediately left the station to make their way onto the streets of Oxford Circus.

A little later on the British Transport Police arrived on the scene to where the two passengers were assaulted earlier by Guillaume. The witnesses had trouble in trying to identify Guillaume as he was heavily disguised. The only thing they could say was that he had dark-skin plus he had a Martial Arts background! The British Transport Police couldn't go on anything as they were unable to obtain much information. On the streets of Oxford Circus Guillaume walked right behind Sahita. "Sahita, there's a sex-shop nearby but, it's only me that's going inside. I want you to go into any nearby shop and remain there until I come out!" instructed Guillaume; Sahita then acknowledged Guillaume's request. When they arrived at the sex-shop, Sahita went immediately into another shop right next-door to it; Guillaume immediately entered into the sex-shop! Whilst inside the sex-shop Guillaume was looking around to see what items he could buy; he then notices both red leather wrist-cuffs & ankle-cuffs. He decided to purchase the two items plus a red ball-gag! Guillaume immediately went to the counter and paid for the items in cash; the shop-assistant just looked at Guillaume without saying a word whilst she was processing the payment. When that was completed Guillaume left the sex-shop to meet up with Sahita. Outside Guillaume stood in front of the shop to where Sahita was at; she then noticed Guillaume in the window. Sahita realized that Guillaume was ready and she immediately left the shop to meet up with him; when Guillaume had noticed Sahita exiting the shop he immediately walked right behind her. "The hotel is about 20 minutes walk away from here." explained Sahita, "Good! We'll go there immediately." said Guillaume; the two of them then walked on making their way to the hotel.

Guillaume & Sahita arrived at the hotel to where the big drugs-deal was going down. Guillaume was observing the hotel from the front. "Sahita just walk past the hotel for a bit, and then go in that small alleyway!" instructed Guillaume; immediately they walked past the hotel and turned straight into the alleyway. "Don't worry we can't be seen here as there are no cameras around. Firstly, I will need from you the hotel number for where the drugs-deal is taking place." requested Guillaume, "The room number is 363; it is right on the top-floor of the hotel." replied Sahita, "Thanks! What I now need you to do is to remain here until I return. Stay well out of sight for your own safety!" instructed Guillaume; Sahita nodded in acknowledgment. Guillaume then exited the alleyway back to the hotel. Whilst observing the hotel Guillaume then pondered to where the

back entrance is and how to get there. All of a sudden he sees
a small lane and so goes down there; further down the lane
Guillaume manages to locate the back-entrance and walks
straight past it. Guillaume then begins to look around and
notices a lot of bushes and so he hides in there and looks
to see if anyone is around. Luckily, no-one was about so
Guillaume immediately went invisible and teleported to the
rear-entrance of the hotel. When he teleported to the
rear-end of the hotel Guillaume stayed invisible and
observed to see how to get inside easily without getting
noticed. Guillaume also wanted to check to see if there are
any security-cameras; there were a number of them. Still
invisible Guillaume looked around to see which room was
which; then his Daemon says to him: "Guillaume
Room-325 is directly opposite room 363. That hotel-room is
unoccupied and no-one is going to take that particular room
for the next 2 days. You got lucky!" When Guillaume heard
this he immediately saw the keys to Room-325; Guillaume
still invisible looked to see if anyone was around. No-one
was around so he took the keys and teleported straight back
to the alleyway to meet up with Sahita.

Upon returning to the alleyway Guillaume stayed
invisible; he notices Sahita there minding her own business.
When Sahita turned her back to Guillaume, he immediately
appeared visible. "Sahita!" said Guillaume; Sahita jumped
in a sense of shock! "Oh my God! You scared me! Where
did you come from? That was quick!" pondered Sahita, "I
came back from the hotel of course. There's a room opposite
363....it is empty so we can go in there and wait." explained
Guillaume; Sahita looked at him with a surprised expression

on her face! "How did you do all of that?" asked Sahita; Guillaume stood there without saying a word. "Well you learn a lot of things in the military plus I learned a lot more when I was in China. Come on lets go we have to do this now!" said Guillaume; immediately both Guillaume & Sahita made their way to the back-end of the hotel! The two of them went down the lane to where the hotel back entrance is; when they got there they stayed out of sight. As Guillaume was observing his Daemon then says to him: "Guillaume go now there's no-one around!" Straight away both Guillaume & Sahita entered the back entrance and went right down the corridor. At the end of the corridor there was an elevator and the two of them went inside of it to go to the top-floor. "Which room are we going to?" asked Sahita, "We're going to Room-325 which is opposite 363!" replied Guillaume as showed Sahita the room key. "How did you know that 325 was free and how did you get the key so easily?" pondered Sahita with a surprised looked on her face! "Let's just say I know these things!" replied Guillaume; Sahita stood there without saying a word. Whilst in the elevator Guillaume went into remote-viewing mode and using the power of his mind he broke the security-cameras on the top-floor so he wouldn't be seen. Eventually, Guillaume & Sahita arrived on the top-floor and they made their way to Room-325; when the two of them arrived at Room-325 there was Room-363 directly opposite it. "So it's now about 10:25 hours and you said that they will have the meeting at 12:00 hours?" asked Guillaume, "Yes that's right!" replied Sahita, "OK, we're lucky! There's no-one around on the top-floor as all of the rooms are unoccupied.

Go in, ladies first." said Guillaume as he opened the door to Room-325; Sahita entered first and then Guillaume afterwards. When they entered the hotel-room Guillaume immediately closed the door and then locked it; next he went to check outside the window to see if there was anyone suspicious around. The coast was clear and Guillaume immediately closed the curtains and switched on the bedside lamp. "OK Sahita! As I explained before I need you to act as a whore. So I need you to take all of your clothes off but, keep your bra & panties on!" instructed Guillaume, "What are you up to?" pondered Sahita worryingly; Guillaume then gave Sahita a stern look! "Just do as I say and I'll explain." Said Guillaume; Sahita complied and took all of her clothes off leaving on her bra & panties as requested. "OK, they're all off!" said Sahita, "Next, I want you to lie on the bed!" further instructed Guillaume; again Sahita complied and she went to lie on the bed. Guillaume then went to get the shopping bag which contained the sex items. He took them all out and put them on the chair. Guillaume then took out one of the wrist-cuffs and went towards Sahita. "OK, give me your left wrists." ordered Guillaume; Sahita raised her left wrist and Guillaume immediately restrained it to the bed-post using the leather-cuff. Sahita had a shocked look on her face! "Hey what are you fucking doing to me?" asked Sahita worryingly! "As I said I'll explain once you are fully restrained to the bed!" replied Guillaume; he then restrained Sahita's right-wrist to the other bed-post. Next, Guillaume restrained Sahita's right & left ankles to the bottom bed-posts; Sahita was now restrained spreadeagled! Sahita couldn't believe her eyes; she was in shock & anger too!

"So let me explain. As you are a whore maybe some of the clients might like their whore to be fully restrained. It's a good distraction for my plan!" said Guillaume; Sahita had an angry look on her face! "You mean I have to stay like this until they arrive?" asked Sahita angrily; Guillaume nodded in return! "You can't do this to me!" screamed Sahita, "Oh yes I can. Oh, I just remembered something!" said Guillaume as he went to get the ball-gag! When Sahita noticed the ball-gag she started to get even more worried! "What are you going to do with that?" asked Sahita angrily, "What do you think? I'm going to shut you up, bitch! You see I remember you very well when I was living in Bedford. You have got a fucking big mouth. Now do as I say or the deals off and you will die!" ordered Guillaume; Sahita complied and she opened her mouth very wide! Guillaume then put the ball-gag in Sahita's mouth and restrained the strap to tighten it. Sahita then began to moan through the ball-gag and she also struggled with the restraints. But, it was of no use to Sahita all restrained to the bed with a ball-gag in her mouth; she had to lie on the bed in that predicament for the next $1^1/2$ hours. Guillaume sat on a chair and he decided to meditate whilst he waits for the three other members of the Indian-Bandits!

It was about 11:50 hours that voices were heard in the corridor; it was the three members of the Indian-Bandits Ayush, Kabir & Dev. They were getting ready for their big drugs-deal with their prospective clients. Guillaume peeped through the mini glass-hole in the door; the three Indian men then entered into their hotel-room. "Oh they're here but their clients are not. We just need to wait a bit longer!"

explained Guillaume; Sahita just lay there on the bed all restrained & gagged. She was none too happy at the predicament she is currently in! All of a sudden the three prospective clients had arrived at Room-363; they knocked on the door and the three Indian-Bandits let them in. Quietly Guillaume left his hotel-room and stood right next to Room-363 and listened on to see what was going down. "Hi guys I'm Ayush. This is Kabir & Dev!" said Ayush, "Please to meet you guys. Do you have the stuff?" asked one of the clients; Kabir pulled out several blocks of cocaine from his bag. The clients then showed the three Indian men the money....there was £50,000 GBP. Their clients then went to check to see if it really was cocaine – it was confirmed that it was the real-deal! Using remote-viewing Guillaume could see what was going down; he then decided to knock on the door to Room-363! Inside Room-363 all 6 men could hear the knock; they wondered who it was! Dev went to check! "Who is it?" asked Dev, "I am looking for Ayush, Kabir & Dev...have I come to the correct hotel-room?" asked Guillaume; Dev then opened the door. "Hi, I'm Dev; yes you have come to the right room." replied Dev, "Oh thank God! I'm here on behalf of Fhazzaar, your boss." said Guillaume, "Oh! What is it?" asked Dev, "Well I'm a pimp hoping to be a part of your gang!" replied Guillaume, "You're a pimp?" asked a bemused Dev, "Yep! What it is he wanted me to send you guys a whore to sweeten the deal you're all doing. By the way she's in the room opposite; I've waited so long for you guys to come!" explained Guillaume, "You've sent a whore for all of us?" asked Dev; all the other men in the hotel-room overheard the conversation and they all felt a little bemused! "Yes, as instructed by Fhazzaar. Oh she's on the bed all restrained spreadeagled wearing a ball-gag. She loves to be tied-up & dominated! So are you interested?" asked Guillaume; all of the men inside the room all looked at one another pondering on what to do next. "Hey guys, let's do this!" suggested Dev; the three clients followed Guillaume to Room-325 and they were let in. The three clients became excited at seeing Sahita all restrained wearing a ball-gag! Sahita's eyes began to widen in shock; when the three Indian men walked in they immediately recognized Sahita! "Sahita, is that you?" asked Kabir frantically; immediately Guillaume slammed the door! Then all of a sudden Guillaume did Martial Arts moves on all six men knocking them down! Even though it was six against one, they had no chance against Guillaume; they were all pounded down really hard. In the end Guillaume snapped five of their necks off to kill them. He then grabbed Ayush's hair and gazed directly at him. "Who are you? What the hell is going on?" asked a distressed Ayush, "I am a French Secret Agent!" replied Guillaume; immediately he snapped Ayush's neck to kill him. Guillaume then left his hotel-room to make his way to Room-363; he went to find the case containing the £50,000 GBP. When he found it he went back to his hotel-room. Upon entering Guillaume put the case of cash down on the floor and went to set Sahita free. "How can you leave me here all restrained & gagged for nearly 2 hours?" asked an angry Sahita; Guillaume looked at her sternly. "Hey stop complaining! Remember I had to do this!" replied Guillaume; Sahita stood there without saying a word! "So what's next?" asked Sahita, "Wash the ball-gag,

I'm going to need it later!" replied Guillaume; Sahita took the ball-gag and went into the bathroom to wash the ball-gag and when she finished she gave it back to Guillaume. All of the sex-gear was placed back into the bag and then Guillaume took the case of money and the two of them went on their way out of the hotel.

Later on in the day the Police had arrived at the crime-scene to investigate the killings of the six men. It was one of the hotel staff who reported it after she discovered the dead bodies. When the Police delve deeper into the investigation they came to a complete dead-end! There were no clues at all on who had committed the murders. Because Guillaume had used his paranormal powers earlier to disable the security-cameras the Police couldn't get any footage. It really baffled the Police on who had done this and what the ulterior motive was.

Guillaume & Sahita met up with the other DGSE Agents and they were informed on what happened. The other DGSE Agents informed Guillaume on what went on with their investigation...they were not 100% sure which members of the Police whom are colluding with the Yugoslavian-6 crime syndicate! "What we need to do first is to find the rest of the Indian-Bandits and then terminate them once and for all; then maybe we can get a strong lead!" suggested Guillaume; all of the agents agreed with Guillaume and they all decided to focus on eliminating the Indian-Bandits making them extinct in the process. Guillaume realized that will be the main priority at this time.

Chapter 24:

Indian-Bandits exterminated!

Later on in the day Guillaume and the other DGSE Agents were discussing on how to approach the rest of the Indian-Bandits. "I have an idea comrades. What we can do is get Sahita to call the leader Fhazzaar and say she's been held hostage." suggested Guillaume, "Yes that is a good idea! Sahita, do have any contact details?" asked Xavier; Sahita then pulled out a piece of paper with Fhazzaar's contact details. "Here they are; he has a lot of them." explained Sahita; Guillaume looked at the list of phone numbers that Fhazzaar has. "OK Sahita, what is going to happen is you & I will look for a telephone-box and then you will contact Fhazzaar. I am going to ask him to do a deal with me but, remember do as I say and everything will be fine!" requested Guillaume; Sahita nodded in agreement. "So Commandant, what are we going to do afterwards?" asked Christophe, "Well when Sahita phones Fhazzaar and tells me the location of his base I can go in and kill him and the rest of the Indian-Bandits. I'll explain more in detail later but, let's do this first." replied Guillaume; both he & Sahita left the hide-out to go and find the nearest telephone-box!

It was a 40-minute walk to the nearest telephone-box when Guillaume & Sahita found it. Guillaume then got out some coins and gave them to Sahita. "Right, what I want you to do is to phone Fhazzaar and inform him that you are well. Then say to him that there is someone who wants to speak to him and immediately pass the phone to me!" instructed Guillaume; Sahita started to put coins into the box and then she telephoned one of Fhazzaar's numbers...Fhazzaar then answered!

Fhazzaar: "Hello!"

Sahita: "Fhazzaar, it's me....Sahita!"

Fhazzaar: "What! Sahita....where are you?"

Sahita: "Just hang on. There's someone who wants to talk to you!"

Immediately, Sahita then passes the receiver to Guillaume!

Guillaume: "Fhazzaar....listen up & listen good....I have your bitch!"

Fhazzaar: "Who the fuck is this?"

Guillaume: "Never you mind! Now as I said listen up!"

Fhazzaar: "OK...I'm listening!"

Guillaume: "Good! Now if you want your bitch returned alive you must do as I say. Now I want to meet you and the rest of the Indian-Bandits later tonight....do you understand?"

Fhazzaar: "OK I'll comply! What is this all about and why are you doing all of this?"

Guillaume: "I'll explain everything when we meet in person. But, remember no funny business or else!" (Call ended!)

Guillaume immediately hung up the phone and the two of them walked back to the DGSE secret hide-out! Whilst they were walking along Guillaume then began to question

Sahita! "So Sahita tell me. Fhazzaar's lair is it heavily secured and guarded?" asked Guillaume, "Yes it is in a way. There are guys who guard it every night. They're all Indians too, they take it in turns to guard the place each night!" explained Sahita, "OK! The reason why I asked is because obviously I need to know how to get in plus I have to kill all of them. Hope you understand that I have to do this!" explained Guillaume, "Including my husband!" said Sahita, "Exactly! Remember I have no choice but, at least you life is going to be spared!" explained Guillaume; Sahita nodded in agreement very meekly. "By the way when we get to the base I am going to have to restrain & gag you again to make you look like a proper hostage!" explained Guillaume; again Sahita began to feel uncomfortable! "That's why you asked me to wash the ball-gag earlier!" said Sahita, "Yes, exactly!" responded Guillaume; the two of them just carried on walking back to the DGSE hide-out!

In the very late afternoon at the DGSE hide-out Guillaume was explaining to his colleagues about the Indian-Bandits hide-out and where it is located. The DGSE Agents decided to plan out a course of action! "Commandant, Raphaëlle & I, we want to try and find out which members of the British Police who are involved with the Yugoslavian-6." explained Thérese, "Yes I am aware of that issue; there have been difficulties. What I suggest is that you & Raphaëlle go & find who they are, and the rest of us will go to the Indian-Bandits hide-out later tonight!" explained Guillaume; the agents were all in agreement with him. The plan will be that the four DGSE Agents will make their way and park their vehicle out of sight about 1-hour

walk away from the Indian-Bandit's hide-out. Then
Guillaume & Sahita will go alone together on foot to meet
Fhazzaar & the rest of the Indian-Bandits!

The time was 18:30 hours and it was very dark outside;
it was the perfect time for the DGSE Agents to disperse to
their duties. Raphaëlle & Thérese immediately went to do
their duties to find out who are the other members involved
with the Yugoslavian-6; Guillaume, Sahita & the rest of the
DGSE Agents went on their way to eliminate the
Indian-Bandits once and for all! The DGSE Agents drove
for about $1^1/2$ hours when they were near the
Indian-Bandits base. They were about 50 minutes walk to
the Indian-Bandits and Guillaume decided to park the van
there! "OK Monsieur's! Sahita & I will go on foot as planned
so all of you stay put just in case." ordered Guillaume; his
colleagues all nodded in agreement with him! "Moreau,
don't forget to turn on your homing device and alert us if
you get into trouble." said Matthieu; Guillaume nodded in
acknowledgement. When Guillaume & Sahita were ready
they got out of the van and then began to make their way
to the Indian-Bandits base. Guillaume & Sahita had walked
on for quite some time until they were about 5 minutes
walk away from the Indian-Bandits base. "Sahita, is that the
place?" asked Guillaume, "Yes it is. That's the place and there
are the guards as you can see." explained Sahita as she
pointed out; Guillaume observed the place using his
supersonic vision. All of a sudden his Daemon spoke to him
again: "Guillaume! You will have to use your paranormal
powers but, make sure Sahita doesn't find out until you are
ready to kill her!" Guillaume then realized that he has no

choice but to use his paranormal powers! "Sahita, go into those bushes there and stay out of sight until I get back. I am going to kill the guards!" explained Guillaume; Sahita nodded at him and immediately went to hide in the bushes! Guillaume then went further down very discretely to get a little closer. Next, Guillaume went into another set of bushes to hide out of sight. Guillaume then went invisible and teleported to the front of the gate on the inside. There were two Indian men guarding the gate; all of a sudden Guillaume appeared visible and the two guards went into shock! Guillaume using his Martial Arts assaulted the two guards and killed them by snapping their necks! Guillaume then looked around to see if anyone was looking...there was no-one! Guillaume then noticed that the two dead guards had a knife each so he decided to take both of them! Guillaume walked on discretely towards the house; he then noticed another guard on top of the surrounding wall and so he hid out of sight. Then using one of the knives Guillaume then threw it and hit the guard in the face....he dies instantly! Then at a far distance Guillaume then spots another guard and uses the other knife on him by throwing it therefore striking his throat. After that Guillaume then looks around to see if the coast was clear...it was all clear; there was no-one around. Guillaume then went to get Sahita! "Hey Sahita it's all clear over here; you can come out now they're all dead!" said Guillaume; Sahita immediately came out of the bushes. "I'm here now! What's next?" asked Sahita, "It's time for you to get restrained again!" replied Guillaume as he showed Sahita the bag with the sex-gears. "Oh that! Yes I do remember!" said Sahita sarcastically; immediately

Guillaume restrained Sahita's hands behind her back and then put the ball-gag into her mouth! Now Sahita was looking like a proper hostage!

Inside the Indian-Bandits lair, there was Fhazzaar & Sahita's husband Joyab standing there both feeling very anxious. "I want my wife back!" shouted Joyab frantically; Fhazzaar looked at him with grave concern. "Don't worry, her kidnapper says if we comply she'll be returned unharmed!" explained Fhazzaar; there were other Indian-Bandits members in the same room as Fhazzaar & Joyab. They were feeling a lot of fear all over their bodies pondering what is going to happen next; they all just stood there in silence. Guillaume with Sahita entered through the front-door and as soon as they did they immediately saw other Indian-Bandits there. Guillaume got out his hand-gun and then shot them all and they all died instantly; Guillaume's Daemon then says to him: "Go to the end of the corridor and then turn right; Fhazzaar and the remaining Indian-Bandits are in that room!" Guillaume complied and made his way to that particular room. When Guillaume arrived at the room he immediately kicked the door open. There was Fhazzaar and the remaining Indian-Bandits standing there in complete shock! "All of you put your fucking hands up right now!" shouted Guillaume; the other Indian-Bandits attempted to go for their weapons! "Hey don't do it! He has my wife!" shouted Joyab; they decided to not go for their weapons. "Well that is smart of you! I take it you're Joyab, Sahita's husband!" asked Guillaume; Joyab nodded at him a 'yes' response. "Who are you and what do you want?" asked Fhazzaar, "I need information. I am in the French Secret Service and I want to know where the Yugoslavian-6 are!" replied Guillaume; all of the Indian-Bandits stood there stunned. "I can't help you with that! What do you want the Yugoslavian-6 for?" asked Fhazzaar; Guillaume then pointed his gun towards Sahita! "My Government wants to apprehend them and we are fully aware that the Indian-Bandits are part of the Yugoslavian-6 syndicate!" explained Guillaume, "Look! We don't know where they are located, honestly!" explained Fhazzaar; Guillaume then sees an empty chair and so he shoves Sahita on it. Then all of a sudden Guillaume shoots the rest of the Indian-Bandits except for Fhazzaar & Joyab...now there are only three of them left! "Why did you do that?" asked Joyab frantically; Guillaume just looked at him with a stern look and said nothing. Guillaume then decided to use his new power again – to generate electricity out of his body. Immediately from his two hands a ball of electricity was generated; the three remaining Indian-Bandits had stunned looks on their faces! Using the ball of electricity Guillaume struck both Fhazzaar & Joyab to the floor at the same time. Next, Guillaume used his new power to electrocute Fhazzaar & Joyab to give them a lot of pain. "Hey what are you doing?" shouted Fhazzaar; Guillaume then decided to stop! "Right you two get on a chair and remain seated or I will kill you both!" ordered Guillaume; both Fhazzaar & Joyab crawled to a chair each and then sat down. "What do you want?" asked Joyab in considerable pain; Guillaume then looked at Joyab sternly. "Like I said before I want information about the Yugoslavian-6...where the fuck are they?" asked Guillaume angrily; Joyab then began to pant

heavily! "We don't know as we said before!" replied Joyab;
Guillaume was now wondering what to do next! "Right you
two fuckers! This is how we are going to do this. My
Government has ordered me to kill all of the Yugoslavian-6
and their syndicates. Now we did a deal with Sahita and
she will stay alive!" explained Guillaume; Joyab then looked
at his wife, Sahita with horror! "What the fuck! You bitch,
how can you do a deal with them?" asked Joyab angrily;
as Sahita was gagged she was unable to reply. "Oh! It gets
better Joyab, I have an interesting proposition! If either you
or Fhazzaar tell me how I can get to the Yugoslavian-6 then
one of you will stay alive. Sahita has already helped us so
she is staying alive. So which one of you is going to tell
me?" asked Guillaume; Fhazzaar & Joyab looked at each
other with glaring eyes! "OK I'll tell! Find the Bum-Lords
of Luton they have a secret hide-out 1 hour from here!"
explained Fhazzaar; Joyab then looked at Fhazzaar angrily.
All of a sudden Guillaume then shoots Joyab in the head...he
dies instantly! "Thank you Fhazzaar, you've been a great
help!" said Guillaume; all of a sudden he then shoots
Fhazzaar in the head....the leader of the Indian-Bandits is
now dead! Sahita sat there looking horrified; Guillaume
then went over to remove the ball-gag from Sahita's mouth.
"Why did you double-cross Fhazzaar...& you shot my
husband!" shouted Sahita, "Look you know the situation
I told you that I had to eliminate the Indian-Bandits!"
explained Guillaume; Sahita then nodded very meekly in
agreement. "So what now; aren't you going to release me?"
asked Sahita; Guillaume then looked directly at Sahita with
a serious look on his face! "No I am not! You see you are too

dangerous to stay alive and I have my orders to complete!" explained Guillaume, "Why? We had a deal!" shouted Sahita, "We lied; it was the only way we could get to the Indian-Bandits. Oh by the way, that school I went to in Bedford I did kill all of the pupils from there & the teachers too!" confessed Guillaume; Sahita's eyes flew wide open in shock! "You murderer! How can you do this to me? I was even willing to be in bondage for your mission!" shouted Sahita; Guillaume said nothing and immediately he shoots Sahita in the head...she dies instantly! The Indian-Bandits have now all been terminated...mission accomplished!

Even though Guillaume had terminated all of the Indian-Bandits he wasn't quite finished yet! He realized that no trace of evidence is to be left anywhere around the place! His Daemon then says to him: "Guillaume, go into the basement there are plenty of cans with petrol in them. It will all be enough to leave no trace of evidence!" As soon as Guillaume heard the instruction from his Daemon he immediately made his way to the basement. When he got to the basement he noticed a lot of huge cans filled with petrol plus a huge boiler. Guillaume then thought that if he sets the house on fire it will explode therefore making it easier to get rid of all the evidence. So then Guillaume immediately gets a can each and teleports to different parts of the house pouring petrol all around it. Guillaume also poured petrol over the dead bodies both inside & outside the house. Also, Guillaume poured petrol outside the house within the perimeter-walls...all of the petrol was used but, it was more than enough. When he was done Guillaume then lit a match inside the house and immediately there were flames all around. Guillaume then immediately teleported away! From top to bottom the house was in flames and there were flames within the perimeter-wall area. All of the dead bodies were also in flames; then all of a sudden there was a huge explosion! It sounded like an atomic-bomb and it could be heard all over London! Guillaume teleported to a bush about five minutes walk from the other DGSE Agents; Guillaume then walked towards the getaway vehicle. "Oh, you've returned Moreau. That was quick!" said Xavier; "Well as I said to everyone I learnt a lot in China!" responded Guillaume, "Yes I can see that, Moreau." said Matthieu, "Anyway, I have terminated all of the Indian-Bandits including Sahita Hana. I have set the building on fire so I could get rid of the evidence!" explained Guillaume, "Oh we wondered where the explosion came from!" said Christophe, "Yes that was me! Anyway, we need to get out of here quickly the Fire-Brigade & Police could be here in any minute!" explained Guillaume; the four DGSE Agents got into the van and sped out to return to their secret hide-out!

Chapter 25:
Find the Bum-Lords!

All over the country the UK media had reported about the huge explosion at the Indian-Bandits residence the previous night. They also confirmed that the dead bodies found were all of the Indian-Bandits. Some of the Police had managed to identify Fhazzaar and had some suspicions that the rest of the dead bodies were the Indian-Bandits! What surprised the Police was that the two men who had knives in their face & neck respectively made them wonder if it was someone who has military experience? They were able to deduce this as the knives were thrown from a distance! However, what baffled the Police was who had done this and why. There were no clues whatsoever that could lead them anywhere!

All six of the DGSE Agents including Guillaume were discussing about the next stage of their mission! "Fhazzaar had informed me that the homosexual gang the Bum-Lords has knowledge about the Yugoslavian-6 location. We need to find them quickly and they are not far away from the Indian-Bandits place; we can get them!" explained Guillaume, "Oh by the way, myself & Raphaëlle managed to find out which members of the UK Police are in cahoots with the Yugoslavian-6; here are their names so far but, we believe there are more!" explained Thérese as she showed the list of names. The DGSE Agents looked at the list of names given and thought of a next course of action. "Oh has anyone got the list of the Bum-Lords?" asked Guillaume, Matthieu then pulled out the list of the Bum-Lords. Here were the names: Silas Peale the leader, Alan Butt the 2nd in command, Thomas Whitfield, Albert Faizan, Perry Thornbird, Wilmot Ellis & Parker Hills. "Everyone, I have an idea. Let me go on my own and I will get them to tell me where I can find the Yugoslavian-6!" suggested Guillaume; the five DGSE Agents all looked at him stunned! "Moreau, are you sure you want to do this on your own?" asked Thérese; Guillaume then nodded with conviction! "Besides this will be a piece of cake compared to the Indian-Bandits. Also, you all need to delve deeper into the UK Police and see what's going on." explained Guillaume; the DGSE Agents with reluctance decided to let Guillaume do the mission on his own. When they finished their briefing all of the agents dispersed to complete the next part of their mission!

Chapter 26:
Bum-Lords killed!

Guillaume had managed to locate the place where all of the Bum-Lords are based; he hid out for a bit and then went into remote-viewing mode. During the remote-view Guillaume could see that all seven of the Bum-Lords are in the abandoned house; there was the ring-leader, Silas Peale standing in front getting ready to talk. Silas Peale was a 6'4" tall man with ginger-hair and his right-hand man Alan Butt who has short brown-hair plus he is fairly fat. "OK everyone we have a big problem. Someone has killed the Indian-Bandits and burnt their place down. Dragan of the Yugoslavian-6 is fuming and he wants us to know who is doing this!" explained Silas; the rest of the Bum-Lords all looked at each other in bewilderment. "Maybe it's MI5; they always do things in secret!" said Thomas, "Are we sure it's MI5?" questioned Albert; the discussion went on for some time! Guillaume could hear every word they are saying and was one-step ahead of them.

It was about 15 minutes later that Guillaume was still hidden out of sight waiting for the right moment to strike! "Oh Silas, what's happening later; are we still going to the gay-orgy tonight?" asked Perry, "Of course we are. Wouldn't miss it for the world!" replied Alan, "Let's see first who killed the Indian-Bandits and then we will go to the gay-orgy!"

suggested Wilmot, "Here! Here!" responded Parker;
Guillaume was still listening on pondering how he was going
to approach them! All of a sudden his Daemon spoke again:
"Guillaume you might as well teleport straight away before
they leave. Just get the information and then kill all of
them!" Immediately Guillaume teleported to the
Bum-Lords residence as instructed by his Daemon! When
Guillaume appeared to the Bum-Lords they all went into
shock! "What the fuck! Where did you come from?" asked
Parker frantically; Guillaume stood there for a bit saying
nothing! "Well Bum-Lords I need information from you
guys!" replied Guillaume, "Hey! How did you know who
we are?" asked Alan frantically, "I know everything! Now
as I just stated I need information. Where is Dragan & the
Yugoslavian-6?" demanded Guillaume; all of the Bum-Lords
looked at each other completely stunned! "We don't know
what you are talking about!" said Silas; Guillaume stood
there looking at all of the Bum-Lords without saying a word!
"OK have it your way! I'll have to extract the information
from you by force!" said Guillaume; immediately using his
powers of telekinesis he threw all of the Bum-Lords around
the place. Then using his latest power he fired electricity
out of his hands towards the Bum-Lords. "OK, OK I'll tell
you! The Yugoslavian-6 are based on the outskirts of this
town called North Weald in Essex!" said Wilmot; Guillaume
stood there with a slight grin on his face! "Parfait! Now it is
time to exterminate all of the Bum-Lords!" said Guillaume;
immediately he went and did Martial Art kicks on each of
the Bum-Lords and killed them by snapping all of their
necks....they all died! Guillaume then took out a

hand-grenade, released the catch and then dropped it. Straight away Guillaume teleported out of the house; a few seconds later the Bum-Lords residence exploded leaving no trace of evidence!

Later on in the day the Police investigated the explosion at the Bum-Lords residence; it baffled them quite a bit. When they observed the crime-scene grenade parts were found; now the Police knew that it was a murder! "Who has done this & why?" asked one of the Detectives, "Beats me! I wonder if it was the same person who killed the Indian-Bandits?" pondered another Detective; it baffled the Police even more! They wondered what is this all about that there were two murders in two days and both places were not far away from each other! The UK media also reported the recent heinous crime on TV; members of the public were now beginning to worry a little!

Chapter 27:
The Yugoslavian-6

Simone Jane Robinson as sleeping away one night at Dragan's base in the town of North Weald in Essex; she was having a nightmare! Simone is dreaming about the time when she was at home with her parents. Both of them were very nasty & cruel to Simone when she was a child. Simone is recalling all of the times that her parents were very abusive towards her....she kept on tossing & turning in her bed as it was all upsetting for her! All of a sudden Simone wakes up realizing that it was all a dream; she went to look at her clock...it was about 01:53 hours in the morning! Simone then lays back on her bed taking a few deep breaths...Simone kept on wondering whether she would ever be set free from her nightmare. All of her life Simone has always gone from one nightmare to another...all she ever wanted was freedom in her life!

It was about 07:30 hours when Simone woke up; she got out of bed and went to the bathroom to wash her face and brush her teeth. When Simone finished her wash she then went to look for Dragan. Simone was walking along and when she got to Dragan's office she then begins to hear voices. "I have been watching the BBC News. Someone has killed two of our syndicates; first the Indian-Bandits and then the Bum-Lords. Someone is after us and we need to find out who it is. Plus, we need to get them quickly or else we've had it!" explained Dragan, "Dragan the Police we have in our pockets are they fully aware of the situation?" asked Novak, "Yes they are. They're going to be on it to see who is doing all of this." replied Dragan; Simone was then wondering who killed the Indian-Bandits and the Bum-Lords. Simone then walked into Dragan's office and knocked on his door! "Simone, I have been expecting you. You're a little late!" said Dragan, "Sorry Sir I overslept; I had a nightmare!" explained Simone; Dragan looked at her with a slightly stern look! "That's no excuse, besides I need to show you something. Take a seat." instructed Dragan; Simone immediately went to sit on a chair. Dragan then played a recording on TV to show Simone; it was the BBC News:

"Police are interested in apprehending this lady, Simone Jane Robinson. She is wanted for working with an International Criminal Organization who are committing all kinds of contraband crimes. If anyone sees her please do not approach her and call the Police immediately!"

Simone sat there in her chair without saying a word! "Well, it looks like the Police are interested in you Simone!" said Dragan, "Please Sir, help me! I want to work for you and I don't want to go to prison!" said Simone, "Well that remains to be seen. You will need to lay low for a while and when things quiet down we'll have more work for you. The Police have been after you for a long time!" explained Dragan; Simone nodded at Dragan in acknowledgment. Simone then returned to her room to be by herself.

It was late morning at the DGSE hide-out and Guillaume explained to his colleagues that he was able to extract information from the Bum-Lords on the whereabouts of the Yugoslavian-6. Guillaume also informed his colleagues that he terminated all of the Bum-Lords and left no trace of evidence. "We need to get the Yugoslavian-6 and rescue Simone Robinson; she needs our help plus she is going to help us in our mission!" explained Guillaume, "Yes we are fully aware! The UK Police are desperately trying to apprehend Simone and things are getting more intense!" said Xavier, "Besides the best next course of action would be to blow up their main base where the other drug-manufacturing place is and kill all of the staff there. Then we can go after Simone." suggested Matthieu; Guillaume then ponders what he should decide to do! "OK everyone! Let's do the building tonight as we are on a tight schedule!" suggested Guillaume; the agents all agreed with Guillaume and decided that they will all blow up the building later that same night!

Chapter 28:
Main Base

It was 21:00 hours and the DGSE Agents had arrived at the Yugoslavian-6 drug-manufacturing warehouse. They could hear all of the machinery sounds coming in from the warehouse itself. "Yes, that is the building as documented by Simone!" said Guillaume; the DGSE Agents continued to observe the warehouse just to check. "So what shall we do next?" asked Raphaëlle, "Well let's get a little closer to the building and check to see what it looks like on the inside!" suggested Matthieu; immediately all of the agents crept over closer to the warehouse keeping a very low-profile! When they got closer they peeked through the windows. All they could see are people manufacturing all of the Class A, B & C drugs. The warehouse itself was much bigger than the one that the Indian-Bandits had when they were manufacturing the drugs. "It may be a big warehouse but, we can handle it!" said Guillaume; the DGSE Agents just observed for a few minutes longer.

About 15 minutes later the DGSE Agents got their guns ready; they were all going to kill the drug-manufacturers in the warehouse. "OK everyone, let's do this!" ordered Guillaume; immediately the DGSE Agents burst into the warehouse and began shooting at all of people there. Everyone in the building started to scream with horror running around trying to escape. However, it was too late; everyone in the building had been shot dead! Next, the DGSE Agents began placing explosives around the building and every time they did the timer was set! Once all of the explosives were placed the DGSE Agents ran out of the warehouse as far as they can. They had managed to get far away enough and then all of a sudden the whole warehouse exploded! There was no trace of evidence left in the warehouse that would have incriminated the DGSE Agents! "We're done here. Let's return to our base!" suggested Xavier; the DGSE Agents all went into the van and then drove off back to their hide-out. The mission itself was a huge accomplishment!

Later on that same night there were Fire-Fighters and Police-Officers at the warehouse investigating the huge explosion. They were all in shock at the amount of dead bodies all over the ground...there were no survivors. It was a nightmare for the Police to carry all of the dead bodies one-by-one putting them into body-bags. Some of the Police had noticed gun-shot wounds on the dead-bodies and they found traces of explosives. "Certainly looks like it wasn't an accident!" said one of the Police-Officers; another Police-Officer nodded in agreement. "Yeah, if you notice the traces of bomb-fragments it looks like the people who committed this are professionals!" explained another Police-Officer; this latest incident really did baffle the Police a lot considering that the timing of it was close to the previous explosions. The UK authorities had no clues on who had done this!

Chapter 29:
Cross-fire!

The following morning Guillaume and the rest of the DGSE Agents had a big meeting on how to infiltrate the Yugoslavian-6 once and for all. However, what is presently overwhelming the DGSE Agents was that there are still a number of syndicate members around London. They wondered what would be the best course of action to take! "Well everyone, how are we going to approach this next part of the mission?" asked Xavier; all the DGSE Agents looked at one another! "To make it easier I can infiltrate the Yugoslavian-6 and rescue Simone Robinson!" suggested Guillaume; his colleagues all looked at him with stunned looks! "Moreau, are you out of your mind?" questioned Matthieu, "No I am not. Believe me I can handle this on my own. As I mentioned before I learned a lot in China!" replied Guillaume, "So Moreau, what do you suggest we do?" asked Christophe; Guillaume then gave his colleagues a sly grin! "Well you see, as there are a possible number of syndicate members around London it would be best if the five of you go around and terminate as many as you can. When I rescue Simone I will get the rest of the details from her. By what she has informed there seems to be bigger fishes to fry!" explained Guillaume; his colleagues then realized it was a good idea what was proposed! When they were ready all six DGSE Agents dispersed and went on to do their duties!

Guillaume was on his own walking around keeping a low-profile so as not to get recognized; he was well disguised! Guillaume then passes a car-dealership and realized that he will need a car soon. His Daemon then says to him: "I know what you are thinking and YES you are correct. You need to steal a car!" Guillaume then looks around to find where he can be out of sight. Eventually Guillaume was able find somewhere secluded and immediately he went invisible and then teleported to the car-dealership! When Guillaume was inside the car-dealership he went to see what car he could steal and then he found one; a Ferrari F430! Guillaume then went to get the car keys and when he did, Guillaume then teleported to inside the Ferrari F430 car still staying invisible. Immediately, the keys were put into the ignition and straight away Guillaume switches on the engine and then he drives the Ferrari F430 through the display window. Everyone in the streets outside could see a car being stolen and the Police were called immediately. A little later on the Police arrived at the car-dealership to investigate the theft of the car by Guillaume; what really baffled them was when they went through the camera-footage they couldn't identify the offender as Guillaume was still invisible at the time. The Police even wondered how did the offender got in without being seen. As the Police had nothing more to go on they took a copy of the recording of the incident and then returned to the Police Station.

As Guillaume was driving the stolen car his Daemon spoke to him again: "Guillaume you are going to have to rescue Simone Robinson soon; the Police & Armed Police are also on their way to Dragan's hide-out. You will have to kill all of them including the Police plus you need to use all of your powers; you have no choice!" Guillaume then realized that he really has no time to lose...the whole of Europe's lives are depending on this part of the mission!

At the Yugoslavian-6 hide-out the leader Dragan was completely irate when he found out that his drug-manufacturing warehouse was completely destroyed including his drugs. "Someone is definitely after us. First they killed the Indian-Bandits, then the Bum-Lords and now someone has blown up my warehouse! Who is doing all of this?" pondered Dragan; all of the Yugoslavian-6 members looked at each other with confused looks on their faces! "However, the big question is how did they, whoever they are, find out?" asked Bogdan, "Well there are only 6 of us plus Simone." said Dragan; all of the Yugoslavian-6 denied that any of them had snitched...so the only one left, Simone is going to be questioned! "Someone tell Simone to come to my office!" ordered Dragan; immediately Vlatko went to get Simone. A few minutes later Vlatko returned with Simone; immediately Dragan gave Simone a cold hard stare. Simone then started to feel very nervous! "Sir, you asked to see me." said Simone, "Yes that's right! I have a very serious question for you!" explained Dragan, "OK, what is the question Sir?" asked Simone, "We have been recently attacked by unknown sources. Now none of us here had snitched to this mysterious group so that only leaves you! So did you tell anyone about

our organization?" asked Dragan sternly; Simone then
began to feel even more nervous! "No Sir, I didn't." replied
Simone; she then started to shake a little! Dragan then
realized that Simone was lying and so he grabbed her arm!
"You lying whore; it was you!" shouted Dragan as he gripped
Simone's arm very tightly; he was beginning hurt Simone.
"Honest Sir, it wasn't me. I'm loyal to you!" begged Simone;
Dragan just gave Simone an evil stare! "Don't lie to me you
fucking bitch!" shouted Dragan; he then stripped Simone's
clothes off! Dragan then ordered two of his men to strip
off Simone's bra & panties and when that was done, Simone
was completely naked! "OK gentlemen, take her to the
punishment-pole and restrain her!" ordered Dragan;
Simone's eyes then flew wide open! "Oh please no Sir, not
the pole. Sir I swear I didn't tell anyone!" begged Simone,
"No use in pleading Simone. Now you're going to pay for
your disloyalty!" said Dragan; his men then dragged Simone
to go outside. All of the Yugoslavian-6 and Simone were
outside the building and it was extremely cold! As Simone
was completely naked it became extremely cold for her and
she immediately began to shiver a lot! "OK restrain her right
now!" ordered Dragan; straight away a metal collar was
placed around Simone's neck with metal wrist & ankle
restraints. Simone was then restrained face-down
spread-eagled to four metal poles; then a chain was attached
to the metal collar which was attached to a metal-plate fixed
to the ground. Simone had nowhere to go; she was now
going to be at the mercy of Dragan. Five of the Yugoslavian-6
stood around a restrained Simone and then Dragan returned
with a leather-whip in his hand. "Now it is time for your

punishment, Simone!" said Dragan as he cracked the whip! Simone then realized that she is going to get whipped. Then all of a sudden Dragan began to whip Simone's back; she screamed in agony! Dragan then whipped Simone again, she screamed even louder! Dragan then continued to whip Simone mercilessly non-stop! Simone kept on screaming & screaming with tears streaming down her eyes; Simone was unable to take the pain given to her. It was extremely painful for Simone as she was restrained outside in the bitter cold weather completely naked. Simone was completely helpless; she just couldn't do anything!

Guillaume was on the road driving the stolen Ferrari; he knew where to go to get Dragan and the rest of the Yugoslavian-6. All of a sudden his Daemon spoke to him again: "Guillaume, Simone is in big trouble. You need to get to Dragan's place quickly. Also, the Police are getting closer; turn right into the forest and leave the car there. Then carry on foot to Dragan's place!" Guillaume acknowledged his Daemon and turned the car into the forests. On the other side of the town the Police were on their way in the Police-Vans to apprehend the Yugoslavian-6 and Simone Robinson. The Police had concluded that not only the Yugoslavian-6 are a danger to society but also Simone! The Police didn't care that Simone was forced to work for Dragan as far as they were concerned Simone Robinson is a dangerous criminal even though she wasn't one!

Guillaume got out of the car and got his hand-gun ready; he was beginning to walk forward until his Daemon spoke again: "Guillaume, don't go too forward. Wait for the Police to arrive!" All of a sudden Guillaume could hear loud

screams; he immediately went into remote-viewing mode!
Suddenly Guillaume could see Simone getting tortured by
Dragan; it sent chills down his spine! Guillaume felt helpless
as his Daemon instructed him not to go forward. All he
could do is witness Simone getting whipped by Dragan; he
was now beginning to feel frustrated and angry!

Dragan was still whipping Simone and she was now
becoming unconscious; her back was severely bruised as
were her bottom and legs! Simone was also bleeding very
badly; her whole body felt numb! All of a sudden the
Police-Vans   arrive   with   the   sirens   sounding;   the
Yugoslavian-6 looked around with shock on their faces!
Dragan immediately stopped whipping and got out his gun
and so did the other Yugoslavian-6 members. All of the
Police came out of their vans armed with their guns! "This is
the Police! Put all of your hands up right now!" asked one of
the Armed Officers; Dragan and his men realized that they
are completely outnumbered. "Well we got lucky. We have
got the Yugoslavian-6 plus Simone Jane Robinson!" said one
of the Police-Detectives gleefully. In the forest Guillaume
was still remote-viewing observing the Police and the
Yugoslavian-6, his Daemon then says: "Guillaume! Go now,
kill them all and rescue Simone!" immediately Guillaume
made a run to the other side of the forest; when he arrived
at the other end there was a big clearing with the Police,
the Yugoslavian-6 and an unconscious Simone Robinson.
Guillaume was now pondering whether he should use his
paranormal powers. Then he pointed his hand-gun towards
Stojan and shot him in the head; Stojan dies instantly!
Everyone looked around to see where the gun-shot came

from...no-one could see anything! Then all of a sudden Guillaume came out of the forest and immediately began using his power of telekinesis on the Police and the Yugoslavian-6. Simone could just about see the Police and the Yugoslavian-6 being elevated by Guillaume, even though she was in a delirious state! When Guillaume put all of them down he then used one of his other powers and generated electricity out of his body and electrocuted everyone continuously at the same time until all of them had died. Afterwards Guillaume then went to release Simone; again he had to use telekinesis to remove all of the restraints. When Simone was released Guillaume then carried her over his shoulder as she was unconscious and too weak to move. But, Guillaume was going to run into more trouble; more Armed-Police arrived and they saw Guillaume with Simone. Immediately Guillaume got out his hand-gun and shot one of the Armed-Police dead. The Police shot at Guillaume but they kept on missing him; Guillaume then ran back into the forest with Simone over his shoulder. The Armed-Police then chased after him but, Guillaume was too quick for them! When Guillaume got further down he then teleported to the other side of the forest with Simone! Guillaume was now near the edge of the forest to where the main road is and about five minutes walk away from the stolen car. All of a sudden Simone began to groan a little! "Simone it's OK, just stay here. I'll be back in a few minutes!" said Guillaume as he laid Simone underneath some bushes; when he did this he then teleported away. The Armed-Police were in the forest still looking for Guillaume; they were unable to see where he is! Then all of a sudden

Guillaume appeared to them; the Armed-Police went into shock at how Guillaume appeared to them. Then all of a sudden Guillaume began to use his Martial Arts to attack the Armed-Officers; then Guillaume killed all of them by snapping their necks; afterwards Guillaume then teleported back to Simone! Guillaume then took Simone and carried her to the stolen Ferrari and drove off at speed...he had to get Simone to safety as soon as possible!

Much later on in the day more Police had arrived at Dragan's hide-out only to find that everyone is dead! The Police were completely baffled at what went on and what had occurred. However, what was more baffling was that they could not see where Simone Robinson is! "Everyone here is dead but, where is Simone Robinson?" asked one of the Police-Detectives; all of the Police looked around for Simone but they were unable to find her! "She has somehow vanished into thin air!" replied another Police-Detective; they all kept on looking still but, Simone Jane Robinson was nowhere to be seen!

Chapter 30:

Simone Unconscious!

Guillaume was still driving for about two hours wondering on what to do next; he felt a deep concern for Simone. Then Guillaume's Daemon says to him: "Simone is going to be fine; there's an abandoned house about 30 minutes drive away and it is very secluded, away from everything. Go in there now, leave Simone in the house then go and get some medicines for her!" Guillaume acknowledged his Daemon and immediately in the far distance he notices a small lane on the left-hand side. Straight away Guillaume turns left into that lane and then drives straight down it; he then sees a very big house which looked more like a mansion. Guillaume then hears from his Daemon telling him that's the house; he stops the car and then gets out. Guillaume makes his way to the front-door and it was locked; so using the power of his mind he manages to open the door. Afterwards, he goes back to the car to collect Simone; he carries her to inside the house and sees a big sofa and so lays her on there. Guillaume then sees a blanket and uses it to cover Simone to keep her warm; he then whispers to her: "I'll be back soon, just hang in there!" Guillaume then leaves the house to make his way into town. Simone was still in an unconscious state!

Guillaume was in Central London driving around searching for the nearest alternative medicine shop. At a far distance Guillaume was able to locate the type of shop he required and so parked the car near there. Immediately Guillaume got out of the car and went straight into the shop! Guillaume was rushing around grabbing different types of essential oils, health foods and drinks! Eventually Guillaume was able to get what he needed and went to pay at the till. Everyone in the shop both customers & staff were all looking at Guillaume oddly at what he had just done. When the shop-assistant finished scanning all of Guillaume's items she then says: "That will be £96.21p." Guillaume immediately paid up and when he was finished he left the shop in a big haste and went to put the shopping bags into the car. Next, Guillaume went to another shop nearby to purchase shower gel, bar-soap, bath towels and shampoo.

As Guillaume was shopping for more items there were two Police-Constables nearby and they noticed the car that Guillaume had stole earlier. They immediately recognized that it is the stolen car and one of the Officers radioed to the Police control-room. "Yes we have the stolen car reported earlier today!" said one of the Officers. In the shop Guillaume's Daemon alerted him: "Guillaume there are two Police-Officers by the car you stole earlier. They have already alerted the Police control-room!" Guillaume then realized that he had to purchase the items quickly and so he did. After Guillaume paid for the items he went straight back to the stolen Ferrari. Near the stolen car the two Police-Constables were looking around and when Guillaume got to the car and unlocked the door the two Police-Constables then went up to him. "Excuse me Sir, what are you doing? This is a stolen car!" explained the first Officer; Guillaume stood there saying nothing! The two Police-Constables looked at each other with confused looks on their faces! Then all of a sudden Guillaume performed Martial Arts on the two Police-Constables and knocked them out! Then all of a sudden there was another Police-car that parked nearby and two other Police-Constables had noticed that Guillaume had assaulted their colleagues. The two other Police-Constables then went for Guillaume but, he managed to somersault over them. Guillaume then did Martial Arts on the two other Police-Constables and then knocked them out as well; onlookers were in complete shock at Guillaume's physical attributes. All of a sudden one of the onlookers decided to play vigilante towards Guillaume. "Hey you stop that! What are you doing?" demanded the vigilante; Guillaume looked at the vigilante and said nothing! Then Guillaume pulled out his hand-gun and pointed it straight at the vigilante; the vigilante then made a run for it! Members of the public had then all became startled; Guillaume then puts the shopping bag into the Ferrari and then drove off!

When Guillaume returned to the abandoned house he got out of the Ferrari and then collected the shopping bags to take inside the house. Inside the house Guillaume went to find the bathroom in which he did; he then entered the bathroom and turned on the water-taps to fill the bath. Guillaume also ensured that the water was not too hot; when the bath was filled he then adds plenty of drops of essential oils to the water. Next, he goes to get Simone; on the sofa Simone was still in a very unconscious state almost to the point of being comatose! Guillaume then carries Simone to make his way to the bathroom and puts her carefully into the bath; he had to do this as the essential oils mixed with water would help heal the horrific wounds Simone received at the hands of Dragan! Simone still in an unconscious state then begins to groan a little; through her eyes all she could see was a big blur! Simone could barely open her eyes! "It's alright Simone everything is going to be fine! I'm going to help you recover from your horrific wounds; you are safe now!" whispered Guillaume; he then went to get the shampoo and washes Simone's hair carefully. Simone was in such a pitiable state that she needed to have a good wash so as not to infect her wounds more! After Simone was properly cleaned up, Guillaume carried Simone to one of the bedrooms and when he got there Simone was thoroughly dried down. Next, Guillaume turned Simone faced down on the bed and using some bottles of tea-tree oils he poured them all over Simone's wounds. Using his hands Guillaume then massaged the oils right into Simone's wounds to get it in deeper. Then Guillaume got out a huge roll of tissues and placed a lot of them over Simone's wounds and then poured more tea-tree oil over the tissues to help heal the wounds more. After all that was done Guillaume first put a dry bath towel over Simone and then a gigantic quilt to keep her warm. All Guillaume had to do was to wait for Simone to fully recover!

In the middle of the night Guillaume teleported to a clothes shop to steal a lot of clothes for Simone and some for himself. It was all easy for him and he had no trouble at all. When it was night-time Guillaume went to sleep as he was completely exhausted from all of the chaos he endured.

During his sleep Guillaume was conversing again with his own Daemon. He said to Guillaume: "Simone needs a lot of help and you are the person who is going to do this. She is a very unique woman who possesses many gifts; by the way she knows you possess many paranormal powers but, she will keep it a secret. When the time comes tell her the whole truth!" Whilst still in a deep-sleep Guillaume realized that he will eventually have to tell Simone everything including the fact that he murdered all of the pupils & teachers from his old school in the UK!

Simone Robinson was unconscious for about three days but, she was making a very good recovery as a result of Guillaume's knowledge of alternative medicine. Guillaume used many kinds of methods including doing Reiki on her; Simone's wounds were healing completely fast! In her unconscious state Simone was having a vivid & clear dream; it was at the point of time when she was restrained to the punishment pole at Dragan's hide-out. Simone's dream revealed very clearly that when the Police & Armed-Police arrived she could see Guillaume using his powers of telekinesis to elevate everyone there. She also saw Guillaume generating electricity out of his body killing all of the Police & the Yugoslavian-6! Simone then recalls Guillaume possessing powers of teleportation to get from one place to another and also she could see the other sets of Police-Officers getting killed in the forest. Simone was feeling all of the pain she received at the hands of Dragan due to his vicious & extreme whipping! Next, Simone begins to recall lying in the back seat of the stolen Ferrari and also being helped in the bathroom getting washed and having essential oils all over her back to heal from her horrific wounds!

Chapter 31:

Simone recovers!

Morning had arrived and a few days had passed since Guillaume had killed all of the Police and the Yugoslavian-6 to rescue Simone Robinson; Police Detectives were still baffled on who had committed all of this. Simone suddenly woke up for the first time in three days; she gets up from her bed and looks around. Simone then wonders where she is and how she got there; she felt very confused! The last thing Simone remembered was getting whipped viciously by Dragan and it had really shaken her to relive that terrible moment. Suddenly beside the bed on a small cabinet was a small note for Simone written by Guillaume. The note said: *I have made breakfast for you and there is a small chair which has a dressing-gown and flip-flops for you.* Simone then wonders who wrote the note; then suddenly she realizes that there are tissues stuck on her back; she removes them and turns her back towards a mirror and to her surprise there were no scars or wounds on her back, bottom & legs! Simone then wonders how it is that possible considering she was completely covered in nasty bruises. Simone sees the small chair with the dressing-gown and she goes to put it on and the flip-flops as well. Also on the chair was a cup with a toothbrush & toothpaste inside of it; they were for her.

Simone then makes her way to the bathroom to have her wash.

Upon finishing Simone then goes downstairs to find the kitchen to have her breakfast. It was the first she sees Guillaume Moreau; he then goes up to Simone. "Good morning Madame! My name is Commandant Guillaume Moreau of the French Secret Service, DGSE!" said Guillaume as he showed his DGSE badge; Simone then looked at Guillaume's badge. "Oh! You are the one who rescued me from Dragan?" pondered Simone; Guillaume then gave her a little smile! "Yes, it was me. I'm glad you have recovered well!" said Guillaume, "Yes I had noticed that; thank you I really appreciate that!" said Simone gratefully. For their breakfast Guillaume made fried eggs, baked beans, bacon, sausages, hash-browns, fried bread & pancakes. "I hope the breakfast that I made for you is fine. I normally don't eat those kinds of foods; I am normally into healthy foods!" explained Guillaume, "No that's fine; besides I am really hungry! Thank you for making breakfast for me." said Simone; Guillaume then gave a big smile and nodded his head in appreciation. Guillaume then puts the food onto the plates and then Simone tucked straight into her breakfast; she was extremely hungry!

During breakfast Simone decided to strike a conversation with Guillaume. "Your English is very good up to the point that you don't sound French." said Simone, "Yes in a way you are right. My parents are from Mauritius which is French-speaking but I was born in England and I lived there until I was 12 years old." explained Guillaume, "Wow! Where did you go?" asked Simone, "I went to China and trained as a Shaolin Monk." replied Guillaume; Simone then had a surprised look on her face! "China? That is a huge step!" said Simone, "Yes what happened I ran away from home as I became fed up with my parents and my old school. I felt it was the only choice I could make but I'm glad I did!" explained Guillaume; Simone then had a realization about something! "I just realized something; I thought I had heard that name before. You were that boy that ran away at the age of 12 years old back in 1989 from a town called Bedford!" said Simone; Guillaume then looked at Simone with a straight face! "Yes that was me! You are spot on, you are a very smart woman!" complimented Guillaume, "I remember it so well; because of that incident you influenced me to run away from home when I was 13 years old. That town Bedford, I know it because of this group called the Indian-Bandits; they are from there! There were part of Dragan's crime syndicate....I heard that they're all dead!" explained Simone, "Yes I killed all of the Indian-Bandits; I was ordered to by my Government!" said Guillaume; Simone then looked at Guillaume with shock on face! "I'm glad you did because they were getting more dangerous. There was this bitch called Sahita Hana, she was a complete psycho!" said Simone, "I know, I remember her from my time in Bedford and the rest of the Indian-Bandits. Sahita had a fucking big mouth! As I had lived in Bedford previously that was one of the reasons why my Government put me on this mission." explained Guillaume, "Yes I can see why! By the way, you need to keep a low-profile as the Police are after you...you're a wanted murderer...I don't want you to get caught. I completely understand why you so wanted to get out of that school and run away; plus I don't blame you!" said Simone, "I know that I am a wanted murderer but, don't worry I am good at staying low. My Government are also aware of this situation and we are always one step ahead!" explained Guillaume; the two of them carried on eating their breakfast!

In the late morning Simone was minding her own business when she then began to have flash-backs! It was at the time when Guillaume was at Dragan's base where he used some of his paranormal powers to kill all of the Yugoslavian-6 and the Police. Simone then realized that Guillaume does actually possess paranormal powers; Simone then wonders what would happen to her if she tells Guillaume that she is aware of his powers. She began to worry a little and decided to keep it to herself for the time being!

Chapter 32:
Revelations!

Simone was trying on some of the new clothes that Guillaume had stolen for her earlier; she was so pleased with her new clothes. "Hey Guillaume! These clothes are amazing; I have never worn any decent clothes at all in my entire life. Thank you so much for them!" said Simone gleefully; Guillaume had a smile on his face due to Simone's elation. "No problem! It is my pleasure, you deserve them. There are also brand new walking shoes for you!" explained Guillaume; Simone felt so happy being free from the Yugoslavian-6 even though she is not out of the woods yet!

A little later on both Guillaume & Simone went to sit at a table together in the abandoned house; Simone was getting ready to reveal everything about the Yugoslavian-6 and their syndicates. "So Guillaume, are you ready for the big reveal?" asked Simone; Guillaume then got out a pen & paper and put them both on the table to show Simone! "Yes I am ready, Simone." replied Guillaume; Simone then took a deep breath! "Where shall I start? Oh yes, to begin when the Yugoslavian-6 started their group and I had just been forced to join, Dragan was wanting to use his contraband business to fund something really big. Dragan and the rest of the Yugoslavian-6 were all ex-military. The Yugoslavian-6 wanted to take over the whole of Europe and team up with

Russia so they could get help and turn the whole continent into an authoritarian rule. Dragan also wanted to get revenge on France because they ended the Yugoslavian war therefore killing all of the separatists including Zarkan, its leader!" explained Simone, "Yes I know about the Yugoslavian war, I was in it when I was a Helicopter-Pilot. It was me who killed Zarkan!" explained Guillaume; Simone had a surprised look on her face! "Wow! That was you! Anyway, let me go on. There are Police Detectives and Police Constables involved with this collusion plus UK Politicians...and I know all of their names!" further explained Simone; Guillaume then stopped writing for a bit! He became subdued at the fact that UK Politicians are involved with this. Guillaume then realized that he has more big fishes to fry! "OK, I'm ready! Tell me all of their names including the UK Politicians." instructed Guillaume; Simone then nodded to indicate that she is ready to reveal all of the names. "So the Police Constables whom are involved are Steven Smith, Paul Birchall, Oliver Williams, Christopher Peters, Derek Davidson, James Cross and Jonathan Hall. The Police-Detectives whom are involved are Michael Paul, Peter Hart, Arthur White, William Woodward and Edward Cane. Now here are the UK Politicians; Simon Pane, Michael Smythe, Peter Dole, Alan McDougall, Martin Klein and Stephen Giles!" revealed Simone; Guillaume looked at the list with shock on his face. "You mean the Foreign Secretary Simon Pane & the Ex-Chancellor Alan McDougall? I don't believe this...that is a big bombshell!" said Guillaume; he sat there with his face in his hands. It gave him a great shock that two well-known

UK Politicians are involved with the Yugoslavian-6 syndicate! "Yes you're absolutely correct! The current Foreign Secretary and the Ex-Chancellor are heavily involved! So what are you going to do next?" pondered Simone, "I will have to sit tight and mull over this situation as this is really deep!" responded Guillaume; he really didn't know what to do! When both Guillaume & Simone had finished they went to have their lunch!

A little after finishing their lunch Simone then went up to Guillaume with a subdued look on her face; Guillaume then realized that something was wrong! "Simone, are you OK?" asked Guillaume with a concerned look on his face. "To be honest...no I'm not!" replied Simone; Guillaume then began to feel a little shiver down his spine! "Why?" asked Guillaume, "Well, you probably know that the Police want to arrest me for the Yugoslavian-6 crimes. They are so desperate to hang me to dry...they really want to get me. The whole Police-force want to set me up and cover-up all of these crimes!" explained Simone; Guillaume then put his hand on her shoulder to calm her down. "Yes I am aware of your very difficult situation, I know how you feel and I want to help you at the same time!" explained Guillaume; Simone then looked at Guillaume eye-to-eye still feeling subdued! "I never really wanted to do this...I had no idea who the Yugoslavian-6 were but, when I found out it was too late. It was either work for them or get killed; I was desperate I didn't know where to turn. I was on the streets for 5 years before I worked for Dragan; I mean I had to escape my old life in Leeds from my horrible school and my evil parents. When I first ran away I felt free within myself and I don't regret doing this, I know I have done the right thing!" explained Simone; Guillaume then paused for a bit! "Believe me as you know I have been there! But, I want to reassure you that I will get you out of the UK into French-Switzerland and no-one will get you! Believe me it won't be that difficult, you're a good woman!" said Guillaume, "Hey thanks! With all of the crimes I'm probably looking at 20-30 years. Oh by the way I don't have a passport!" said Simone, "Don't worry I'll get one for you!" responded Guillaume; it really is going to be quite a challenging mission for Guillaume and the DGSE.

In the very late afternoon Simone decided to go up to Guillaume again; she desperately wanted to talk to him! "Guillaume, sorry to bother you I have a couple of questions." said Simone; Guillaume looked at Simone for a bit. "OK, so what is the first question?" pondered Guillaume, "What is going to happen about the UK Politicians?" asked Simone, "Well after careful thought the only option I have is to terminate all of them. They are far too dangerous to stay alive and the whole of Europe is at stake! So what is the second question?" further pondered Guillaume; immediately his Daemon then says to him: "Guillaume, it is time!" Guillaume then pondered what his Daemon meant! "Well it's kind of hard to explain. I had a lot of flash-backs over this including in my dreams. Do you have paranormal powers? I swear I saw you use telekinesis & teleportation!" explained Simone; Guillaume then realized what his Daemon meant! "You know, you are absolutely correct! I do possess these powers plus many more!" responded Guillaume; Simone then realized why she was receiving all of those flash-backs. "Wow that's big! How did you get all of these powers?" pondered Simone, "Well when I was a Shaolin Monk in China we do a lot of Martial Arts and meditation. Normally we go to the mountain-caves and meditate in there as it increases our intuition more. On one particular day when I was still 12 years old and a few months into being at the Shaolin School I was meditating in the caves I suddenly had an out-of-body experience and spoke to a being called a Daemon sometimes it can be referred to as your Higher-Self. My Daemon helped me developed all of these paranormal powers!" explained Guillaume; Simone had the look of awe on her face! "Wow that's amazing! I would love to possess all of these powers!" joked Simone; Guillaume then smiled at Simone a little at her amusing remark. "There are 2 things that I need to tell you. For one, nobody knows that I possess paranormal powers; you are the first person to know. And two I used my paranormal powers to kill all of the pupils & teachers from my old school!" confessed Guillaume; Simone then looked at him without any reaction! "For some bizarre reason, I knew somehow that you did! However, I don't blame you I can see why you did this! Remember what I said to you before; when I heard about your story you influenced me to do the same. My parents were so bad to me that I had to leave!" explained Simone; Guillaume had suddenly felt a big sense of relief all over his body. "I'm so glad that I influenced you and thank you for the compliment." said Guillaume, "Every time I heard on TV that a Timothy Morely pupil or teacher got murdered by you for some bizarre reason I had somehow wished that you would never get caught...now I know why

I felt that way. Oh by the way I will keep this all a secret just between the two of us!" said Simone, "Thank you, I appreciate that!" responded Guillaume; Simone then went over and gave Guillaume a hug. The two of them then realized that they seemed to have so much in common and a very special bond! Both Guillaume & Simone realized that they needed each other in more ways than one!

Chapter 33:

Simone's revenge!

Morning had arrived both Guillaume & Simone went to have their breakfast; Simone had recovered a lot more from her injuries at the hands of Dragan. Simone was going to inform Guillaume about the D-Turks who are another syndicate of the Yugoslavian-6. "So Guillaume the D-Turks are based in a Central London town called Holland Park, as they are the eyes & ears for the Yugoslavian-6; they hide out of sight quite well." explained Simone, "I see; sounds intriguing! What do the D-Turks actually do for the Yugoslavian-6?" asked Guillaume, "Well when the drugs are produced they are sent to the D-Turks and they sell them on the streets of London." replied Simone, "Do they do anything else?" questioned Guillaume, "Yes, they sell weapons and hold some of them for the Yugoslavian-6." explained Simone, "Luckily my Government had given me the photos & names of the D-Turks; good thing you remembered them, Simone." complimented Guillaume; Simone smiled in appreciation! "Oh by the way, the apartment building they're in is abandoned and it hasn't been used in years before the D-Turks occupied it. No-one knows that the building is occupied; everybody thinks it's still abandoned!" explained Simone; Guillaume then realized that he could be onto something which would make his task easier!

It was late morning Simone was in the bedroom contemplating on something; she was having deep thoughts! Simone then left the bedroom to look for Guillaume. When Simone found Guillaume she went up to him and had a sullen & subdued look on her face; Guillaume then realized that something was wrong! "Simone, are you OK? You don't look very happy at all." said Guillaume with concern; Simone just gazed at him and then took a deep breath! "Yes you're right Guillaume; there's something that I need to get off my chest and it is very personal. I have held this for a very long time!" explained Simone; Guillaume looked at Simone pondering what she is going to say. Then Guillaume's Daemon says to him: "Listen to Simone & then help her!" Guillaume then realized it is something big! "OK Simone, tell me!" responded Guillaume, "Well my trashy school in Leeds as I explained was very corrupt. It was also a very dangerous place to be in...we were all treading on our toes...yes it was that scary. What happened there were these 6 boys and they were completely evil to the core. They were a gang who always stuck together and they did all kinds of evil things together but, the school turned a blind-eye to all of it. There was speculation that they killed people but, nobody could prove any of this!" explained Simone; Guillaume had a slightly shocked look on his face! "Wow, that's heavy!" said Guillaume; Simone looked at Guillaume and gave him a slight nod! "Well it gets worse & worse! Firstly, there was this boy at my school who was in the same year as me and he was completely harmless. He was born in England to

Nigerian parents and these boys attacked & murdered him due to the colour of his skin; it was racially motivated! My teachers knew about this and who committed the murder but, they were all racists too and they covered up the whole crime! My teachers were pleased that the Nigerian boy had died and even the local Police covered up the crime! Now onto the second bit! I had this best-friend and her name was Belinda; we had so much in common! Like me she was an only child and also like me she had serious problems with her parents. We made a pact that we were going to runaway from this shit-hole as soon as possible and go to wherever we could go. Unfortunately, what happened those same 6 boys abducted Belinda and gang-raped her! Then afterwards those evil bastards killed her!" explained Simone; she sat there with great sadness on her face! Guillaume couldn't believe what he had just heard! "So what happened after that incident?" pondered Guillaume, "Well like the other murder my evil teachers just covered up the whole thing even though they knew who committed this heinous crime! Not only I lost my best-friend I also lost my sister. Belinda was the sister that I never had!" explained Simone; Guillaume had great sadness on his face and had great empathy for Simone! "I'm so sorry to hear of this; your old school was really that evil! So where are we going with this story?" asked Guillaume; Simone then looked at him with a slightly stern look on her face! "Well I need your help. I want to see those boys dead...all 6 of them! I want revenge for the Nigerian boy & Belinda! Can you help me kill them?" asked Simone; Guillaume then gave Simone a nod! "Of course I'll help you. What we need to do first is that you & me will remote-view together as I need their descriptions. When we're both more relaxed we'll be able to remote-view together easier!" explained Guillaume; Simone nodded a little without saying a word!

A little later on in the day Simone was more relaxed after the horrors of what she had told Guillaume about her old school in Leeds. Guillaume was also more relaxed; earlier he felt worried about Simone's state of mind! "Simone! Are you ready to remote-view with me?" asked Guillaume; Simone then turned her head towards Guillaume and then nodded a 'yes' response to him! "Let's do this!" replied Simone; Guillaume then instructed her to sit cross-legged facing him and so she complied! Guillaume also sat cross-legged facing Simone. "OK! What I need you to do is to take a few deep breaths to relax your whole body more so you can get into the alpha state." instructed Guillaume; Simone complied and took a few deep breaths continuously until she was completely relaxed! Guillaume did the same thing as well. "Next, lay your hands on top of mine and then close your eyes." further instructed Guillaume; Simone immediately laid her hands on top of Guillaume's hands and then she closed her eyes! Guillaume also closed his eyes! "OK Simone, firstly I need you to open your mind so I can get the identities of the 6 boys from your old school in Leeds, then I will need to go deep inside of your mind and then we can seek them out!" explained Guillaume; Simone relaxed herself more & more and Guillaume was easily able to get inside Simone's mind! As Guillaume delved deeper & deeper into Simone's mind he managed to get the identities of the 6 men; he could hear Simone's Higher-Self saying to him:

"These are the 6 boys from my old school!" This made it easier for Guillaume to go even deeper. In their minds both Guillaume & Simone were tracking the location of the 6 men, then all of a sudden an invisible voice says to them: "Later on the 6 men are going down to their local pub to have a few drinks. You can get them there!" All of a sudden both Guillaume & Simone came out of their trance; Simone hyperventilated a little! "Wow, that was so powerful! I know that pub; it's in my home-town. Looks like they all never left Leeds. Can you do it, Guillaume?" asked Simone; Guillaume then looked at Simone with utter silence on his face! "Yes I can. It won't be a problem all I need is a balaclava. What will happened is when I teleport to that pub I'll have to kill them with my bare-hands. I won't be able to us my hand-gun as it will arise suspicions and it could possibly be traced back to the Government of the Republic of France!" replied Guillaume; Simone acknowledged him understanding what he meant. Guillaume was more or less ready to go in for the big kill!

Evening had arrived and Guillaume was fully ready to kill the six men from Simone's old school; Simone had noticed that he was all set to go. "Simone I am going in for the kill, I'm ready!" said Guillaume, "Good! Thank you for doing this; I want retribution for the 2 victims!" responded Simone; Guillaume then nodded at Simone and then put the balaclava over his head to conceal his identity! Immediately Guillaume then teleported to the pub in Leeds. Guillaume teleported to the men's toilets of the pub and immediately went into invisible mode. Luckily there was no-one in the men's toilets and so Guillaume went visible

and made his way out of the men's toilets. When Guillaume
arrived in the drinking area the customers were all
wondering what a man wearing a balaclava is doing inside
a pub; they all became nervous. Guillaume ignored them
and went to look for the six men; eventually he was able to
locate all six of them sitting at a table together. The six men
were all laughing & joking among themselves; Guillaume
stood there looking at them closely. One of the six men
then noticed Guillaume standing still observing them. Then
the other five men then noticed this too; they all looked
at one another completely bemused. One of the men then
asks Guillaume: "Hey! You got a problem mate?" Guillaume
didn't respond; everyone in the pub became baffled! All of
a sudden Guillaume then goes into Martial Arts mode and
attacked all six men knocking all of them down. Everyone
went into shock at Guillaume's physical abilities; then when
all of the six men were beaten down viciously Guillaume
then proceed to snap all of their necks off! All of the six
men from Simone's old school were now dead...Guillaume
had achieved Simone's retribution! All of a sudden a man
then tried to attack Guillaume but he was no match for
Guillaume as he was eventually knocked down out cold.
Many people in the pub ran out in horror and one of the
bar-staff went to telephone the Police. Guillaume went
straight back into the men's toilets and immediately
teleported back to the abandoned house. Upon returning
Guillaume told Simone about the success of killing the six
men from her old school. "You know, that has given me a
great sense of relief...justice has been served!" said Simone
gleefully; Guillaume was himself pleased that he was able to

help Simone get revenge for what the six men did at her old school.

At the pub where Guillaume killed the six men, Police-Detectives were there investigating the crime by interviewing the witnesses. They couldn't get much information as Guillaume was wearing a balaclava at the time of the incident; it was a little difficult for them to get any clues whatsoever. What was worse for the Police was that there was no trace of DNA found at the crime scene! Then a bombshell hit them; they found out that the six men had attended the same school as Simone Robinson! The Police were fully aware who Simone is as she is one of the most wanted person in Britain! The Police were also wondering if it was a strange coincidence!

Chapter 34:
Escape!

It was the middle of the night that both Guillaume & Simone were fast asleep; the two of them decided to go to bed a little earlier as they both still felt very exhausted! It was about 03:00 hours in the morning and Guillaume was receiving another message from his Daemon: "Guillaume, I really need to warn you because you & Simone are in grave danger. At first light you & Simone must leave the house and make your way to Central London. The Police later on will find out where you & Simone are; then they will get ready to apprehend the two of you. Do what you have to do even if it means killing the Police...you have no other option! Pay attention to what I am about to show you!"

Even though Guillaume was fast asleep he was fully aware of his own Daemon speaking to him. His Daemon then showed some images and Guillaume paid attention; at first there was the London Police delving into the investigation of the incidents involving Guillaume. The Police-Detectives then realized that he was hugely responsible for the killings of the Indian-Bandits, the Bum-Lords & the Yugoslavian-6! However, the Police were having great difficulties as they were unable to identify Guillaume as he was heavily disguised. The Police even wondered who Guillaume really is and what his motives are unaware that he is a on a mission for the French Government. Some of the Police-Detectives were getting worried as they are the ones whom are heavily involved with the Yugoslavian-6. Guillaume in his sleep is receiving the information very clearly; he is aware of what the Police are investigating. As usual Guillaume is one step ahead of the Police. Going deeper into the investigation the Police wondered if the abandoned house that Guillaume & Simone are residing at is still there! Some of the Police didn't even know that there was an abandoned house on the outskirts of Greater London! The Police-Detectives then decided to check if there is an abandoned house; they were all in a state of confusion! All of a sudden the images began to distinguish and then there was a blank space! Guillaume's Daemon then says to him: "There you go! I have given you enough information. Now it is time for you to take action!" Guillaume then suddenly woke up from his sleep hyperventilating a little; he then went to check his watch...it was 03:20 hours! Guillaume realized that he & Simone have to escape very soon; he got out of bed and rushed to wake Simone!

When Guillaume arrived at Simone's bedroom he immediately went to wake her; Simone suddenly woke up! "Sorry to wake you so early Simone but, we're going to have to leave soon!" explained Guillaume; Simone then rubbed her eyes a little! "Hey! What time is it?" asked Simone in a sluggish state! "It is about 03:25!" replied Guillaume; Simone had a surprised look on her face! "What! 03:25?" said Simone frantically, "Yes, exactly! I had a message from my Daemon; the Police will be here soon. We need to escape as soon as possible!" explained Guillaume; Simone's eyes suddenly flew wide open in shock! "What time will they get here?" asked Simone frantically, "It will be much later in the morning. Don't worry we will have time to eat breakfast and do other stuff!" explained Guillaume; immediately Simone got out of bed and went to the bathroom to have her wash. Guillaume then went to do the same!

It was about 05:00 hours that Guillaume & Simone were having breakfast; Guillaume needed to go over the plans with Simone. "OK what we need to do is booby-trap the house so when the Police arrive the place will blow up and kill all of them. Also, you will need to disguise yourself more Simone as you're wanted by the Police. We'll escape by the car first and then we will carry on by foot; I won't be able to teleport physically as there are too many cameras around when we get closer towards Greater London!" explained Guillaume; Simone acknowledged him and gave a nod. "How are we going to booby-trap the house and how am I going to disguise myself more?" pondered Simone; Guillaume then got out a woman's wig and a pair of spectacles to show Simone. "This brown wig here will cover your blond hair and these fake spectacles will make it harder for the Police to recognize you more. I have some make-up so you can cover your face more." explained Guillaume as he gave a box of make-up to Simone. "Wow, you certainly came prepared!" complimented Simone; Guillaume appreciated her comment. "To booby-trap the house there are plenty of petrol in the basement. First we must pour as much petrol all around the house and then turn on the gas-supply system. I found a very long piece of rope; we need to soak it with petrol and then tie it somewhere to the house. Next, we will go in the car and drive as far away down into the forest. Then I will use telekinesis to bring the rope over to us and I will light the rope...and the rest they say is history!" explained Guillaume; after the plans were briefed to Simone the two of them carried on eating their breakfast. It was going to be a long and difficult road ahead!

At 07:00 hours Guillaume & Simone went to put the first part of the plan into action! Guillaume went to fill the bathtub with petrol so he could soak the rope in it. Next, both Guillaume & Simone went to pour petrol all around the abandoned house from top to bottom and also on the outside. The two of them had to wear latex gloves at all times so they wouldn't leave their finger-prints anywhere. There were plenty of cans of petrol so they had more than enough and they used every drop of it. Lastly, the rope was then tied to the house. When they finished that part of the plan Simone had to put her disguise on as instructed by Guillaume. Simone had to put on a different shade of pink to make herself unrecognizable; then lastly she put on the brown wig and fake spectacles. Simone then went to look for Guillaume to show him her new image. "Hey Guillaume how do I look?" asked Simone as she showed Guillaume. "Well you certainly don't look like Simone Jane Robinson!" joked Guillaume as he smiled a little! Simone smiled back at Guillaume's response! Guillaume & Simone packed their rucksacks with all of their personal belongings and when they were all set it was time to leave. It was nearly 08:00 hours and surprisingly it was still very dark outside. "It is a good thing that it's still dark. This will make it easier for us

to get undetected!" explained Guillaume; the two of them
then got inside the car and drove as far as they can deep
into the forest. There was a small-clearing and Guillaume's
Daemon instructed him to stop the car immediately and
so he complied. Both Guillaume & Simone got out of the
car and immediately Guillaume went into remote-viewing
mode. Using remote-viewing Guillaume focused on the rope
soaked with petrol; he then uses telekinesis to bring the rope
over to him and he was successful. "So what are we going to
do next?" pondered Simone, "All we have to do is sit & wait
for the Police to arrive...then there will be the BIG BANG!"
replied Guillaume; the two of them then sat in the car and
waited.

At the Police station Detectives were still wondering
whether there is an abandoned house where Guillaume &
Simone were staying at. Then they received the
breakthrough; one of the Police-staff found out that there
is a house there and no-one has lived in it for many years.
However, they found out from gas, electric and water
companies that it had been recently used. Now the Police
realized that very likely Guillaume & Simone had been
staying there; an even bigger breakthrough! The
Police-Detectives then went to call for the Armed-Police
and when they were summoned all of them made their way
to the abandoned house. They were all getting ready to
apprehend Guillaume Moreau & Simone Jane Robinson!

Back in the forest Simone was asleep in the car but,
Guillaume was wide awake; all of a sudden he could hear
Police sirens. He immediately knew the Police are on their
way to capture him & Simone! "Simone, wake up!"

whispered Guillaume as he jerked Simone; she suddenly wakes up! "What is it?" asked Simone, "The Police are here...it's time!" replied Guillaume; Simone could also hear the sirens! "Oh yeah! I can hear the Police sirens!" said Simone; the two of them then got out of the car. As they got out Guillaume went into remote-viewing mode and observed the Police, Armed Police & Detectives from a distance. He could see all of the Police entering the house with their guns looking for the two of them. However, the Police couldn't locate them; Guillaume then realized it was time to go in for the kill! "Simone, I'm going to do it now. Get ready for a massive explosion!" explained Guillaume; immediately he went into remote-viewing mode to locate the gas-supply systems and when he did he switched on the gas-levers using telekinesis. Gas emitted out of the pipes and all of the Police inside were completely unaware of this! Guillaume then generated electricity out of his body and used it to light the petrol-soaked rope! "Simone, lets go!" ordered Guillaume; immediately they got into the car and then Guillaume drove off at high-speed! The rope was alight with fire and as soon as the fire reached the abandoned house there was a huge explosion! It was the equivalent of a nuclear bomb explosion which could be heard in many parts of London. Every member of the Police had perished and as the explosion was so huge the abandoned house completely disintegrated; plus there was a huge hole created in the ground. There were many dead bodies lying around...it looked like a massacre!

Further down the road Guillaume was driving along looking for somewhere to dump the stolen car. He then sees a river which leads towards the Thames; his Daemon then instructs him to dump the car in the river. "Simone, we need to dump the car there in that river to get rid of the evidence!" explained Guillaume; Simone nodded at him in agreement! Guillaume then drove the car off-road towards the river-bank and then the two of them got out of the car. "Simone what we need to do is push the car into the river and then I will throw a grenade into it. As soon as I do this move out of the way!" explained Guillaume; Simone obliged and went to help him push the car into the river. As soon as the car got into the river Guillaume then immediately threw a grenade into the car; both he & Simone took cover and all of a sudden the car exploded into many pieces. "So what shall we do next?" asked Simone, "We need to make our way to the nearest coach-station and then take a coach to Central London. I need to find my colleagues; they will be wondering what has happened to me." replied Guillaume; Simone then nodded a little. "How long will it take to get there?" asked Simone, "It is about a 40-minute walk to the nearest one!" replied Guillaume; immediately the two of them went on their way to the coach station staying in the forest to keep out of sight. Whilst the two of them were walking along Guillaume had to go over some new plans with Simone. "What we need to do next is when we get nearer to the coach station we need to keep a distance between us so as not to arouse any suspicions. But, don't worry I'll be right behind you where I can see you. When we get to the coach station go straight into the book-shop and buy a book for yourself; I will do the same. When we get on the coach we'll sit in separate seats; by the way you get on the coach first before I do and again I won't be far away from you!" explained Guillaume; Simone nodded in acknowledgment at Guillaume. The two of them then carried on walking.

At the abandoned house that Guillaume blew up there were Police & Fire-Fighters looking at the carnage of it all. All of them were in complete shock; the Fire-Fighters had spent many hours extinguishing the flames. It was a complete horror to see all of the dead bodies; they didn't know what to do. "It certainly looks like that Simone Robinson was here with possibly that mysterious man whoever he is!" said Detective Arthur White, "Yep! I agree. This man is also wanted for multiple assaults in many places. There could be other crimes as well but, we don't know what he looks like. What's more disturbing is that he is some kind of Martial Arts expert from all of the footage we've seen. The weird thing here is that he is smaller than a lot of them...how does he do it?" pondered Detective William Woodward; it really was baffling the Police a lot on how they were going to solve this complex case and at the same time apprehend Simone Jane Robinson!

Chapter 35:
Onward to Central London

The UK media reported the huge explosion at the abandoned house that Guillaume & Simone were staying at. They also reported that Simone Robinson as the main culprit with a mystery man whom is not recognized as Guillaume Moreau. Some of the people in Leeds who knew Simone before she ran away paid particular attention as it was her. They were fully aware that Simone has been a wanted woman for a long time!

Guillaume & Simone had managed to reach a small shopping mall with the coach station attached to it. The shopping mall was on the outskirts of Greater London and it was going to be a fairly long journey to Central London. The two of them were far apart from each other as instructed by Guillaume. They both entered the shopping mall and they first went to buy a coach-ticket each from the ticket-office. Afterwards Simone had noticed a bookshop and entered it first; when Guillaume had noticed this he waited for a few minutes and then he entered the bookshop as well. Inside the bookshop still keeping a distance both Guillaume & Simone were browsing around looking for a book to read. The book that they each picked out were both fiction; Simone went to pay for her book first and immediately left the bookshop to make her way to coach-bays for the Central

London route. Whilst Simone was walking along the shop-floor she notices many of the advertisement boards with her photo displayed on each of them. The advertisement boards goes on to explain that Simone Robinson is a wanted woman; Simone felt a little nervous. However, at present she is unrecognizable from her brown wig and fake spectacles; when Simone arrived at the coach-station she made her way to the required bay and sat in the waiting-room reading her book.

A few minutes later Guillaume was walking along the shop-floor and noticed Simone's face advertised everywhere. He realized that Simone had to be protected at all costs even if it meant he has to kill someone! Guillaume's Daemon suddenly speaks to him: "I know that you are a little worried about Simone but, don't worry! Just stick to your plan & everything will be fine. Stay very vigilant!" Guillaume had managed to calm down a little at what his own Daemon told him. When Guillaume arrived at the coach-station using remote-viewing he manages to locate the required coach-bay and Simone too at the same time. Guillaume then entered the waiting-room and noticed Simone sitting there reading her book; she also had noticed Guillaume. He then went to sit down at a distance from Simone but, where he could see her. About twenty minutes later the coach was ready to leave for Central London; the coach-driver opened the door to the coach and then went to sit in the drivers' seat. One-by-one each passenger boarded the coach and showed their ticket to the driver; Simone had shown her ticket and then went to find a seat. When Guillaume went to show his ticket, the driver became a little nervous considering he is wearing a wig, sunglasses and a hoodie! After his ticket was checked Guillaume then went down the aisle and saw where Simone was sitting. Guillaume then went to sit at his seat which was three rows away from where Simone was sitting; he took his seat and began to read his book. Some of the passengers looked at Guillaume in a strange way; they all thought it was unusual for someone to read a book whilst wearing their sunglasses! When all of the passengers boarded, the coach was now ready to leave for Central London; Guillaume sat there feeling a little nervous as he felt something BIG is going to happen!

At the Police station in London Police-Detectives were thinking of where and how they are going to locate Simone & the mystery man with her. Police-Detectives went through all of the camera-footage of the incidents involving Guillaume; however, it was extremely difficult for the Police as they were unable to know what he actually looks like! "Man! This mystery guy with Simone is so hard to recognize who he is!" said Detective Arthur White, "Yeah! Tell me about it. You can see why he is so heavily disguised!" said Detective William Woodward; all of a sudden a Police-Constable entered the room. "Detective, we have a breakthrough! At a coach-station we have camera-footage of the mystery man; it's definitely him! But, we are unable to locate Simone Robinson!" explained the Police-Constable; the two Detectives looked at each other in astonishment! "Do you have any more information about this?" asked Detective White, "Yes we do. The coach the suspect boarded is heading towards Central London!" replied the Police-Constable, "Good work!" complimented Detective

Woodward; the two Detectives then alerted all of the Police-staff. They were going to drive and locate the coach to apprehend Guillaume!

Back on the Central London coach, Guillaume was still reading his book whilst wearing his sunglasses. Some of the passengers nearby were still looking at him strangely at what he was doing! Then one of the passengers asks him: "Hey! Wouldn't it be better to read without your sunglasses?" Guillaume refused to answer the question and completely ignored the passenger! Some of the other passengers looked at one another in astonishment! Suddenly Guillaume then gets contacted by his Daemon: "Guillaume, I really need to warn you! The Police are on their way and they know what coach you are on. They are mainly after you but, not Simone as she's in disguise. You know what you've got to do!" Guillaume paused for a bit and realized that he is going to be in a predicament! Guillaume then puts his hand underneath his hoodie to check to see if he has his hand-gun on him; he had to do it discretely so no-one knows that he has one. Guillaume then took a deep breath and then carried on reading his book to calm himself down!

About thirty minutes later the coach that Guillaume & Simone were on was suddenly stopped by a lot of Police vehicles. When the coach-driver stopped the coach, he became bemused at why this is happening; then all of the Police and Armed-Police came out of their vehicles. The passengers on the coach began to get worried; Guillaume's Daemon then warns him that the Police have arrived. Guillaume played it cool and remained as relaxed as possible! Detective White entered inside the coach with two

Armed-Police Officers! "Sorry to halt you; we are looking for a suspect. We believe he is a passenger on this coach!" explained Detective White; one of the accompanying Police asked all of the passengers to remain in their seats...everyone complied! Detective White and the two Police-Officers went down the aisle with their hand-guns looking for Guillaume. As they went further down Detective White noticed a woman with brown-hair & glasses...he realized it was Simone! "Hang on Officers! Well...well, if it isn't Simone Jane Robinson!" said Detective White; immediately the two Police-Officers apprehended Simone. Guillaume then realized he had to think quickly and using telepathy he orders Simone not to say anything! The passengers went into complete shock that the country's most wanted individual is on the same coach as them! One of the passengers then says: "Oh my God, that's Simone Robinson!" Detective White had a slight smile on his face! "Well Miss Robinson that's quite a disguise. You can fool everyone but you can't fool me. Now tell me who is that man that was with you and where is he?" demanded Detective White; as requested by Guillaume, Simone refused to answer! Detective White then gives Simone a very stern look! As Guillaume was still sitting down his Daemon then tells him: "Guillaume go now, you know what you've got to do!" Guillaume then got up from his seat and immediately went towards the two Police-Officers & Detective White. "Hey excuse me! I said to remain in your seats!" shouted one of the Officers; immediately Guillaume put the Officer into a Martial Arts grip and then he did a Martial Arts kick on the other Officer and Detective White knocking both of them to the floor.

The Officer that Guillaume had in a Martial Arts grip had his neck snapped by Guillaume killing him instantly! Everyone on the coach became horrified; then Guillaume got out his hand-gun and pointed it at both the Police Officer & Detective White. "Don't fucking move, Monsieur's!" shouted Guillaume; they just laid there in total shock! "Who the hell are you?" asked Detective White; Guillaume refused to answer! Simone stood there right next to him feeling nervous! "What shall we do next?" asked Simone in a slightly frantic state! "That Officer there. He has got another hand-gun in his left-ankle. Remove it quickly, Madame!" ordered Guillaume; she managed to locate the other hand-gun in the Officers left-ankle and removed it. "Here you go!" said Simone as she handed the hand-gun to Guillaume. "Now Monsieur I want you to turn and eat the fucking floor!" demanded Guillaume; the Officer complied and turned to face the floor laying down. "Hey! Are you a French Secret Agent?" questioned Detective White; like before Guillaume refused to answer. "Now you, Monsieur! Fucking get up!" ordered Guillaume; Detective White complied and rose to his feet! "Hey, what is this all about?" asked Detective White; Guillaume then looked at him sternly. "You know what this is all about. I know you're a member of the Yugoslavian-6!" replied Guillaume angrily, "Hey I am not a member of the Yugoslavian-6!" said Detective White; Guillaume felt he was lying! "Don't fucking lie to me, Monsieur!" shouted Guillaume; there was a stand-still on the coach...everything went silent! "You're at stalemate, Monsieur. You have nowhere to go!" said Detective White sarcastically; Guillaume stood there in silence for a bit! "Not really! Now I'm going to tell you this. I want you to go outside and tell your colleagues to move out of the way or I'll blow his fucking brains out!" ordered Guillaume as he pointed his gun to the Police-Officers head. Detective White didn't know what to do; he felt very stuck! "Hey! Be reasonable you can't do this!" said Detective White; he was now getting worried! "Just do as I fucking say or I'll blow his brains out!" shouted Guillaume; Detective White then left the coach to inform his colleagues. As Detective White was outside conversing with his colleagues Guillaume ordered Simone to get the ignition key from the coach-driver. This was so he couldn't drive away just yet! "Hey mate! What is this all about? Why are you doing this?" asked one of the passengers; Guillaume began to feel a little agitated but, he didn't get deterred! "Shut the fuck up Monsieur or I'll put a fucking bullet in your head!" shouted Guillaume; the passenger immediately went silent and said nothing further! Everyone else in the coach just sat there and waited.

A few minutes later Detective White returned and approached Guillaume. "OK, you've got your wish. My colleagues are moving out of the way." said Detective White; Guillaume then looked at him! "Good!" said Guillaume; immediately he snapped the Police-Officers neck killing him instantly! Everyone on the coach went into complete shock! "Hey you promised no-one will get hurt!" said Detective White; Guillaume said nothing. All of a sudden Guillaume kicks Detective White in his testicles and then snaps his neck killing him instantly! All of the passengers couldn't believe what Guillaume had just done; they were all too scared to say or do anything. Guillaume then went into his rucksack and pulled out a sniper-gun; some of the passengers eyes flew wide open in shock; they were wondering what he is going to do next? Guillaume then said to Simone: "Just stay here; I'll be back in a few minutes." Guillaume then climbed onto one of the passenger seats and punched the sunroof open. Very discretely Guillaume then climbed onto the top of the coach with the sniper-gun; Guillaume then ran towards the front-end of the coach. When he got to the front-end he immediately shoots all of the Police including Detective Woodward in a surprise attack! The passengers on the coach all witnessed what had occurred; what surprised them was how Guillaume was able to kill all of the Police on his own with complete ease! "Is that guy a French Secret Agent?" asked one of the passengers; the other passengers all looked at one another and shrugged their shoulders. When Guillaume got back into the coach he instructed Simone to give the ignition keys to the coach-driver and to order him to drive on. Simone complied and returned the keys to the driver and requested him to immediately drive; the coach was now on it's way to Central London. Outside on the road where all of the Police-Officers were shot dead there was one Officer who was barely still alive compared to the rest of them. He reached for his radio and notified the Police Control-Room and said: "Officer down! Officer down! All Officers are dead; male suspect has shot all of the Police!" Everyone in the Control-Room were looking at each other in astonishment! Then one of the Control-Room staff asked: "Where is the suspect?" The wounded Officer then said:

"He has gotten away on the coach. I think there are still passengers on the coach & Simone Robinson is also on the same coach. Need reinforcements!" The Officer then breathed his last breath and died! The Police in the Control-Room attempted to radio the Officer but, it was to no avail they all realized he had perished! There was complete silence in the Control-Room they all went completely numb; immediately more Police were ordered to find the coach that Guillaume & Simone are on so they could apprehend them!

It had been about an hour since the incident involving Guillaume and the Police; the coach was still on the road on its way to Central London. There was a complete silence on the coach; no-one wanted to say or do anything! Guillaume's Daemon then says to him: "Guillaume, the Police are sending reinforcements get ready for them! You know what you've got to do even if it means using extreme measures!" Guillaume then looked around at all of the passengers; he wanted to find a solution to escape without hurting anyone! He then went over to Simone to warn her at what is going to happen next! "Simone, there is going to be more Police on their way...they have already sent in reinforcements! Just wait for further instructions!" whispered Guillaume; some of the passengers were all wondering what Guillaume had whispered to Simone! A few minutes later Guillaume could hear the Police sirens sounding; he realized they were coming for him! Guillaume then looked at Simone and nodded at her; Simone instantly knew what he meant. "What shall we do next?" asked Simone, "Tell the driver what is happening and then tell him to drive on!" replied

Guillaume; Simone then made her way to the front of the coach to inform the driver; the driver complied and drove on. The Police cars & vans got closer & closer to the coach; Guillaume then signaled to the driver to stop! At a distance the Police parked their vehicles and the Armed-Officers came out with their guns ready! Then one of the Police-Officers came out with an electric megaphone saying: "This is the Police! You are surrounded and have nowhere to go. Please give yourselves up!" Guillaume & Simone heard the announcement and looked at each other; however, Guillaume knew he was one step ahead! Guillaume then said to all of the passengers: "Madame's & Monsieur's please pay attention to what I am about to say. Now firstly I am not here to hurt any of you at all. Secondly, I want you all to know that many members of the UK Police and some UK Politicians are involved with an International Terrorist group called the Yugoslavian-6. They are a big danger to the whole of Europe!" All of the passengers gasped with horror! They were all shocked at the revelations being told. Guillaume then went on: "Lastly, I will let all of you go, one-by-one. Driver I want you to go first on my mark; and when you all leave please get as far away from the coach!" Everyone all looked at each other in a confused state wondering what Guillaume is up to. For the time being everything was at stale-mate!

Twenty minutes later Guillaume had decided it is now time to release all of the passengers. He gave the signal to let the coach-driver leave first and so he did; then a few more passengers left as well. When some of the passengers left the coach they all immediately went as far as possible,

well away from the coach. Guillaume then looked at all of
the passengers without saying a word; people were now
wondering what he is planning. Then Guillaume released
more passengers and the coach was now half-full; he then
went to talk to Simone. In her ear Guillaume whispered: "I
have grenades in my rucksack. We'll entice the Police into
the coach and then we will teleport together out of here!"
Simone looked at Guillaume and gave him a nod in
agreement; the remaining passengers were wondering what
they were whispering about! Guillaume then released more
passengers and now there was only ten passengers left. "OK
you lot! As you are the last set of passengers, when you leave
the coach inform the Police that there are only the 2 of us!"
instructed Guillaume; the ten passengers nodded at him in
compliance! Five minutes later Guillaume released the last
ten passengers; as they left Guillaume got out some grenades
and gave a few of them to Simone! "When I say so; pull
the pins out and just throw them anywhere on the coach.
We definitely have enough to cause a huge explosion to kill
most or all of the Police!" explained Guillaume, "Good plan,
let's do this!" agreed Simone; one of the passengers then
informed the Police that only Guillaume & Simone are left
on the coach. Some of the Police went towards the coach
immediately; Guillaume's Daemon then warns him of the
incoming Police. "Simone, pull all the pins out now. They're
coming!" ordered Guillaume; immediately both Guillaume
& Simone pulled all of the pins from the grenades and then
threw them everywhere on the coach. Simone then grabbed
her rucksack and so did Guillaume; Simone then held onto
Guillaume and immediately they teleported together!

Seconds later many of the Armed-Police entered inside the coach however, they couldn't see either Guillaume nor Simone. Then all of a sudden there was a huge explosion; all of the Armed-Police perished and some on the outside were killed as well. There were only a few Police-Officers left; they couldn't believe that they all got sucked into Guillaume's trap. Both Guillaume & Simone teleported to the bushes on the side of the road at a distance from where the passengers and remaining Police are. Using his remote-viewing powers Guillaume was observing and noticed that there are still Police-Officers around; he realized that they needed to be terminated! "Simone, wait here for a bit. I am going to terminate the rest of the Police." explained Guillaume as he teleported away on his own. Guillaume teleported behind another set of bushes and hid out of sight so no-one would suspect that he possesses paranormal powers. Suddenly Guillaume came out of the bushes and immediately went to shoot the rest of the Police; he was able to achieve his objectives! The passengers and the coach-driver all became extremely nervous of Guillaume; they wondered how did he manage to escape the coach unhurt unaware that he possesses many paranormal powers! "Sorry Madame's & Monsieur's. I had to do this; I had no choice!" explained Guillaume; he then ran off in a haste and when he was out of sight he teleported back to Simone! When Guillaume teleported back, Simone was pleased to see him. "OK! It's all done, let's go!" said Guillaume; the two of them took their rucksacks and held on to each other and then teleported away again!

Chapter 36:
Hideaway!

Guillaume & Simone had managed to teleport to a small alleyway in the Central London town of Ealing Broadway; luckily for both of them there were no cameras around. "Do you think anyone has noticed us?" asked Simone; Guillaume using his remote-viewing didn't see anyone around. "No! We got lucky. We'll wait here in the alleyway until it gets a little dark; then we will rendez-vous with my fellow DGSE Agents." said Guillaume; the two of them just stayed out of sight in the small alleyway.

The UK media reported the incident that Guillaume was involved in earlier with the Police & Detectives on the coach. The passengers on the coach and the coach-driver himself gave their statements to Scotland Yard Police about what happened. They even mentioned Simone Robinson and that she is in disguise but, they couldn't pinpoint what Guillaume looks like. Scotland Yard Police then realized that it was the same individual who was involved in the killings of the Yugoslavian-6 and the Indian-Bandits! "Detective, one of the passengers mentioned that the male suspect could well be a French National. They even said that he could be a French Secret Agent!" explained one of the Police-Officers; the Detectives all looked at each other feeling bewildered! "If it is a French Secret Agent, what the hell is he doing in London. What does the French Secret Service want?" asked Detective Peter Hart; as they were pondering on the question suddenly one of the other Detectives had a brainwave! "I've just realized something. It has to do with the Yugoslavian-6; remember they instigated the Yugoslavian Civil War and it was the French Army that ended it all! There must be a connection between the two!" said another Detective, "Shall we contact the British Intelligence Services?" asked one of the Police-Officers; they all nodded a 'yes' response. Scotland Yard Police decided that upon returning to the station they will immediately inform British Intelligence of what had occurred earlier.

It was 17:00 hours and London was beginning to get very dark; Guillaume still in the alleyway with Simone was wondering whether it is the right time to move. "Simone, it's now getting very dark. We can move out now and locate my fellow agents. Plus as it is dark people will not be able to recognize us but, be very discrete or we will get caught out!" explained Guillaume, "Yeah, I can see what you mean. I can understand your logic behind this!" responded Simone; immediately the two of them concealed their identities and began to leave the alleyway onto the streets of Central London. It was going to be very difficult for both Guillaume & Simone as they have painted a big bullseye on their foreheads! As they were walking around London for quite some time Guillaume had managed to locate the other five DGSE Agents. Guillaume introduced his colleagues to Simone. "Moreau, we heard there was a commotion on a coach and they're saying it is possibly the French Secret Service involved with this." explained Xavier; Guillaume looked at him and nodded a little. "Yes you're right! Somehow Detective Arthur White knew that I'm a French Secret Agent but, I didn't confirm this...I remained silent." explained Guillaume, "What shall we do now?" pondered Matthieu, "We still stick to the plan but, we are going to have to do this in a different way!" replied Guillaume; all the five DGSE Agents looked at one another wondering where Guillaume was going with this! "What do you propose Commandant Moreau?" pondered Christophe, "Well the first thing I want to ask is were you all able to achieve your objectives?" questioned Guillaume, "Yes we all did!" replied Christophe, "Good! So I take it that all there is left are the D-Turks and the UK Politicians?" questioned Guillaume, "Yes we can confirm this, Moreau!" replied Raphaëlle, "That will make my job a lot easier. So let me tell you this; Miss Robinson here has given me the names of all 6 UK Politicians whom are are involved with the Yugoslavian-6 syndicate. So, Simone & I will deal with the D-Turks; I need to order the rest of you to immediately return to France!" instructed Guillaume; the DGSE Agents looked at him with surprised looks on their faces! "Moreau, why? You're committing suicide!" said Thérèse; Guillaume then looked at her eye-to-eye! "The big problem is that the UK Police will contact the British Secret Service and they'll be after us in a heart-beat! When you all get through the UK-Borders I'll be able to wipe off any records of you all being here in the UK. Don't worry I know how to do this!" explained Guillaume, "Are you sure you want to do it that way?" pondered Thérèse; Guillaume immediately nodded a 'yes' response to her. "Besides your own safety & security are at risk. The sooner you all return the safer you'll be; and when you return to France someone inform our boss of what happened and to get Simone & I two tickets for the Eurostar back to Paris. Deliver the tickets to the French Embassy in London." ordered Guillaume; they all disbanded and the five DGSE Agents went on their way to get ready to leave the UK to return to Paris, France.

Later on in the evening Guillaume & Simone found an abandoned squatters flat in London; it was on the top-floor of a 3-storey building. The place itself was perfect for them; it was fairly secluded even though it is in Central London. "I know it's not perfect but, at least we're safe here for the time being." explained Guillaume, "No it's all fine." responded Simone, "Besides it does have a bathroom with running water." explained Guillaume, "So what shall we do next?" pondered Simone, "Well we need to locate to where the D-Turks base is and how we are going to locate the 6 UK Politicians." replied Guillaume, "Well I can help you with both, especially with the UK Politicians." said Simone; Guillaume looked at her bemused! "Oh! What do you mean exactly?" pondered Guillaume, "I just realized that in 3 days time there's going to be a big posh event in Bank, London. All 6 of them are going to be attending the event. I remember Dragan talking about it; him & the rest of the Yugoslavian-6 were meant to be attending this as well. I need to show you where it is." replied Simone. "Oh I see. What we'll do tonight is that I need to ask you to take me to both places just to show me and then I will go on to plan to kill the D-Turks first then the 6 UK Politicians." explained

Guillaume; they then went on to plan together for the remaining parts of the mission!

It was very dark outside both Guillaume & Simone left the squatters flat and made their way into town. They went to find the nearest bus-stop and waited for one of the London night buses. When the bus arrived the two of them boarded and paid for their tickets; both Guillaume & Simone sat in separate seats on the bus so as not to arouse any suspicions. The journey itself took twenty minutes when they arrived at the required bus-stop for Holland Park and the two of them got off the bus. Simone walked on in front first and Guillaume just followed on; five minutes later Simone suddenly stopped! "Guillaume, that building across the other side is the D-Turks lair. They are all abandoned flats over there, the Yugoslavian-6 did a lot of dirty dealings with some of the Police a while ago." explained Simone, "Perfect! It won't be too difficult to kill them!" explained Guillaume; when they finished they returned to the same bus-stop and waited for the next bus. Simone was going to show Guillaume to where the event will be hosted; a few minutes later another bus arrived and the two of them boarded. Like before both Guillaume & Simone sat in separate seats to remain very discrete! The next part of the journey took 45 minutes when the night-bus arrived at the required destination of Bank, London; Simone got up first and then Guillaume followed on. Five minutes from the bus-stop Simone stops at a big events hall and then Guillaume stopped as well. "That's the place where they're going to hold the event." explained Simone, "OK! What we'll need to do is when the time comes we need to dress up really posh. I am going to assume that it is going to be a black-tie event." pondered Guillaume, "How will we get in? We're not on the guest-list!" pondered Simone, "We have no choice we have to teleport inside." replied Guillaume; after they had finished the two of them went to return to the squatters flat at Ealing Broadway.

Chapter 37:
Moreau observes

Morning had arrived when Guillaume & Simone woke up from their sleep; Guillaume was taking a peek outside to see if everything was clear. All Guillaume could see was people walking around going to work...it was the morning rush-hour! "Everything OK, Guillaume?" asks Simone observing; Guillaume then turns to look at Simone and he gives her a little smile! "Yes, everything is fine. I just wanted to check just in case if anyone is spying on us, but everything is clear." replied Guillaume; Simone then breathes a sigh of relief! "Well at least that's reassuring. Everyone is after us...we have painted a big bullseye on our foreheads." explained Simone, "Yes I know but we will get through this. I really want to get you out of the UK to French-Switzerland." said Guillaume, "You know, you're the first person I've met who I really trust." complimented Simone; Guillaume then gave Simone a big smile. "Thank you! It's because you're a good woman and I really want to help you; you deserve better. By the way did you sleep well?" queried Guillaume, "Yeah I slept fine; besides I'm used to sleeping rough!" replied Simone with a slight smile. The two of them then went to have their wash and then eat breakfast.

After breakfast Guillaume & Simone went on to discuss more about the D-Turks; Guillaume wanted to terminate all of them first. "Guillaume, I just realized something! Two of the D-Turks Volkan Durnaz & Ahmet Diyadin; they like to hang out at this Turkish bar-restaurant on most evenings. The place itself is in Sloane Square." explained Simone, "Oh really? Very likely this could make it easier for me...I can kill these two first and kill the rest of the D-Turks on another day! Sloane Square is on the District Line." said Guillaume; Simone then nodded. "Yes, I remember because I have been there a few times. Dragan used to do his shady business dealings with those two." explained Simone; "What I'll do tonight is that I will kill the two D-Turks you mentioned. I want you to stay here when I do this for your own safety." explained Guillaume; Simone then went on to explain more about the Police-Detectives whom are involved with the Yugoslavian-6 syndicate. When everything was established Guillaume was more or less ready to execute his plan later in the evening.

At Scotland Yard Police-Detectives were racking their brains out trying to work out who the male assailant was, which is Guillaume Moreau. Even though they ran his identity through the computer-systems it kept on returning a result of NOT RECOGNIZED. The Police were so baffled on why this has occurred! "Has British Intelligence managed to identify this mysterious man?" asked Detective Michael Paul, "They said that there was no identification. They even said that they've checked all of those who are in French Intelligence but, he's not on their systems." explained Detective Peter Hart, "What we'll do is put out under-cover Police-Detectives all over London. This man with Simone Robinson must be somewhere in London!" suggested

Detective Edward Cane; Scotland Yard then ordered to put out undercover Officers to search for Guillaume Moreau & Simone Robinson.

When early evening had arrived Guillaume left Simone at the squatters flat to go on his mission to seek out the two members of the D-Turks Volkan Durmaz & Ahmet Diyadin. Being very discrete Guillaume made sure that the coast was clear and when it was he was on his way. As it was so dark Guillaume was able to conceal his identity and he wore dark clothing which made it more difficult for anyone to notice him. Guillaume was walking along as usual making his way to Ealing Broadway tube station; when he arrived there he immediately went down the flight of stairs to catch the train. As soon as Guillaume got down the stairs there were two undercover Police-Detectives who noticed him; they realized that it is the suspect they are looking for. The two undercover Detectives then decided to follow Guillaume but, they kept a distance from him so as not to arouse any suspicions. One of the undercover Detectives then used his cell-phone to inform Scotland Yard about the situation; as Guillaume was walking along his Daemon then warns him: "Guillaume, you have 2 undercover Police-Detectives following you. They believe you are the suspect for the recent events involving the Yugoslavian-6 syndicate!" Guillaume was now fully aware of the issue at hand and he just walked on to catch a District Line tube train. Whilst waiting on the platform for the train Guillaume then realized the two undercover Detectives; he just decided to play it cool. The tube train had arrived and Guillaume immediately boarded it; the two undercover Detectives also boarded the same train. The two Detectives sat down on the seats but Guillaume decided to stand; he could see the two Detectives in the glass reflection observing him! His Daemon then says to him: "Yes, those are the 2 undercover Detectives. Just go and kill them; don't worry no-one will recognize you! You are well disguised!" Guillaume remained calm and again just played it cool. The tube train stopped at South Kensington tube station and when the doors opened Guillaume then stepped out of the train; the two undercover Detectives then stood up! Guillaume then stepped back onto the train; everyone on the train were baffled at what he had just did! The train doors closed and the two Detectives stood there and looked at each other completely puzzled! All of a sudden Guillaume turned around and attacked the two undercover Detectives using his Martial Arts skills. The passengers on the train were shocked to see what Guillaume had just done; then Guillaume went in for the kill and snapped the two undercover Detectives necks....the two undercover Detectives died instantly! The horrified passengers all moved as far away as possible fearing for their lives! Guillaume just stood there cool & calm as you like; when the train arrived at Sloane Square tube station he just got off the train to carry out his mission.

A little later on the Police were called in to investigate the murders of the two undercover Detectives committed by Guillaume. The Police then realized that it was the same suspect that has been sought after for the previous incidents. It was really scaring the Police a lot considering how dangerous and skilled Guillaume Moreau is. They were even unsure whether it is a French Secret Agent and are still unsure what he actually looks like!

Meanwhile, Guillaume was out on the streets of Sloane Square seeking out the Turkish bar-restaurant that Simone mentioned to him earlier that same day. A few minutes later Guillaume had managed to locate the Turkish bar-restaurant; he then sees two Bouncers outside guarding the entrance-door. Guillaume then goes to find a secluded area and when he does he then teleports physically to the men's toilets of the Turkish bar-restaurant immediately. After Guillaume teleports to the men's toilets luckily for him there was no-one around; he then leaves the toilets and goes straight into the bar area to look for the two D-Turks. Guillaume was going around looking to see where Volkan & Ahmet are located; as there were so many people around it became crowded. Guillaume tried not to let it bother him too much; though he was getting a little desperate. Then at a far distance he sees the two D-Turks in the executive lounge-suite; Guillaume then goes up to them. When Guillaume got a little closer to the two D-Turks he just begins to observe them; they were getting a little high on cocaine. "Hey Volkan, this stuff is really good!" said Ahmet gleefully; Volkan was getting a little too high on cocaine and Guillaume could see this. "Hey man I think it's time for the heroin!" suggested Volkan, "Are you sure man? I think you have taken too much coke!" joked Ahmet, "Yeah, I'm totally sure!" replied Volkan; Ahmet just sat there looking stunned! Guillaume then decided to go straight to the executive suite; as he arrived there Guillaume just stood there looking at the two D-Turks! "Hey man! Who are you? What do you want?" asked Ahmet; Guillaume didn't reply. Suddenly he gets out his hand-gun and shoots a few rounds of bullets at both Volkan & Ahmet; they both died instantly! Everyone at the bar-restaurant screamed and ran for their lives; then when the manager saw this he attempted to approach Guillaume. "Hey what are you doing?" asks the manager frantically; Guillaume said nothing and immediately he shoots the manager dead! Outside the bar-restaurant the two Bouncers heard the gun-shots and went straight inside to check it out; when Guillaume noticed the two bouncers he immediately shoots both of them dead! Guillaume then exits the bar-restaurant so he could return to the squatters flat. As Guillaume departed the bar-restaurant he could hear loud Police sirens; he knew immediately that it is to do with him! The Police got out of their cars and immediately Guillaume shoots many of them dead; next he gets out a hand-grenade and throws it towards the remaining Police...they all died instantly! Guillaume then goes to find a secluded place and when he does Guillaume teleports straight away!

Guillaume had managed to return to the squatters flat and went to talk to Simone straight away. "I managed to kill the 2 D-Turks." said Guillaume, "Good! So when do we get the rest of the D-Turks?" asked Simone, "First thing in the morning. Then after that we need to get the Police-Detectives whom are involved with the Yugoslavian-6." replied Guillaume; Simone then nodded in agreement. The two of them then went to get ready to go to sleep as they have got a long day ahead of them; so far for Guillaume it was all going according to plan!

Chapter 38:
Kill the D-Turks

In the early hours of the morning the UK media reported the killings of the two undercover Police-Detectives and of the two D-Turks on the previous night. They knew it was the same perpetrator but, as Guillaume was well-disguised it was virtually impossible to see what he actually looks like. The news-reader went on:

"Last night after the killings of the 2 Police-Detectives and the 2 Turkish men it has been established by the Police that it was the same individual behind many recent killings. It has been speculated that the individual may possibly be a French Secret Agent; but the question we all have to ask ourselves is, what is this all about?"

The UK public were all baffled and worried at many of the recent killings by Guillaume; they all felt that they had hit a brick-wall! Earlier Guillaume had found out by chance that two of the corrupt Police-Detectives Peter Hart & Edward Cane are going to meet up with a mysterious man at Greenwich Museum who is heavily involved with the Yugoslavian-6. The two corrupt Police-Detectives are going to give the mysterious man a file containing documents in relation to the plans to take over the whole of Europe. Guillaume realized that he has to kill them & get the file at the same time.

A little later in the morning Guillaume & Simone were having something to eat for breakfast; they were also discussing about the next stage of the plans. "So what is the next course of action?" asked Simone, "Well, firstly we need to kill the rest of the D-Turks. Then we need to find the Police-Detectives whom are involved with the Yugoslavian-6 and then I will kill them too!" replied Guillaume; Simone nodded at him in acknowledgment. "I have a query. You know that you're a marked man, how are we going to get through this issue?" pondered Simone, "We will get through this. We just need to keep a low profile and keep wearing our hoodies & sunglasses. That way we will not get recognized!" replied Guillaume; both Guillaume & Simone then carried on eating their breakfast.

It was about 08:30 hours that both Guillaume & Simone went to get ready for the next part of the mission. When they were fully dressed both Guillaume & Simone put their hoods over their heads and then put on their sunglasses. "Are you ready?" asked Guillaume; Simone nodded a 'yes' response to Guillaume. Immediately the two of them left the squatters flat and then went on their way.

Back at Scotland Yard Police-Detectives were again racking their brains out over the recent killings the other night. "Who is this guy? They all say he's a French Secret Agent! And how the hell is one guy is able to kill so many people?" asked Detective Paul; all of the Scotland Yard Police looked at each other feeling completely helpless! Even though they ran Guillaume's identity through the computer-systems, as he was well-disguised it still gave responses of 'NOT RECOGNIZED!' Scotland Yard Police just didn't know what to do!

Guillaume & Simone arrived at Ealing Broadway tube station and waited for the Central Line tube train to arrive. At the time it was the rush-hour as people were going into work; however, it would be easy for Guillaume & Simone to conceal their identities behind so many members of the public. The train then finally arrives so both Guillaume & Simone boarded on; the two of them stayed close together but remained silent throughout. On the tube-train some of the passengers were looking at both Guillaume & Simone in a weird way; they all wondered why they were dressed the way they are. Then a man came up to them and joked: "Did you two go to a Halloween party last night!" The passengers all laughed on the train; Guillaume then looked at the man and said nothing! Then all of a sudden Guillaume did Martial Arts moves on the man and in the process knocked him out! The passengers were all horrified at what Guillaume had just done! Then another man came up to him and said: "Hey, what's your problem man? It was only a joke!" Guillaume said nothing and immediately did a Martial Arts side-kick on the second man. The man went flying across; again people were horrified at this! When the tube train arrived at Holland Park Guillaume & Simone then got off to make their way towards the D-Turks lair.

A few minutes later Guillaume & Simone arrived at the D-Turks lair and went somewhere nearby out-of-sight so none of the D-Turks would see them. "So what do you know about this building?" asked Guillaume, "Well there are security-cameras but, they are all hidden out of sight; what do you suggest we do?" asked Simone, "Let me remote-view first and see where the cameras are." replied Guillaume as he immediately goes into remote-viewing mode. Whilst Guillaume was remote-viewing he could see where all of the security-cameras are located inside the D-Turks lair. Using his telekinetic-powers Guillaume was able to dismantle the security systems. "Great news Simone! I was able to cut-off the security systems. We will be able to get in but, we must still do it discretely." explained Guillaume, "Brilliant! On the side is the entrance-door to the D-Turks lair, we can get through there." explained Simone; immediately the two of them made their way to the D-Turks entrance!

At the tube station where Guillaume assaulted the two men on the train earlier, Police were investigating the incident. When they went through the camera-footage they had a shock! "It's that French Secret Agent!" said one of the Officers; when all of the passengers overheard what was said they all went into complete shock! The passengers couldn't believe that it was a French Secret Agent who assaulted the two men that morning. Back at the D-Turks lair Guillaume & Simone quietly crept in through the door and the coast was clear. "Go up those stairs; most of the D-Turks are there!" whispered Simone, "OK! Just stay right behind me for your own safety." said Guillaume; he then took out his hand-gun! Both Guillaume & Simone quietly crept up the stairs to the first-floor; the two of them felt a little nervous! When they arrived on the first-floor Guillaume looked around; there was no-one there. All he could see was a big landing with separate apartment buildings. "Apartment number 1 is the leader Serkan Dincher. I can't remember the other D-Turks apartment numbers." whispered Simone; Guillaume then had a message from his Daemon again: "Guillaume! In apartment number 1 Serkan is doing a business deal right now. Kill him first and do the others afterwards!" Guillaume then stood there thinking on how he is going to approach the situation. "Simone, I'm going to kill Serkan first and the rest afterwards." explained Guillaume; Simone then nodded at him. Guillaume & Simone then crept up to apartment no.1 where Serkan Dincher is; inside Serkan's apartment he was doing a big drugs deal with his guests. All of a sudden Guillaume then bursts through Serkan's flat and shoots him and his clients....they were now all dead! The apartment opposite to Serkan's one, gun-shots were heard and immediately the door is opened...it was Mustafa Demir! As soon as Guillaume saw Mustafa he shoots him straight away killing him in the process! All the other D-Turks came out of their apartments and Guillaume then begins to shoot all of them as well. Guillaume also shot the other guests in the building; all of them had now died. "Is it safe now?" asks Simone nervously, "Yes it is. All we need to do is place the bombs all around here." replied Guillaume.

The Police were called from a member of the public about gun-shots being heard from the abandoned apartment-building. When the Police heard of this immediately Armed-Police were called in to report to the building. At the apartment building Guillaume got out a lot of hand-grenades and passed some of them to Simone. "Simone, what we're going to do is put these grenades around the building so we can blow it up. I've set each one

on a timer for 15 minutes so it will give us time to get away."
explained Guillaume; they both went around the whole
building placing hand-grenades in different spots. All of a
sudden they could hear Police-sirens...they both realized that
the Police are after them! "Can we still get away?" asked
Simone frantically, "We have to teleport together. It is the
only way!" replied Guillaume; all of the grenades were now
placed around the apartment building. The Armed-Police
parked their vans outside the abandoned building and
immediately entered it with their guns. Guillaume &
Simone could hear them coming up the stairs; Simone then
begins to hold on to Guillaume and immediately they
teleported away just in time! When the Armed-Police
arrived they noticed all of the dead-bodies lying around!
Then all of a sudden the bombs exploded...all of the
Armed-Police had perished!

Guillaume & Simone had teleported to another alleyway
about twenty minutes walk from the D-Turks lair; luckily
the alleyway itself had no security-cameras. "Are you OK,
Simone?" asked Guillaume; Simone had just managed to
catch her breath! "Yes I'm fine, thanks!" replied Simone,
"Let's make our way to Greenwich Museum; are you ready?"
asked Guillaume; Simone then nodded a 'yes' response to
him. The two of them then went back on to the Central
Line tube-train to make their way to Stratford. On the tube
train both Guillaume & Simone kept a low profile by bowing
their heads down so they could conceal their identities more.
They still had their hoods over their heads and still wearing
their sunglasses! It was quite a long journey for them but,
the tube-train did eventually arrive at Stratford train station.

Guillaume & Simone both felt very nervous as their identities had been reported all over the media over the many recent incidents. They got off the Central Line train and made their way to the Docklands Light Railway line so they could take a train to Greenwich Museum.

As they were walking towards the DLR line both Guillaume & Simone were being followed again by two undercover Police-Officers; however they were unaware! Guillaume's Daemon suddenly summoned him again: "Guillaume! You have 2 undercover Police-Officers following you & Simone. Don't do anything drastic until you get on the train, then you'll know when to strike!" Guillaume then immediately whispers to Simone: "Simone, we have 2 undercover cops following us. Just keep going & walk in front of me!" Simone remained calm and complied with Guillaume's request; they then arrived at the Stratford DLR line and then waited for the train. "Guillaume, how did they know we'll be here?" asks Simone frantically, "They must have undercover cops at every London underground station. It's very likely the undercover cops are part of the Yugoslavian-6 syndicate; they must know that my Government are on to them and their crooked schemes!" explained Guillaume; Simone started to feel to slightly worried! The DLR train arrives at Stratford and the two of them boarded on; the two undercover cops also boarded the same train keeping their eyes on both Guillaume & Simone!

On the DLR train from Stratford Guillaume & Simone sat right next to each other and even though the two undercover Police-Officers were in the same carriage they sat away from them so as not to arouse any suspicions! As

Guillaume was sitting down he immediately went into remote-viewing mode and his Daemon then shows him who are the two undercover Police-Officers. Now Guillaume was fully aware who they are! Guillaume then puts his hand over his mouth and whispers to Simone: "I know the identities of the undercover cops; what we'll do is just before the DLR reaches Greenwich we'll get up and wait at the train-doors. We're going to hug each other but, my back will be facing towards the undercover cops and then I will kill them before we get off. Don't say anything just give me a nod if you understand." Simone then nodded her head a little to confirm that she fully understood. The two of them then remained silent throughout! Just before the train reach Cutty Stark station Guillaume & Simone got up from their seats and made their way towards the train-doors. They then began to hug each other; the two undercover Police-Officers then got up and stared at Guillaume & Simone. "I think they're the undercover cops." whispered Simone, "Yes, you're right!" replied Guillaume. The train then stops at Cutty Stark station and the two undercover Police-Officers were now wondering if they are going to get off there...they didn't! The two undercover Police-Officers then stared at each other with baffling looks! Guillaume then reaches down his trousers for his hand-gun and immediately turns around shooting the two undercover Police-Officers dead! Everyone on the train panics fearing for their lives. When the train arrived at Greenwich station Guillaume & Simone then got off hastily making their way to Greenwich Museum!

As Guillaume & Simone left Greenwich station they made their way up a hill to the Royal Observatory part of

Greenwich Museum. "This place takes me back for when I was in London." said Guillaume, "Oh! You remember this place?" queried Simone, "Yes, it was a school trip for when I was in Primary School." replied Guillaume; eventually they managed to arrive at the top of the hill to where the entrance is. "Simone, go in and pay for your entrance ticket; I'll go in a few minutes later. We must stay separate but, in view." explained Guillaume; Simone immediately entered the museum and then pays for her entrance-ticket. About five minutes later Guillaume then enters the museum and pays for his entrance-ticket. Both Guillaume & Simone walked around the Royal Observatory but, remained separate from each other. Guillaume went around around looking for two of the corrupt Police-Detectives and who they are meeting with; there was no indication that they are at the museum. All of a sudden Guillaume's Daemon then says to him: "The 2 corrupt Detectives, Peter Hart & Edward Cane are going to arrive soon in the museum. Get ready!" Guillaume then paused for a second; he wondered how he is going to approach the situation in a very public place!

Guillaume was still looking around the shops in the museum when a mysterious man wearing sunglasses, a smart suit & hat entered. Guillaume's Daemon then says to him: "Guillaume the man that just entered; he is going to meet the 2 corrupt Police-Detectives. Kill all 3 of them and get the documents!" Guillaume then notices the mysterious man and his Daemon pointed to him; he then sees Simone nearby and goes up to her and whispers: "That man over there with the sunglasses, suit & hat. He is going to meet up with the 2 corrupt Detectives; he's one of the Yugoslavian-6 syndicates!" Simone then looks up and nods in acknowledgment. Five minutes later the two corrupt Police-Detectives Peter Hart & Edward Cane then entered the museum. Simone then whispers to Guillaume: "Those are the 2 Police-Detectives!" Guillaume could then see the documents in Detective Peter Hart's right arm guarding it with his life. "Just stay out of sight until I deal with this." whispered Guillaume; immediately Simone distance herself from him. When the two Detectives saw the mysterious man they all went to the very top of the museum on the outside balcony at the point where east meets west which is known as the Greenwich meridian line. "Hey, we have a big problem. I think the French Intelligence Services are onto us." whispered Detective Hart, "Yes I am aware of this; and you're absolutely correct the French Intelligence Services are onto us and our plans." explained the mysterious man, "What shall we do next?" asked Detective Cane, "Do you have the file?" asked the mysterious man; Detective Hart then nodded and gave him the file. Guillaume noticed what was going on and then his Daemon tells him: "Do it now; you have no time to lose!" Immediately Guillaume goes towards all three men and attacks them using his Martial Arts skills. He then pulls out his hand-gun and shoots all three of them dead and immediately takes the file. Guillaume then signals to Simone to get ready to leave; Simone complies and immediately they leave Greenwich Museum to return to Greenwich station.

Guillaume & Simone arrived at Greenwich station and they noticed a massive Police presence at one of the entrances. It was to do with when Guillaume shot the two undercover Police-Detectives earlier on the DLR train. "Simone, there's another entrance we can go through to catch the train back to Stratford." said Guillaume; the two of them then made their way to the back entrance of Greenwich station. Guillaume & Simone had managed to get to the platform to return to Stratford; the DLR train where Guillaume killed the two undercover Police-Detectives was stationary so the Police could investigate the incident further to see what went on. They took statements from witnesses; the Police knew it was Guillaume Moreau that committed the murders. All of a sudden the Police were notified about the three murders at Greenwich Museum and the same description of the offender was given. "It's that fucking French Secret Agent!" said one of the Officers; the witnesses overheard what the Officer had just said! They all went into shock and wondered what a French Secret Agent is doing in the UK and what this is all about. The DLR train back to Stratford had arrived; both Guillaume & Simone boarded the train quickly and the train was now on its way back to Stratford.

The train arrived back at Stratford; Guillaume & Simone got off straight away and made their way to the Central Line. At Stratford station there was a strong Police presence; they were urgently looking for Guillaume & Simone. The Police were everywhere around the station and Guillaume had noticed this; Simone was feeling tensed at all of this. Simone even wondered on whether she'll be free once & for all; suddenly Guillaume receives a message from his Daemon: "Guillaume! Don't go to the Central Line, the Police are there looking for you. Take the Jubilee Line!"

Guillaume then realized that he would be completely trapped if he goes to the Central Line. He then whispers to Simone: "Simone, change of plans. We need to get to the Jubilee Line. My Daemon tells me that the Police are there!" Simone got even more worried! "Oh fuck, we're trapped! There are Police everywhere!" said Simone frantically; the two of them just walked on. A few minutes later an Armed Police-Officer had noticed two people wearing hoodies; the Officer wonders if it is the two suspects. The Armed Officer then goes and follows them; Guillaume's Daemon then warns him about the Armed Police-Officer trailing him from a distance! As the Armed-Officer was still following Guillaume & Simone he decided to call out to both of them! "Hey you two wearing the hoodies. Can I have a word with you both?" called the Officer; Guillaume & Simone ignored the Officer and walked on! "Excuse me! Didn't you two hear me!" called the Officer; crowds of people had noticed the Armed-Officer calling out to Guillaume & Simone. The two of them just carried on walking regardless; they knew that if they get caught it was more or less all over! The Armed-Policeman then decided to chase after Guillaume & Simone; when he got closer to them the Armed-Officer then puts his hand on Guillaume's shoulder! Immediately Guillaume put the Officers hand into a Martial Arts grip; the Officer screamed in agony and then Guillaume did an Aikido throw on him. Members of the public were shocked at what Guillaume did; next Guillaume did Martial Arts kicks on the Officer and then he went in for the kill and snapped the Officer's neck killing him in the process!

Guillaume & Simone then made a run for it; members of the public stood there in complete shock!

A few minutes later Guillaume & Simone got near to the Jubilee Line; all of a sudden there were more Armed-Police going after them. Guillaume gets out his hand-gun and immediately shoots some of the Police dead. Everyone at the station screamed with fear and started running around; it caused problems for the remaining Police they couldn't get through! Guillaume & Simone managed to get away but, unfortunately for them more Armed Police had arrived but, Guillaume was able to kill them using his hand-gun! At times he had to use his Martial Arts to kill the Armed Police; members of the public couldn't believe at Guillaume's physical attributes. The Armed Police that Guillaume & Simone met a few minutes earlier were now onto them. Guillaume & Simone kept on running and at the right moment Guillaume got out his hand-gun and shot all of the Armed-Police; they were now all dead! Guillaume & Simone had managed to get onto the Jubilee Line train from Stratford. Considering all of the chaos, Guillaume & Simone had managed to overcome it all! Simone was a little more relaxed but, still fearful! Guillaume & Simone took the Jubilee Line train to Green Park; then they took the Victoria Line to Oxford Circus and lastly took the Central Line from Oxford Circus back to Ealing Broadway.

Chapter 39:
Political Slaughter!

The incident involving Guillaume and the Police at Stratford station was reported all over the UK media; there was complete shock all over the UK! The UK authorities still could not identify Guillaume as the perpetrator considering he was well-disguised. However, the authorities suspected that the woman with him is Simone Jane Robinson even though she was well-disguised too!

At the squatters flat Guillaume & Simone were resting a bit that evening; even though Simone was safe for the time being she still felt extremely nervous and Guillaume could see this. "Simone, are you OK?" asked Guillaume, "A little bit; it's just that after the fiasco at Stratford the Police are going to be combing the area!" replied Simone; Guillaume then realizes that he had to reassure her safety. "Don't worry Simone, everything is going to be fine. Bear in mind I am always 10 steps ahead of the Police with my paranormal powers & I have my Daemon." explained Guillaume, "Yes I realize this; I really do need to relax. I'm worried that once I get caught by the Police I'm going to be spending the rest of my life in prison!" explained Simone; Guillaume then looked at Simone with concern. "Yes I am aware of your difficult situation but I am going to help you get to Switzerland safely. Oh by the way we need to teleport later on to a clothes-shop so we can get a smart dress for you & a tuxedo for me for when we go to that posh event tomorrow night!" explained Guillaume; Simone looked at Guillaume and breathed a small sigh of relief.

It was 23:00 hours and it was extremely quiet all over London; Guillaume thought that would be the right time to teleport to a clothes-shop. "Simone, are you ready to go?" asked Guillaume; Simone nodded at Guillaume to indicate that she's ready. "Yes I am, let's do this!" replied Simone; she then held onto Guillaume and together they teleported to a clothes-shop. When Guillaume & Simone teleported to the clothes-shop they were in one of the fitting rooms. Guillaume had to teleport to a fitting room as were no security-cameras there. "Let me use my telekinetic powers to switch off all of the security-cameras. Then we can look around the shop for suitable clothing." explained Guillaume; immediately Guillaume closed his eyes and used remote-viewing to see where all of the security-cameras are located. When Guillaume located all of the cameras in his minds eye he immediately used the power of his mind to switch off all of the security-cameras. "Simone, it's all done. We can go & look around." said Guillaume. The two of them then went from the fitting-rooms area onto the shop-floor.

The clothes-shop itself was specifically for the upper-class people so Guillaume & Simone were spoiled for choice for the appropriate clothing. Guillaume had eventually found a tuxedo to wear plus very smart shoes to go with it; Simone had managed to find a descent dinner-dress suitable for the upcoming event. "Hey, are these shoes OK?" asked Simone as she showed Guillaume; in her hand she had a pair of posh high-heeled shoes. "Yes that's perfect for the event. We have to look as posh as possible." replied Guillaume; when they had finished they both teleported back to the squatters flat in Ealing Broadway quickly so they could get plenty of sleep.

The time had arrived for Guillaume & Simone for the last part of the mission...to kill the six UK Politicians: Simone Pane, Michael Smythe, Peter Dole, Alan McDougall, Martin Klein & Stephen Giles. Guillaume & Simone got dressed into their respective clothing; the two of them had to wear new wigs to conceal their identities and put on fake spectacles. Guillaume had to color his face white to conceal his identity more and Simone this time wore a long black wig. "Well Simone, this is the final push." said Guillaume, "Yep! I so cannot wait when this is all over and then I can begin my new life. I really do want a fresh start!" explained Simone, "Yes I know. Let's go!" said Guillaume; they held on to each other and teleported straight away to the London town of Bank....it really is now or never!

Guillaume & Simone teleported to a small shop in Bank, London opposite the event itself; Guillaume wanted to observe a bit more before doing anything else. At the entrance door they could see two Door-Supervisors; they were checking to see if all of the guests had their tickets to enter. "Simone, I just wanted to wait until all of the 6 UK Politicians enter the building and then I can go in for the kill." explained Guillaume; Simone understood Guillaume's logic. From a distance they could see through the display window all of the guests arriving at the event. Then one of the UK Politicians arrives...Simone Pane; he is being accompanied by a young woman. He showed his invitation and was permitted to enter the building. "I wonder where all the other 5 are?" pondered Simone, "Well it is early days at this moment in time. They're probably biding their time but, they will get there. There is obviously something going down." explained Guillaume; they both continued to observe carefully! Twenty minutes later Michael Smythe & Peter Dole arrived at the same time both with a young woman each by their side. "Good grief! All the 3 Politicians we've seen so far all have ladies young enough to be their daughters!" said Simone; Guillaume then gazed at her and smiled a little. "It's more likely that they are Escort-Girls; to make themselves look good." explained Guillaume; they continued to observe. After one hour of observing the last three UK Politicians had all arrived: Alan McDougall, Martin Klein & Stephen Giles. Like the other three UK Politicians they all had young ladies accompanying them to the event. Guillaume assumed that they are also Escort-Girls. "Simone, they are all in at the event; we can teleport now. What we need to do first is that I'll teleport you to the ladies toilets & then from there I'll teleport to the men's toilets." explained Guillaume; he then closed his eyes and began to remote-view. Guillaume scanned the whole building and went to observe the ladies toilets; he could clearly see it was empty. Now Guillaume & Simone were ready to teleport; Simone held on to Guillaume and they teleported to the ladies toilets straight away!

Guillaume & Simone teleported to the ladies toilets and luckily there was no-one around. "Simone I'm going to the men's toilets now, I'll meet you outside." said Guillaume;

Simone then nodded a 'yes' response to him. Immediately
Guillaume teleported to the men's toilets; alone in the ladies
toilets Simone was beginning to feel a little nervous. When
Guillaume teleported to the men's toilets like Simone he was
all alone there; it was empty! Guillaume then made his way
out of the men's toilets; upon exiting he then sees Simone
and the two of them went together arm-in-arm. As both
Guillaume & Simone were walking around they noticed all
of the guests dancing around and having a good time.
"Simone, what we'll need to do is split up for a bit. That way
they'll think you're alone." explained Guillaume; the two of
them then split up. Guillaume was walking around observing
everyone looking for the six UK Politicians to kill. Then all
of a sudden he sees Peter Dole at a distance sitting in the
VIP lounge; he was laughing & joking with other guests.
Then Guillaume's Daemon says to him: "It is now the right
time to kill Peter Dole. You know what you've got to do!"
Very discretely Guillaume then gets out his hand-gun and
attaches the silencer to it. Not one of the guests had even
noticed that Guillaume possesses a hand-gun! Guillaume
with his gun concealed behind his tuxedo then begins to
walk a little closer towards the VIP lounge and decides to
wait for the right moment! "Well ladies & gentlemen when
you become a Politician you have all the power to do
whatever you want & no-one would even care!" joked Peter;
the other guests laughed along with Peter! One of Peter's
guests then asks him: "Hey Peter! This thing with the
Yugoslavian-6 & the Police, who is doing all of the this?"
Peter then looks directly at the guest! "Well isn't it
obvious...it's the fucking EU! They don't want us taking over.

But, we'll fucking stop them!" replied Peter; Guillaume could hear all of the conversations going on. He realizes in his mind that he has to kill Peter Dole very quickly; the only thing lingering in his mind is when can he kill him? About ten minutes later as Guillaume was still observing Peter Dole & his guests, two of them got up from their seats. "Peter, I need to go to the toilet....I've had too much to drink!" explained one of the guests; the other guest wanted to go to the toilet too! "No problem take your time I'll be still here when you get back!" said Peter; all of the other guests including Peter Dole's Escort-Girl also got up from their seats to make their way to the toilets. Peter was now on his own; Guillaume then realizes this is his opportunity! Guillaume then looks around to see if any of the party-goers are looking and so he makes his way to the VIP lounge area.

As Guillaume stepped into the VIP lounge he comes face-to-face with Peter Dole; Peter then wonders what Guillaume is up to. "Hey! Who the fuck are you?" asked Peter in a drunken state; Guillaume then stays silent for a bit! "The fucking EU!" replied Guillaume; he then immediately gets out his gun and shoots Peter Dole straight in the head! Peter Dole dies instantly; Guillaume then checks to see if anyone is looking. Luckily for Guillaume no-one had noticed that he shot Peter Dole; immediately Guillaume leaves the VIP lounge area to search for his next victim. A few minutes later as Guillaume was walking along he notices Simone sitting alone at the bar; she was just minding her own business. All of a sudden another Politician Martin Klein sees Simone alone and decides to approach her; Guillaume just stands there observing! "Why hello there, let me buy you a drink." said Martin, "Not interested, I don't drink!" responded Simone as she turns her head away! "Hey come on! I'm just being nice!" said Martin sarcastically; Simone continued to rebuff him! Guillaume could see that Simone was having problems with Martin Klein; he was waiting for the right moment to strike. "What about that fucking bimbo you're with tonight? Why don't you buy her a drink?" suggested Simone sarcastically, "Hey there's no need to be like this! Besides she's nothing she's only a call-girl!" said Martin; Simone just ignored him! Suddenly Guillaume notices the bartender leaving the bar for a bit and sees that no-one else is at the bar except for Simone and Martin Klein. Guillaume then decides to go in for the kill; he goes up and from behind Guillaume does a karate chop on the back of Martin Klein's neck. It took Martin by surprise and straight away Guillaume snaps Martin's neck. Martin Klein was now dead; it was a case of two down four to go! "Just go Simone; I'll meet you later!" instructed Guillaume; immediately Simone leaves the bar to go somewhere else! Before Guillaume left the bar he takes a cocktail-knife from the counter and went on his way.

Thirty minutes later Peter Dole's guests arrived back at the VIP lounge area from the toilets. They noticed Peter was lying on the couch; they all thought he was drunk! "Well it looks like Peter had one too many; definitely more than me!" joked one of the guests; they all tried to wake Peter Dole but, to no avail. "Come on Peter, wake up!" said another guest; all of a sudden Peter Dole's dead body fell on the floor with his face looking upwards. All of a sudden the guests noticed Peter Dole's bleeding forehead; when they looked closer they realized that it was a bullet in Peter's forehead. "Oh my God! Who has done this? Someone alert one of the staff!" said one of the guests. About ten minutes later Guillaume was walking around searching for the four remaining UK Politicians....then he sees Simon Pane! Immediately Guillaume pulls out the cocktail-knife and throws it directly in Simon Pane's face....he immediately dies! Guillaume immediately walks off to search for the remaining three UK Politicians! Minutes later one of the party-goers then notices Simon Pane's dead body on the floor; then other party-goers had noticed this too. They all went into shock!

Guillaume was walking around looking for his next intended victim; he then sees Michael Smythe with his Escort-Girl. Guillaume then gets out his hand-gun; he is getting ready for the kill! "Oh! The Right Honorable Mr. Smythe!" called Guillaume; suddenly Michael Smythe turns around and sees Guillaume. Then immediately Guillaume shoots Michael Smythe and he dies instantly; the Escort-Girl screams in horror and attempts to run away but it was too late! Guillaume shoots a couple of bullets and the Escort-Girl dies straight away! Some of the party-goers had witnessed what Guillaume had done and they ran away in terror. The Door-Supervisors were alerted at what occurred earlier and they immediately alerted the Police! Guillaume immediately goes to seek out the three remaining UK Politicians; he realizes that it needed to be done quickly before the Police arrives. One of the other UK Politicians Simon Pane was dancing around and flirting with other women unaware that three other UK Politicians have already been killed and that he is an intended target! From a distance Guillaume sees Simon Pane dancing away and immediately goes towards him getting his hand-gun ready. When Guillaume gets closer to Simon he pulls out his hand-gun and shoots the next UK politician...Simon Pane was now dead! People then screamed and ran away in fear. A few feet away the other UK Politician Alan McDougall had witnessed that Guillaume killed Simon Pane; he then realizes that it is a French Secret Agent. Guillaume then locks his eyes on Alan McDougall; he had no time to lose! "Oh my God you're a French Secret Agent!" shouts Alan McDougall; but it was was too late Guillaume immediately shoots Alan dead! Now there was only one left to go.....Stephen Giles!

There was panic all around and Guillaume was having difficulty searching for Stephen Giles, the last remaining UK Politician. As he couldn't focus due to all of the panic Guillaume was unable to connect to his Daemon! Meanwhile Simone was walking around trying to hide away when all of a sudden she bumps into Stephen Giles! "Hang on! I recognize you; you're Simone Jane Robinson!" said Stephen as he grabs Simone's arm; Simone became more nervous. "Get your fucking hands off me!" demanded Simone, "You're not getting away that easily! It's a good disguise but, you don't fool me; now who are you working for?" asked Stephen aggressively, "Fuck you! You're going to die anyway; it is all over!" shouted Simone; all of a sudden Guillaume appeared! "She's working with me!" responded Guillaume; immediately Stephen turns around to look! Immediately Guillaume throws a Martial Arts punch at

Stephen to daze him. Then Guillaume does Martial Arts kicks on Stephen and knocks him to the ground; next Guillaume goes in for the kill and snaps Stephen Giles' neck! All six UK Politicians are now dead....Guillaume & Simone had achieved their big objectives! "Let's go, we're done!" said Guillaume as he grabbed Simone's hand. As they were running Guillaume's Daemon suddenly says to him: "The Police have arrived; kill them all by any means!" Guillaume & Simone then stopped at the door of the men's toilets. "Stay down, the Police are coming. I need to kill them all!" ordered Guillaume; immediately Simone crouches down for her own safety. The Armed-Police arrived in the building and Guillaume immediately begins shooting at all of them killing them in the process! Some of the Armed-Police attempted to shoot at Guillaume but he was able to dodge the bullets and shoots more Armed-Police in return. Then Guillaume pulls out a hand-grenade from his tuxedo and and lulls it at the remaining Police. Guillaume then grabs Simone and they go into the men's toilets; immediately the two of them teleport out of the building. Soon after Guillaume & Simone had teleported away the the grenade suddenly explodes!

Guillaume & Simone teleported to an alleyway just behind the building; luckily there were no security-cameras around! "We're done! Let's get out of here to go somewhere safe to teleport back to the squatters flat!" said Guillaume; Simone gave a slight nod to Guillaume in acknowledgment. All of a sudden Guillaume's Daemon speaks to him again: "Guillaume, more Police are arriving. Kill them all for your own safety & Simone's too!" Guillaume then suddenly stops! "What's wrong?" asks Simone, "My Daemon says there are more Police arriving. What we should do is walk arm-in-arm casually and when the Police arrive I will then kill them all!" instructed Guillaume; immediately the two of them walked arm-in-arm and made their way towards the end of the alleyway. All of a sudden they could hear the sounds of the Police-sirens; Guillaume got out his hand-gun and conceals it behind his back. When they arrived at the end of the alleyway immediately Guillaume begins shooting at the Police as soon as he sees them. Then Guillaume gets out another hand-grenade and throws it towards the Police; both he & Simone ran for cover. The grenade explodes and all of the Police perish! Guillaume & Simone then went to find a place to teleport discretely and when they did Simone then holds onto Guillaume and together they teleported back to the squatters flat! Freedom soon awaits for Simone Jane Robinson...she has longed for that particular desire!

Chapter 40:
Close to freedom!

Morning had arrived at DGSE in Paris, France; Générale Lévesque was unhappy that the DGSE Paris-based agents left Guillaume on his own with Simone in London. "Générale, Commandant Moreau ordered all of us to return to Paris immediately for our own safety & security. He said he'll handle the rest!" explained Matthieu; Générale Lévesque then gazed at Matthieu with a very stern look! "Moreau is my agent and you all left him in the lions' den. Do you not realize the big risk you are all putting him in!" shouted Générale Lévesque; she constantly argued with all of the DGSE Paris staff. She was beginning to worry deeply about Guillaume!

In the squatters flat both Guillaume & Simone were now planning their final part of the journey to King's Cross International Station to take the Eurostar to Paris. Even though Simone knew that she is ever so close to freedom she was still feeling nervous about everything considering that she is wanted by the UK Authorities. "As you have never been abroad I take it that you've never had a passport if I do recall on what you had told me?" pondered Guillaume, "Yes that is absolutely true." responded Simone; Guillaume then realized that he has a dilemma! "Right! What we need to do first is get you some passport photographs. We need to find

the nearest photo-booth so you can take photos of yourself."
explained Guillaume, "The thing is that we have the UK
Police all over London looking for the both of us. They want
to hang us to dry." explained Simone; Guillaume perfectly
understood Simone's logic. "I know, I had that thought too.
We need to be extra discrete and yes we need to disguise
ourselves but it will be easy. We just need to keep a very low
profile." explained Guillaume, "Do you think that anyone
will recognize us?" pondered Simone, "Not if we disguise
ourselves more discretely." responded Guillaume, "Thanks!
You know I never got the chance to achieve anything big in
my life. I have always been running & hiding from everyone.
I don't want to miss the opportunity to have a descent life."
explained Simone, "You will Simone, you will." said
Guillaume; Simone then felt more relaxed & reassured.

It was late morning, Guillaume & Simone were both
getting ready to go into town to purchase passport
photographs. What they did this time was to disguise
themselves more so no-one will recognize them for when
they go. "Voila! Now not one person will recognize us." said
Guillaume, "I agree!" responded Simone; as soon as they
were ready Guillaume & Simone went on their way. The two
of them had to walk and take public transport as Guillaume
did not wanted to risk using his power of teleportation. As
usual they took the tube train from Ealing Broadway to the
nearest photo-booth; luckily for them they only had to take
one line which is the Central Line. They were going to
London Liverpool Street station as the nearest photo-booth
is there. Compared to the other days on the tube it was an
easy journey as Guillaume & Simone didn't run into any

trouble at all. The passengers on the tube train didn't even suspect that there are two wanted individuals on the same train!

When the train arrived at London Liverpool Street station both Guillaume & Simone got off and made their way to the shop-floor. London Liverpool Street was not only a station but, also a shopping complex all rolled into one. On the shop-floor Guillaume had noticed a few Police-Officers around but, he wasn't deterred by any of them. Immediately Guillaume & Simone had found the nearest photo-booth which was only a few steps away. "OK Simone! What is going to happen is that I will take 12 passport photographs of you which is 4 per strip. When you get into the booth take your wig & sunglasses off and then wipe off your make-up. Then straighten your hair as best as you can; when you're ready give me the thumbs-up and I'll put the money in." instructed Guillaume; immediately as Simone got inside the photo-booth she first removed her sunglasses & wig, then using the wet-wipes she removed all of her make-up from her face. Simone then tidied herself up more and straightened her hair; she was now ready. Simone then stuck her hand out of the curtain and gave Guillaume the thumbs-up. Guillaume then put money into the machine and the photos were then taken. When that was completed Guillaume then stuck his head into the photo-booth to talk to Simone. "It'll be ready soon. Reapply the make-up back onto your face and then put your wig & sunglasses back on. Don't rush, take your time." instructed Guillaume; Simone immediately reapplied the make-up to her face and then put her wig & sunglasses back on. As Guillaume was waiting the twelve passport photographs then came out...it was all perfect! Guillaume then puts the passport photographs into his pocket immediately; minutes later Simone comes out of the photo-booth back in her disguise! "Brilliant you're ready! The photos came out perfectly; lets get out of here before anything else happens." suggested Guillaume, "Yeah, I see what you mean. There are some Police around; the sooner we get out of here the better!" said Simone; the two of them then went to take the tube train back to Ealing Broadway!

The UK media reported the incident at the event in Bank, London the previous night where all six of the UK Politicians were killed. It was all over the newspapers as well; people were in complete shock at it all. The reporter on TV goes onto say:

"Last night at the event 6 well-known Members of Parliament were murdered & they were Simon Pane, Michael Smythe, Peter Dole, Alan McDougall, Martin Klein & Stephen Giles. Scotland Yard Police reported that all 6 MP's were targeted but are unsure on what the motive was. It has been speculated that it was the same French Secret Agent who was also responsible for various killings on the other previous days. This French Secret Agent is accompanied by Britain's most wanted woman Simone Jane Robinson who is wanted for many contraband crimes."

Many members of the public were in fear about Simone Robinson considering what has gone on in the past few days. They feel she's the most dangerous individual around unaware that she is completely innocent of it all and that she has been set-up all along! The UK Authorities were still unable to recognize Guillaume Moreau as the perpetrator considering he was in disguise all of the time. The computer-systems still could not recognize him at all.

It was 22:00 hours and Guillaume was getting ready to teleport to the passport office to prepare a passport for Simone. "Luckily I have a photocopy of your birth-certificate with me. My Government has the original copy. It will make it easier for me to make your passport." explained Guillaume, "Yeah what happened before I ran away from my parents I managed to find my birth-certificate and took it with me just in case. Looks like it was a good idea in the end." explained Simone, "It was a good idea. I'm getting ready to teleport, see you later." said Guillaume as teleported away. When Guillaume arrived at the passport office there was not a soul in sight – no-one was around! Guillaume then went straight to the computer-systems and switched on one of the computers. As Guillaume logged on he immediately hacked into the Police computer-systems and found the file on Simone Robinson. Guillaume deleted Simone's file ensuring that she is no longer a wanted individual by the Police. Next, Guillaume goes on to produce Simone's passport using details from her birth-certificate. Guillaume's Daemon gave him careful instructions on how to make Simone's passport; he managed to make it fairly quickly. When Guillaume had finished he made sure that Simone's details were wiped off the systems so no-one will ever know about it. Guillaume then switched off the computer and teleported back to the squatters flat.

Upon teleporting back to the squatters flat Guillaume sees Simone; she was pleased to see him! "I've got your passport done. On a more positive note I managed to hack into the Police computer-systems and wipe off all of your records. You're no longer a wanted criminal. But, when we go we cannot get complacent." explained Guillaume as he gave Simone her new passport. Simone was so impressed at her new passport; she felt complete elation! "So what's next?" pondered Simone, "Well as it is getting late we need to get some sleep as we have a long day tomorrow. I will need to go over the plans with you before we move out; the Police will still be combing the area looking for us." replied Guillaume; Simone understood Guillaume's explanation. "Wow! I can't believe that I'm going to be free soon; your Daemon is awesome!" complimented Simone, "Yes that is so true. Daemons are very unique beings." said Guillaume, "I wonder how they do it." pondered Simone, "Well I can explain...they are dimensionless. When I was in China I learned about multiple universes & that we are all immortal. I found out that I am not a virgin-lifer but, in my virgin-life I time-traveled and changed my past for the better. It affected the other versions of myself in a good way so I am always going to have an abundant & prosperous life." explained Guillaume, "Wooo! That is so powerful but interesting too!" said Simone; it was getting late and they both decided to get a lot of sleep as they are going to have a tough day ahead of them. Simone Jane Robinson is now one step away from freedom!

Chapter 41:

It's time!

Guillaume beforehand had to change his plans slightly;
the French Embassy in London informed him that a
French Secret Agent from DGSI will meet him at Kings
Cross International to hand him the train tickets to go to
Paris. Luckily for Guillaume it was someone he knew very
well who served with him in the French Army.

Morning had finally arrived for Simone and it was going
to be her last ever day in the UK. Simone had felt she was
dreaming that she is going to finally leave her traumatic past
behind forever. To Guillaume he just couldn't wait to leave
the UK; the country itself gave him too many bad memories
and no good ones at all. "This is it Simone, you're finally
going to be free!" said Guillaume; Simone had a slight smile
on her face! "I know we're not out of the woods yet but I
can finally taste it! What do we need to do?" asked Simone;
Guillaume was now ready to reveal his plans. "Well firstly we
need as usual to disguise ourselves so no-one will recognize
us especially the Police. Now with the Police they are still
going to comb the area and search at every train station all
over London. So what we'll do is when we get to Kings Cross
station go into the toilets & change your clothes because
you're going to need to reveal your face when the
Border-Guards check your passport. I will use my powers to

turn off all of the computer-systems so no-one will see us on the security cameras. What we must do is not to walk together but I will be right behind you. On a serious note I will need to destroy my hand-guns because I won't be able to take it through security. All I've got to use are my head & hands." explained Guillaume; Simone nodded in agreement! Immediately Guillaume took hold of his two hand-guns and using his telekinetic powers he held the guns afloat in between his two hands. Then he generated a ball of electricity between his hands and destroyed his hand-guns; it all turned into dust! It was necessary for Guillaume to do this so he could get rid of the evidence.

Later on in the morning Guillaume & Simone were all geared up and ready to leave; they put their rucksacks on their backs and made their way out of the squatters flat for the last time. When Guillaume & Simone arrived at Ealing Broadway tube station they waited for the tube train and they remained apart so as not to arouse any suspicions. When the tube-train arrived both Guillaume & Simone boarded in separate carriages just in case. They took the train first to Oxford Circus and from there they then took the Victoria line tube-train to London Kings Cross. Around London there were many Armed-Police & Detectives at each station searching for Guillaume & Simone; it was proving to be very difficult for them as their two suspects have worn many different disguises! When the tube-train arrived at Kings Cross both Guillaume & Simone got off and made their way to Kings Cross International to take the Eurostar back to Paris. Immediately Guillaume used his powers of mind-control to disable all of the computer-systems to throw all of the UK Authorities off the scent. As Guillaume & Simone were taking the long walk to Kings Cross International one of the corrupt Police-Officers whose name is Paul Birchall was suspicious of them and pondered if they are the two culprits. PC Paul Birchall then alerted his other colleagues about Guillaume & Simone as possible suspects. Guillaume's Daemon then warns him: "There's a Police-Officer who is suspicious about you & Simone. Take every precaution necessary and use extreme prejudice!" Guillaume was now aware and decided to walk on behind Simone; he then goes up to Simone and whispers: "Simone, the Police are on to us. Just stick to the plan & head straight to the toilets and get changed!" When they arrived at Kings Cross International Guillaume then sees the DGSI Agent he knows; the two them then went to a pay-phone each right next to each other. They were both going to pretend to talk to someone on the other line, when really they are going to talk to each other. "I take it you have the train-tickets?" asked Guillaume, "Yes I do, here they are." replied the DGSI Agent as he very discretely handed Guillaume an envelope containing the train-tickets. "Merci! Now get on the train & get out of here quickly. The Police are on to us but, don't worry I have managed to disable all of the computer-systems. No-one will capture us!" explained Guillaume; the DGSI Agent nodded at him and went on his way to the border-checks to board the train back to Paris. Guillaume then made his way to look for Simone and he had to do this in a rush as she was far ahead of him! When Guillaume had managed to locate Simone he took Simone's ticket out of the envelope and discretely slipped it to Simone! The two of them then arrived at the men's & women's toilets and made their way inside to get changed.

Meanwhile on the main-floor of Kings Cross International some of the other corrupt Police-Officers Steven Smith, Oliver Williams, Christopher Peters, Derek Davidson, James Cross, Jonathan Hall & Detective Michael Paul were frantically looking for Guillaume & Simone all over. They couldn't see them at all; they were now beginning to panic! "Has anyone asked the control-room to see if they were spotted on the cameras?" asked Detective Michael Paul, "Sir, there's a big problem. The whole network is down!" explained PC Steven Smith, "What? That's all we need!" said Detective Michael Paul. In the women's toilets Simone was in a toilet cubicle getting changed into different clothes; she took her wig off and straightened her hair. When Simone was ready she put on a hat to disguise her hair and then flushed the toilet to make people think she was using it. Simone came out of the toilet-cubicle and went to wash her hands; there was another woman next to her who was also washing her hands in the sink. She noticed Simone in the mirror and had the thought that she had seen Simone somewhere before. However, the woman couldn't pinpoint where she actually had seen Simone; all of a sudden Simone then began to fear that the woman had seen her in the newspapers and quickly dashed out of the women's toilets! In the men's toilets Guillaume was doing the same thing by getting changed into different clothes and when he was fully changed he put on a cap & sunglasses to conceal his identity! Guillaume then flushed the toilet and went to wash his hands, then he immediately dashed out of the men's toilets.

As Guillaume departed the toilets he could see Simone at a far distance making her way to the UK border-checks; Guillaume then made his way to the border-checks too. The Police & Detective Michael Paul were still rushing around looking for the two suspects until Detective Paul spots a woman resembling Simone. "Hey look over there, it looks like Simone Robinson!" said Detective Paul; all of the Police then rushed over to Simone. When they got close to Simone PC Birchall then grabs her arm; Simone then realized that she has been caught and so the other Police-Officers then surrounded her! "Well, well! If it isn't the famous Miss Simone Jane Robinson!" said Detective Paul gleefully; Simone suddenly felt trapped and some members of the public were wondering what is going on. As Guillaume was still walking along his Daemon then suddenly says to him: "Guillaume, Simone is in trouble the Police have now captured her!" Immediately Guillaume rushes to find Simone, until he manages to see her! "So Miss Robinson, where is your accomplice? Who is he?" demanded Detective Paul; Simone refused to answer. All of a sudden Guillaume dropped his rucksack and immediately went to attack the Police. Firstly, Guillaume flipped over PC Birchall to the ground and then snaps his neck; next several Police-Officers attempted to apprehend Guillaume but using his Aikido skills Guillaume was able to thwart the oncoming Police and then he killed them by snapping all of their necks off. Guillaume then says to Simone: "Just go & stick to the plan!" Immediately Simone made a dash towards the border-checks! The onlooking crowd were all in shock at how one person is able to kill that many people all at once; only Detective Paul was left. "Who the hell are you?" asked Detective Paul frantically; Guillaume said nothing and immediately he did Martial Arts moves on Detective Paul and then kills him by snapping his neck off! At a far distance there were two Armed-Police Officers who witnessed Guillaume killing all of the Police and they went straight for him with their guns ready! "Hey you!" shouted one of the Armed-Police Officers; Guillaume realized who they are and immediately his Daemon says to him: "Go into the cafe-restaurant next to you, then go into the toilets & teleport away!" Guillaume then sees the cafe-restaurant and immediately dashes into it with the Armed-Police chasing him. When Guillaume gets into the cafe-restaurant he sees two sharp knives on the counter and so grabs both of them with one in each hand; the Armed-Police then get closer and at the same time Guillaume throws both knives and instantly kills the two Armed-Officers. The customers in the cafe-restaurant were all horrified not only at the killings but, also how Guillaume was able to do this so easily. Guillaume then runs into the toilets behind the cafe-restaurant and immediately he teleports away!

Guillaume was able to teleport to another men's toilets near the border-checks; he came out and saw Simone queuing up waiting for her passport to be checked. Guillaume immediately went to the French section as he is French; the French Border-Guard checked his passport and Guillaume removed his cap & sunglasses. The French Border-Guard was satisfied at the checks and let Guillaume through. When Simone was ready to have her passport checked the Border-Guard looked at it; he was satisfied and let Simone through. Both Guillaume & Simone then went through the security-checks to have their luggage examined through the cameras. Once everything was completed Guillaume & Simone then made their way to board the Eurostar train. Simone went straight inside the train from the end-carriage and made her way to the very front of the train as a first-class ticket was purchased for them. Guillaume walked on the outside platform to make his way to the very front of the train; as he was walking he constantly looked to his left to check on Simone and he could see her through the train windows. Guillaume had managed to reach the first-class carriage before Simone did; he boarded on and found his seat. Immediately he put his luggage into the overhead-compartment; minutes later Simone then arrives in the first-class carriage. Guillaume went to assist Simone by putting her rucksack into the overhead-compartment. "Just keep your hat & sunglasses on just to conceal your identity." instructed Guillaume; Simone nodded and complied with the request. Guillaume had also kept on both his cap & sunglasses. About thirty minutes later the Eurostar train was now ready to depart; the train-conductor blew the whistle and all of the train doors were shut. The train-conductor then signaled and the train moved making its way to Paris. For Simone Jane Robinson one chapter of her life had ended but a new one is going to begin!

Scotland Yard Police had arrived on the scene at Kings Cross where Guillaume had killed all of the Police & Detective Michael Paul earlier. They were all in shock at what happened; they knew it was the same perpetrator as all of the other incidents. However, they could not pinpoint what the perpetrator looks like; they took so many witness statements but had reached a dead-end! "No-one knows what this guy looks like. He's obviously a French Secret Agent but, why are the French Government so interested in this case?" asked an investigating Detective; what was worse for them was that as Guillaume disabled the computer-systems the Police were not able to obtain any shred of evidence. Scotland Yard decided to leave it as that and return to head-quarters; at the same time they were contemplating contacting British Intelligence over the matter as it was a French Secret Agent!

Chapter 42:
Return to Paris

The Eurostar train had arrived in Paris on time; Simone was now feeling ever more liberated. She realized that it was no longer a dream but, a reality! "Well Simone we're here now in Paris." said Guillaume; Simone nodded in agreement and breathed a huge sigh of relief! "Yes I know! I can't wait to be finally free." responded Simone. The two of them then brought their rucksacks down from the overhead compartment and made their way from the train to the border-control to get checked.

Générale Lévesque and the DGSE staff were waiting on the other side for Guillaume & Simone. Générale Lévesque was feeling a little anxious; she wondered if Guillaume was successful in his mission! "Stéphane! I'm wondering if Moreau was successful in the mission. He is on his own plus I'm also wondering if Simone Robinson has been caught by the UK Authorities. If she gets caught we can kiss the whole of Europe goodbye!" explained Générale Lévesque; Stéphane Bastien looked at Générale Lévesque with a somber look on his face. "Well Générale the DGSI Agent who gave Commandant Moreau the train tickets said that both he & Miss Robinson were safe & sound." explained Stéphane; the two of them then continued to wait for Guillaume & Simone hoping for the best.

At the French Border-Control it was Guillaume's & Simone's turn to be checked; they went together to the Border-Guard. When they got there Guillaume gave his passport and showed his DGSE badge; Simone gave her passport as well. Guillaume explained to the Border-Guard that he works for the French Government and that Simone is urgently requested by them. He said this to make the process go a little quicker; the French Border-Guard understood the situation and went to work on it straight away. The passport checks took only a few minutes and when it was all successfully completed both Guillaume & Simone were allowed to go through the border. As Guillaume & Simone made their way through they walked on and at a far distance Guillaume saw Générale Lévesque & Stéphane Bastien. "Look over there; it's my boss of DGSE (Q) & the main head of DGSE." said Guillaume; as they walked towards them, all of a sudden Générale Lévesque noticed Guillaume & Simone. She had a big sense of relief on her face. "Commandant Moreau, it is so good to see you. Miss Robinson, it is a pleasure to meet you. I am Commandant Moreau's boss Générale Joëlle Lévesque." explained Générale Lévesque as she shook Simone's hand. "Générale, the mission was a success." said Guillaume as he handed over the documents to her. "Well done Commandant. We have transport ready to take Miss Robinson to Switzerland." said Générale Lévesque; immediately they all made their way out of the train station to their vehicle to take Simone to Switzerland.

When they departed from the train station there was a people-carrier vehicle waiting for them; there were other

French Secret Agents assigned to give Simone extra protection. They all got inside the car and one of the DGSE Agents switched on the ignition to start the engine; now they were all off to Switzerland. Inside the car Générale Lévesque wanted to discuss the mission in some detail with Guillaume. "Moreau, we're on a time-scale so I'll need you to brief me on the whole mission so we can be prepared next time." explained Générale Lévesque; Guillaume suddenly felt perplexed at what was being told to him. "What do you mean we're on a time-scale?" asked Guillaume, "I need to get you to another mission straight away in Germany. You're needed there & we are desperate for extra agents." replied Générale Lévesque; Guillaume nodded in agreement. Guillaume then went on to give full details of this most recent mission; both Générale Lévesque & Stéphane Bastien took full notes down.

It was quite a long journey but, they eventually arrived in the French-part of Switzerland; the car arrived at a castle-type building which belonged to the French Embassy in Switzerland. When they all got out of the car they made their way into the Chateau. Inside the Chateau Simone was taken to a room to stay for the time-being; it contained a bathroom, bedroom & lounge. The whole room itself was quite spacious; Simone was in complete awe! "Miss Robinson, for your own safety & security you will need to stay here until further notice. My people will keep an eye on things to check to see if Interpol are not looking for you. Also give us all of the full details about the Yugoslavian-6 & their syndicate." requested Générale Lévesque; Simone nodded in agreement. "Générale, may I say a proper goodbye to Simone before we go?" asked Guillaume, "Of course you can, Moreau." replied Générale Lévesque; Guillaume then went up to Simone. "Thank you so much for your help, Guillaume. I will never forget you!" said Simone gleefully; she then gave Guillaume a big hug & then she kissed him on his cheek. "My pleasure! You're finally free now. You have your whole life ahead of you." said Guillaume; when they finished saying their goodbyes Guillaume immediately went with Générale Lévesque to the car and the DGSE Agent then drove off to another place. In her room Simone sat down with a big smile on her face; she had to take it all in that she is now a free woman!

Chapter 43:
Scandal revealed!

S imone had spent a lot of time giving details of the
Yugoslavian-6 and their evil plans to take over the whole
of Europe. The DGSE Agents took down every detail plus
they had the secret documents that Guillaume gave them
which helped their case even more. The DGSE had
instructed Simone to stay out of sight so she doesn't get
caught by the Interpol Authorities. As expected the DGSE
were fully aware that Interpol was searching for Guillaume
Moreau & Simone Robinson; however, when Interpol were
informed by the UK Authorities that the male suspect is a
French Secret Agent they immediately paid the French
Intelligence Services a visit. When French Intelligence were
questioned about whether they sent one of their agents to
the UK they denied the whole incident. They replied that
they had no knowledge whatsoever about London Inferno.
When the UK Authorities & Interpol searched the
computer-systems to see whether DGSE Agents had entered
& departed the UK they both came to a dead-end. There was
no record of any DGSE Agent and Simone Robinson on the
computer-systems; Guillaume was able to use his
mind-power control to wipe off all of the records. DGSE
knew Guillaume Moreau was responsible for wiping off all

of the records but, they were unsure on how he was able to do this so easily.

When DGSE had gathered all of the information from what Simone had given them they produced a document and printed out several copies of them. DGSE are planning to send each copy to every UK newspaper so it gets reported to the general UK public. They had to do this to throw the UK Authorities & Interpol off the scent. When all of the documents were printed out the French Intelligence Services then got out A4-size envelopes and placed every copy into each envelope. On each A4-size envelope the addresses of some of the major newspapers were written on them. The French Intelligence Services then sent out one of their agents to go to London by Eurostar train and to very discretely post the envelopes into a letter-box; that way no-one would suspect that it all came from the French Secret Service. It went all according to plan; no-one suspected anything!

The major UK newspapers got hold of the documents and when journalists had read them they all went into shock! They couldn't believe that the UK Police and some of the UK Members of Parliament whom were heavily involved with the Yugoslavian-6 and what they were planning. Each of the major UK Newspapers decided to print the story about this and let it go to press. When the story about the Yugoslavian-6 was printed out there were many pages about it on every UK newspaper; it horrified the British public that people in high authority were involved with a fascist regime. When the Commissioner of Scotland Yard read the newspapers about the Yugoslavian-6 he had egg on his face! The House of Commons also had eggs on their faces when they found out that UK Members of Parliament were heavily involved with the Yugoslavian-6. There was a public outcry over what was revealed in the newspapers and they called for an investigation over the whole Yugoslavian-6 fiasco! The UK media also reported about the Yugoslavian-6 on TV and people were wondering if this is all a nightmare even though it wasn't! The whole fiasco had painted a bad picture of the UK.

Scotland Yard Police decided to hold a press-conference over the Yugoslavian-6 revelations in the newspapers. They expected to get heavily grilled about the whole fiasco! The Scotland Yard Commissioner sat at a table with other senior officers around him. A reporter then asked: "So Commissioner, why is it that some of your own officers were involved with the Yugoslavian-6 & yet you did nothing about it?" The Commissioner then replied: "I was unaware that some of our Officers & own Members of Parliament were involved with the Yugoslavian-6!" The reporter then said: "How can you not know? You are the Commissioner, you should've known!" The Commissioner sat there in his seat feeling helpless; he didn't know what to do! In the House of Commons there was a lot of arguing about how & why that UK Politicians were involved with the Yugoslavian-6 and what they had to gain from all of this. In the end they were all backed into a very big corner!

It was reported to many of the national newspapers about Simone Robinson's old school in Leeds about the corruption that went on there. Many revelations were told about the school including about the gang that murdered Simone's best friend Belinda and the racist murder of the

Nigerian boy. Many of the teachers of that school in Leeds were questioned by Police about the cover-up and some of the Police-Officers who were there at the time were also questioned. In the end many of the teachers & Police-Officers were indicted & arrested plus UK School-Inspectors had to call in a special emergency meeting about the matter at hand. The School-Inspectors decided that appropriate action will be taken against the school and long-term measures will be put into place.

When Interpol found out about the UK Police & Politicians involvement with the Yugoslavian-6 they decided to abandon their search for Guillaume Moreau & Simone Robinson. Interpol in France, Germany & various other European countries were all fuming at all of the scandals revealed. They decided to not pursue the case at all as retribution. Simone Robinson was informed by DGSE that Interpol had no interest in her at all & that they decided to close the case permanently; Simone was now completely free to live her new life!

PART 2:
NEW
GERMANY

Chapter 44:
Arising!

In another part of French-Switzerland the DGSE Agents stopped at a French Château in a very secluded area. The Château itself is owned by both the French-Swiss & French Governments; it is primarily only for the French Intelligence Services. Guillaume got out of the car; he was still thinking about Simone after the London Inferno mission as it took a lot out of him. He was concerned for Simone hoping that she will never get caught by the UK Authorities. "Moreau! Just go inside & freshen yourself up before the next briefing." instructed Générale Lévesque; immediately Guillaume made his way to the wash-room to freshen up.

When Guillaume had managed to freshen himself up he went straight to the briefing-room to find out what the next mission will be. Guillaume is going to be working with the same five DGSE Agents from the London Inferno mission. The DGSE were short of agents due to other important missions so they had to make do with what they have got at present. The meeting was now ready to commence and Générale Lévesque was going to explain the mission at hand. She then goes on to say:

"OK everyone, this mission is of great importance & it is imperative that this must be successfully completed as soon as possible. This will affect the whole of Europe & in particular the EU. Unfortunately we are short of Agents and all of the Quebec based Field-Agents are on a big mission in the USA. This is what we have got right now....you people! So what this mission is all about is to do with the former East Germany; even though back in 1990 when East & West Germany unified to become one country there are some who have resented the unification. There is a group from the former East Germany that want to resurrect it again and this time call themselves New Germany!"

All of the French Agents looked at one another with stunned looks on their faces; Générale Lévesque stood there motionless. She was determined for the mission to become a complete success. "Générale. Does the German Government know about all of this? And if so, why aren't they doing anything about it?" queried Xavier, "Well, put it this way the German Government are completely unaware of this situation plus they have their own big problems to deal with at this time. It is up to us to complete this mission." explained Générale Lévesque, "Générale, you stated that this is going to affect the whole of Europe including the EU. In what way?" queried Guillaume, "Good question Moreau! What it is Russia is helping this group. They want an easy way to get into Europe & destroy the EU first, then take over the whole of European continent." replied Générale Lévesque; the DGSE Agents were all stunned at the revelations. "It feels like the Cold-War all over again!" said Matthieu, "Yes, you are absolutely correct!" responded Générale Lévesque; she then handed out files to each agent. In the files there were documents of the groups plans to help Russia take over the whole of Europe. Also included in the files are the list of names who are part of the group; the leader is named as Jürgen Schwarz. It shocked the DGSE Agents at the number of names on the list; they realized that they are going to have their hands full! "Générale; I am a bit concerned that there are only 6 of us & many of them! How are we going to deal with this?" pondered Christophe; Générale Lévesque had a concerned look on her face. "I know; I understand your point of view. The best way to deal with this is to be very discrete & lay low as possible. All 6 of you must stay alive for this mission to be a success." explained Générale Lévesque; all of the DGSE Agents looked at one another and nodded a 'yes' response in agreement.

Later on in the day Guillaume and the other DGSE Agents were discussing plans on how to terminate the 'New Germany' group. It went on for some time; they realized that they're going to have a big fight on their hands! "What we need to do is stick together and when we need to we will split up and kill the members one-by-one. But, we only split up if absolute necessary!" suggested Guillaume; his fellow Agents all looked at him with serious looks on their faces. They all agreed with Guillaume's plans but, they are unaware that he is planning to use his paranormal powers to achieve the DGSE's objectives. After their meeting had finished the six DGSE Agents then left the Château and made their way to the country of Germany.

Chapter 45:
The Group

There was Jürgen Schwarz in a private room with the rest of his 'New Germany' group; he's planning a meeting and he is getting ready to talk. "Comrades, this is our opportunity & moment. I want revenge on the former West Germany for not helping us. They treat us like East Germans, not like Germans at all; it is time to resurrect the old East Germany but this time we will call ourselves NEW GERMANY!" explained Jürgen with enthusiasm; a man called Hans Koch who just recently joined the New Germany group was listening on. Since the reunification of Germany Hans became disillusioned due to the way the former East has been treated. "Herr Schwarz; is it true that Russia is going to help us achieve our objectives?" asked Hans; Jürgen then looked at him and smiled a little. "Yes Hans it is very true; Russia will help us. We realize that we can't do this alone but, it will come at a price. Russia wants to take over the whole of Europe & run it as an authoritarian rule; then they will get rid of the EU altogether. We must help them achieve their objectives; nothing will stop us now. The old USSR had helped us before many times especially during the Cold-War." explained Jürgen; everyone nodded in agreement with Jürgen.

Jürgen then went on to explain of the benefits of colluding with Russia and the formation of New Germany; he went on to say that there would be huge financial gains for them once New Germany is formed. When the whole group understood the benefits of the formation they all had big smiles on their faces. They all realized that they are no longer going to be prisoners of the former West Germany. In the end the whole New Germany group agreed with Jürgen and decided to work with each other to help form the country of New Germany. Jürgen then passed along champagne glasses to each member and a bottle of champagne; once all of their glasses were filled Jürgen then went on to say: "Here's to New Germany & our new future!" Everyone cheered and raised their glasses at the same time. They all realized that there is no turning back!

Chapter 46:
Spy & Kill!

The DGSE Agents arrived somewhere in a secluded area of Germany so they could put their plans into action. The secluded place was an abandoned house away from everything; it was the perfect place for them. Earlier the DGSE Agents found out that two members of the New Germany group are close-by; Guillaume decided to take it upon himself to kill the two members. His fellow agents agreed to Guillaume's request to do the mission on his own.

In the late morning Guillaume was in a German town called Bautzen which is in the former East and he finds the two New Germany men. Their names are Tobias Huber & Jonas Scholz; he then goes invisible and follows the two men. As Guillaume gets closer to the two men he then overhears them conversing. "Tobias! Does anyone suspect that we're trying to resurrect the old East Germany?" pondered Jonas, "No! Nobody knows. The German Secret Service are having their own big problems. No-one suspects anything; not even the Americans." replied Tobias; the two men then smiled at each other in satisfaction! Little did they know that Guillaume was right behind them listening to every word. He knew of their big plans!

About twenty minutes later Tobias & Jonas entered a clothes-shop to look for new suits to buy; Guillaume decided not to follow them and went into a small lane next to the shop. Still invisible Guillaume looked around to see if anyone was in sight and luckily there was no-one. Guillaume then appeared visible and came out of the small lane; he then decided to enter the same clothes-shop as Tobias & Jonas. Inside the clothes-shop Guillaume was pretending to browse around when he was actually spying on Tobias & Jonas. At the same time Guillaume was able to browse & spy on the two New Germany members; Tobias & Jonas had now noticed that Guillaume was constantly gazing at them. They then began to get suspicious of Guillaume! "I noticed that there's a man over there who is constantly looking at us!" said Jonas, "Yes I know. This smells very fishy!" responded Tobias; the two of them then began to get a little worried! "Who is that guy?" asked Jonas in a slightly frantic way; Tobias didn't know how to respond. "Never mind, let's just get out of here!" suggested Tobias; the two men immediately departed the clothes-shop and went on their way. Guillaume remained in the clothes-shop and continued to browse around so as not to arouse any suspicions!

Tobias & Jonas were walking in a hurried way considering what they had encountered earlier; they were starting to feel frantic. "Is that man a spy? If so, from which country?" asked Jonas, "He could well be a spy. The only thing is that I have no idea which country he is from. I don't think it is the USA!" replied Tobias; the two of them continued to walk on in a rush! Back in the clothes-shop Guillaume was still in there browsing around until his Daemon spoke to him again: "Guillaume! It's time to kill the two New Germans. Leave the clothes-shop & go into that small lane. Then teleport & kill them!" Guillaume then immediately leaves the clothes-shop and goes into the small lane; he then went into remote-viewing mode to look for Tobias & Jonas. When he located the two New Germans Guillaume then teleports away. Tobias & Jonas were in a small park when Guillaume suddenly appeared; the two men went into complete shock! They thought that they had just seen a ghost! "Hey! Who are you?" asked Jonas frantically; Guillaume just stood there saying nothing! "Are you a spy?" asked Tobias; Guillaume then looked at both Tobias & Jonas a little. "I am in the French Secret Service. I know of your plans to resurrect the former East Germany; and we are not going to let it happen!" said Guillaume; both Tobias & Jonas looked at each other completely stunned! Then all of a sudden Guillaume immediately knocked them both down using his Martial Arts. He continued to beat the two New Germans viciously and when they were completely worn out Guillaume went on to kill them by snapping both of their necks! Afterwards, Guillaume teleported away leaving no trace.

Much later on in the day German Police were investigating the two murders of Tobias Huber & Jonas Scholz. It horrified the Police at the state that they were in; the German Police also had no idea what the motive was. They ruled out robbery because both men had a lot of money still in their wallets. As there were no witnesses to the crime it made it increasingly difficult for the Police to gain any leads. There was no evidence at all that the German Police could find which would've led them to the killer; they had reached a dead-end!

Chapter 47:
Take them all out!

B ack at the temporary hide-out in Germany, Guillaume had informed his fellow DGSE Agents of the successful termination of Tobias Huber & Jonas Scholz. They were all pleased at the outcome; however, the other DGSE Agents are unaware that Guillaume used his paranormal powers! The DGSE Agents then had a meeting to decide what the next step is going to be to exterminate New Germany. "We need to kill this group as soon as possible before it gets out of hand!" explained Raphaëlle, "Also we have to keep a very low profile so no-one suspects that it is our Government behind all of this!" said Thérèse; they continued to plan & plan as much as they can.

After all of the intensive planning the DGSE Agents realized that it was going to be more difficult than expected. They found out that a number of the New Germans are spread-out in some parts of the former East Germany. "So how are we going to get them all?" suggested Thérèse; they all looked at one another bemused. "Well we will find the ones that are nearby now and then we can kill them. The others we can kill another time." suggested Guillaume, "Who are the ones that are nearby?" asked Xavier; Matthieu then got out the list of all of the New Germans nearby. "Here they are?" said Matthieu showing the list. They were:

Günther Krüger, Lukas Schmitt, Elias Jung, Walter Fuchs, Stefan & Petra Köhler, Monika Hahn, Gisela Möller & Emilia Günther. "Now we know the names, I suggest that we all split up into pairs and kill the ones on the list." suggested Guillaume; the DGSE Agents all agreed with him so they paired up and then went on their way to terminate more of the New Germans. As difficult as it is going to be for the six DGSE Agents they were all very determined to achieve their objectives; they are doing this for the whole of Europe! Guillaume paired up with Christophe.

Chapter 48:
Better than expected!

The time had come for Guillaume and the rest of the DGSE Agents to commence killing some of the German Separatists. The DGSE Agents all paired up first and then went on their way; immediately Guillaume & Christophe went together to find who to kill first. "Well Commandant, who do want to go after first?" asked Christophe; Guillaume then pondered on the question. "Whoever we'll see first." replied Guillaume; Christophe then nodded back in response.

Guillaume & Christophe arrived into the town and were looking around; the other DGSE Agents were further away. The two agents were looking around and all of a sudden Guillaume saw Stefan & Petra Köhler of New Germany. The two of them are husband & wife plus they are completely dissatisfied with the German reunification. They are hard-core East Germans who desperately want to go back to the old East Germany. "Hey look over there. It's Stefan & Petra Köhler." said Guillaume, "Well spotted Moreau; let's keep tabs on them. When the time is right we'll strike!" said Christophe; from a distance the two French Agents followed Stefan & Petra Köhler. Guillaume & Christophe followed the Köhler's for about thirty minutes and all of a sudden Guillaume's Daemon spoke to him: "Guillaume, it

278

is time to kill them. There's an alleyway on the left further down; you can kill them there. Don't worry you won't get caught!" Guillaume acknowledged his Daemon and went to talk to Christophe. "There's an alleyway on the left we can kill the Köhler's in there." suggested Guillaume; Christophe was able to see the alleyway from a distance. "Are you sure, Moreau?" questioned Christophe, "Yes I am sure, trust me it is the only way. Besides we have no time to lose." replied Guillaume; immediately the two of them went up to the Köhler's. When the two French Agents got closer to the Köhler's, Guillaume went to Stefan's right-side & Christophe when to Petra's left-side. Very discretely they got out their hand-guns and pointed them to their hips. "OK you two, don't try anything funny. Get in that alleyway right now & don't say a word!" ordered Guillaume; the Köhler's remained silent and complied with the request.

A few minutes later when they all got to the alleyway Guillaume noticed a giant dumpster and ordered the Köhler's to stand right next to it; like before they complied. "Who are you? We don't have any money!" begged Petra; Guillaume & Christophe stood there saying nothing! "We don't want your money Petra Köhler!" replied Christophe; the Köhler's looked at each other completely stunned! "How do you know my name?" asked Petra frantically, "We want to ask you both about New Germany, Petra!" replied Guillaume; immediately there was a look of shock on the Köhler's faces! "What! How do know all of this?" asked Stefan; Guillaume then got out his DGSE badge and showed it to the Köhler's. "We are with DGSE. We are French Secret Agents and we need information." explained

Guillaume; the Köhler's now felt trapped & helpless! "What does the French Secret Service want with us? Why?" asked a frantic Stefan, "You know why! If New Germany is created it is going to affect the whole of Europe. Oh by the way we are fully aware that you're working with the Russians. We have all of the evidence!" explained Guillaume, "OK! We are working with Russia. Look, all we want is a better life; we are getting nothing here in East Germany!" explained Petra, "OK, we will spare your life if you tell us everything you know. And if you help us we can help you two get a better life somewhere else." said Christophe; the Köhler's agreed to cooperate. "Where do you want to begin?" asked Stefan, "Tell us where your main base is?" requested Guillaume, "It is 50 miles east of Berlin. It is in an abandoned mansion in the middle of nowhere." replied Stefan, "OK, now we want to know about why Russia is helping you!" demanded Christophe, "Well this group, they're called Dark-Russia. They are situated on the outskirts of St. Petersburg and are working secretly with the Russian Federation to help their agenda." explained Petra; Guillaume & Christophe looked at each other and then nodded! "OK, that's all we need to know." said Guillaume; both Stefan & Petra breathed a huge sigh of relief, both Guillaume & Christophe then put their hand-guns away. All of a sudden Guillaume did Martial Arts moves on the Köhler's and knocked them both down to the ground. Then Guillaume went in for the kill and snapped both of their necks; the Köhler's were now both dead! "Christophe, open the dumpster lid." ordered Guillaume; Christophe complied and opened the lid of the dumpster. Guillaume & Christophe then put the two dead bodies into the dumpster and closed the lid. Luckily no-one was looking around. The two French Agents then made their way out of the alleyway!

When Guillaume & Christophe came out of the alleyway, Christophe suddenly spotted Lukas Schmitt; he is also a member of New Germany. "Hey Moreau, look over there! It is Lukas Schmitt!" said Christophe, "Oh yes it is! Well spotted; let's get him now whilst the going is good!" said Guillaume; immediately the two French Agents began to follow Lukas Schmitt. They had tailed Lukas Schmitt for quite some time until he arrived at a small park. Guillaume suddenly had a brain-wave! "You know if we can get him into the bushes we can make our next kill." suggested Guillaume; Christophe agreed with him. Deep into the park there was a very secluded bushy area where Lukas was; Guillaume then realized this is the opportunity to strike! In the secluded park area there was only Guillaume, Christophe & Lukas Schmitt present there. The two French Agents then looked around to see if anyone else was there as well; luckily there wasn't! "Hey Lukas Schmitt over there!" shouted Guillaume; Lukas Schmitt then turned around and noticed the two French Agents. "Who are you two? How do you know my name?" asked a puzzled Lukas; Guillaume then smiled a little a Lukas sarcastically! "We are French Secret Agents & we know you are a member of New Germany. We are here to kill you!" replied Guillaume; Lukas Schmitt's eyes suddenly flew wide open. He made a run for it but he had no chance; due to Guillaume's athleticism he was able to catch up with Lukas Schmitt. Guillaume then grabbed Lukas and with one hand he picked up Lukas and threw him against a big tree. Lukas then became dazed due to the force he was thrown at; then Guillaume went in for the kill and snapped Lukas' neck...he was now dead! Afterwards both Guillaume & Christophe carried Lukas Schmitt's dead body and hid it under a bush so no-one could see it. Guillaume & Christophe then went about their duty.

The other DGSE Agents had great success with their tasks; they were able to eliminate a large number of New Germany members one-by-one without any drawbacks. The DGSE Agents were also able to conceal all of the killings without anyone knowing. The DGSE Agents didn't think that it would have been that easy! Later on in the day all six DGSE Agents had another meeting; they realized that there are only seven New Germany members left including the leader Jürgen Schwarz. Guillaume & Christophe informed their colleagues of what the Köhler's had told them about New Germany and the Russian group Dark-Russia. "So what is the next plan?" asked Xavier; Guillaume then put up his hand! "Everyone! I can take out all of the seven New Germany members on my own; it won't be that difficult at all." suggested Guillaume; his colleagues all looked at him stunned! "Moreau, are you mad?" asked Matthieu, "No! Besides it's easier that way. I'll be able to cover our tracks if I do this on my own. Also, the rest of you need to look more into Dark-Russia." said Guillaume; the other DGSE Agents deliberated for some time at Guillaume's request. However, in the end even though they were not happy with Guillaume's request they decided to agree to it. Now Guillaume was on his way to terminate New Germany once and for all!

Chapter 49:
New Germany thwarted!

Nightfall had arrived and the abandoned mansion on the outskirts of Berlin was occupied by the remaining seven separatists including their leader Jürgen Schwarz. The separatists had found out earlier that many of their members were murdered; however they wondered who is committing all of the murders. They were beginning to even wonder whether the German Authorities or even German Intelligence know of their big plans. "Jürgen, what shall we do? They are onto our plans!" said Ursula Schulz; Jürgen looked at Ursula and nodded a little. "We stick to our plans. We must go ahead & create New Germany!" responded Jürgen; all of the remaining separatists agreed with Jürgen.

Outside the abandoned mansion Guillaume was in the bushes listening on to New Germany's plans using his remote-viewing powers. Earlier Guillaume had used remote-viewing to locate the abandoned mansion and when he found it he immediately teleported to there. The New Germany group are unaware of Guillaume's presence outside; Guillaume was always one-step ahead of them. He then listened on. "OK everyone we have no time to lose we are ready to create New Germany & we must do it now!" ordered Jürgen, "We need to tell the Russians about what's going on or our plans will fail!" explained Uwe Schroder;

everyone realized that Uwe had made a good point! In the bushes Guillaume could overhear all of the plans New Germany are executing. Suddenly Guillaume's Daemon spoke to him: "Guillaume! Just teleport right now & kill all of the members of New Germany. You have no time to lose just do it! You have the power!" Immediately Guillaume then teleports to the abandoned mansion.

The seven members of New Germany were still discussing their plans and all of a sudden a bright light appeared to them...it nearly blinded them! Guillaume had suddenly appeared; all of the New Germany members went into shock; they wondered how someone could appeared just like that from out of nowhere! "Who are you?" asked a frantic Jürgen; Guillaume just stood there in silence. "I am Commandant Guillaume Moreau from the French Secret Service!" responded Guillaume; everyone gazed at each other completely stunned! "What does the French Secret Service want with us?" demanded Jürgen, "Oh we know all about New Germany & we are going to stop it right now before Europe descends into chaos!" explained Guillaume, "And how are you going to stop us?" demanded Jürgen, "It doesn't matter how; all that matters is that it is time for all of you to die!" replied Guillaume; immediately he used his powers of telekinesis to throw all of the New Germany members around. They all became petrified at Guillaume's paranormal powers; when they were all dazed Guillaume then killed them by snapping all of their necks one-by-one! Guillaume succeeded in destroying New Germany; it was a case of mission success! Immediately Guillaume took out some hand-grenades and threw them around the place and straight away he teleported out of the mansion. The abandoned mansion exploded and it was heard in some parts of Germany.

Later into the night the Fire-Brigade were called in and Fire-Fighters had managed to extinguish the fires out of the abandoned mansion. The German Police were also present at the mansion investigating the huge explosion. When the dead bodies were all pulled out the Police had noticed that they were murdered considering their necks had all been snapped. They also noticed the hand-grenades; they realized that it was done deliberately! They then found some burnt documents which had the inscription NEW GERMANY shown; it baffled the Police on what it all meant. They also had no idea who committed this heinous crime! The German Police had nothing to go on!

Chapter 50:
Final briefing

Guillaume and the rest of the DGSE Agents returned to Paris, France the next day to brief DGSE Headquarters on what occurred on their recent mission to prevent the rising of New Germany. During the briefing the DGSE Agents mentioned the Russian Group 'Dark-Russia' whom are working closely with the Russian Government. The French Intelligence Services listened on with slight concerns on their faces. The DGSE Agents were all wondering what they are all thinking!

The final briefing had gone on for quite some time and the DGSE Agents concluded that they want to find the group Dark-Russia and terminate them. "Unfortunately we cannot comply with your request!" explained Stéphane, "But Monsieur, Dark-Russia are an extremely dangerous group & we need to terminate them. If we don't God knows what they'll do next!" explained Xavier, "Yes I do understand your logic but, we cannot take any risks!" responded Stéphane; the DGSE Agents were not at all happy with Stéphane Bastien's request not to pursue Dark-Russia. Guillaume stood there in complete silence; he was also not too happy at the outcome!

Later on in the day Guillaume had another message from his Daemon: "Guillaume! Your fellow Agents are correct;

Dark-Russia has to be terminated before Europe descends into chaos. Kill them on your own & don't tell anyone. You know how to do this!" Guillaume then decided to get ready and go after Dark-Russia on his own; he realized that there is no other option!

Chapter 51:
Dark-Russia located

Guillaume was still at DGSE Headquarters in Paris wondering how he is going to terminate Dark-Russia. Very discretely Guillaume went to get hand-grenades and a hand-gun for himself; he made very sure that no-one knew on what he is about to do! When Guillaume was ready he went immediately into remote-viewing mode to locate Dark-Russia. When Guillaume located Dark-Russia he took an in-depth look at the building inside. He realized looking inside the building that there are quite a lot of people who are part of Dark-Russia. Guillaume then suddenly decided that he was ready and immediately teleported to Dark-Russia's building; he was now ready to go in for the big kill!

Guillaume teleported inside the Dark-Russia building on the ground-floor; there was no-one around. Guillaume then took out his hand-gun and went around looking for the Dark-Russia members to kill. He then sees a man coming along and immediately he is shot by Guillaume; suddenly another man appears and immediately Guillaume does Martial Arts moves on him and then snaps his neck to kill the other man. As there was no-one else around on the ground-floor Guillaume then takes the stairs to the first-floor. When Guillaume arrived on the first-floor he immediately notices a lot of people there and straight away he begins shooting at them. Guillaume was able to terminate all of the people there on the first-floor! However, there was still a lot more of Dark-Russia to kill.

Guillaume went on every floor of the Dark-Russia building killing all of the members; eventually he was able to kill every single one of them. Upon killing all of the members of Dark-Russia Guillaume then got out the hand-grenades and set the timer on each one. Guillaume teleported quickly to each floor of the building placing the grenades around every time. On the ground-floor Guillaume then put the rest of the hand-grenades there. Immediately upon completion Guillaume then teleported back to DGSE Paris; the whole of the Dark-Russia building exploded into pieces and it was heard in many parts of St. Petersburg. Guillaume had fully accomplished his big mission....Dark-Russia had been eliminated once and for all!

Later on that same day the Russian Authorities investigated the huge explosion of the Dark-Russia building; the KGB were also present at the crime scene. It had baffled both the authorities and the KGB a lot; they had no idea on who committed this act. There were no clues whatsoever they could find which connected to the mass killings. It was reported on both the Russian media and on the international stage. The KGB knew who the people were, the only thing which baffled them was who had killed them all!

The French Government & Intelligence Services had found out about the mass killings of the Dark-Russia group and especially about the explosion itself. It really baffled them on who had committed the heinous crime; they even thought it was the KGB had committed this crime. However, both the French Government & Intelligence Services were pleased at the outcome as they knew how very dangerous Dark-Russia are to the whole of Europe. To them it was a case of mission accomplished!

PART 3:
NORTH KOREA
ARISES!

Chapter 52:

Dangerous mission

Générale Lévesque was in her office doing some paperwork whilst waiting for Guillaume Moreau to report so that she could send him on his next mission. After the New Germany mission Générale Lévesque had given Guillaume three weeks respite as he had two missions back-to-back. Guillaume had really needed the big rest and Générale Lévesque was fully aware of this.

Later on in the morning Guillaume had arrived at Générale Lévesque's office; he was fully fresh & ready for his next mission! "Ah! Commandant Moreau it's good to see you. I hoped you had a good rest." said Générale Lévesque; Guillaume smiled a little. "Yes I did Madame, merci." responded Guillaume, "Glad you did! Are you ready for your next mission, Commandant?" asked Générale Lévesque, "Yes I am Madame. Before you tell me, is it OK to ask if Simone Robinson is doing well?" pondered Guillaume; Générale Lévesque looked directly at him motionless. "I can happily report that Miss Robinson is doing well. She has settled very nicely in Switzerland & the UK Authorities have given up on her after what was revealed all over the UK media. She is well & truly free, she won't be touched." replied Générale Lévesque; Guillaume felt very relieved and pleased at the outcome. "That's great to hear. Simone is a good woman, all she needed was an opportunity. Anyway, I am now ready for the next mission." said Guillaume, "Good! So this next mission I am sending you & other DGSE (Q) Agents to Korea. I chose you because you know Korea very well as you had studied Martial Arts there." explained Générale Lévesque, "Oh! That would be nice to go to Korea. I have good memories of that country." responded Guillaume, "Glad you remember because we have a major problem. There's a group who are all Communists & they want to split Korea into 2 countries; hence one will be called North Korea & the other will be called South Korea. Now North Korea will be the big problem not the South!" explained Générale Lévesque; Guillaume suddenly had a puzzled look on his face. "Générale, why is North Korea going to be a big problem for us?" asked a bemused Guillaume; Générale Lévesque then looked at him with a subdued look on her face. "Well Moreau, North Korea will become a Communist country but, also it will become a dictatorship. This will be very dangerous to the whole of North America, both Canada & the USA. Once North Korea has been established they will develop all kinds of weapons of mass destruction and threaten many countries especially all of us here in North America. It is up to us to stop this from happening before it's too late!" explained Générale Lévesque; Guillaume had a slight shocked look on his face! "My God! This is so shocking to hear. When I was doing Martial Arts training in Korea I had always found it be such a peaceful, loving & happy nation." explained Guillaume, "Well sometimes things do change. There is this Korean man & his name is Sung-Hoon Gwan who is the leader of this Korean Communist group; he is a total tyrant. Later on I will introduce you to the DGSE (Q) Agents whom you will be working with for this mission." explained Générale Lévesque; after the briefing Guillaume then left Générale Lévesque's office.

It was in the early afternoon that Guillaume was on his own in the canteen contemplating on his upcoming mission to Korea. He was feeling very sad at what could happen to the country of Korea if it splits into two separate countries. He had many fond memories of his time in Korea when he studied Martial Arts there. Whilst Guillaume was eating his lunch his Daemon then spoke to him: "Guillaume! Don't worry about your upcoming mission to Korea, you will be successful. Just do as I say & you have all the power to do this!" Guillaume suddenly felt a surge of tingling all over his body; he realized that he could prevent North Korea from being established. He is determined to make this particular mission a complete success!

Chapter 53:

Korean Communists

S ang-Hoon Gwan, the leader of the Korean Communists was in a secret building holding a meeting with his fellow Communists. He stood there looking at everyone with very serious looks. Sang-Hoon Gwan is known to be an evil & sadistic man who strongly believes in extreme-torture! One of Sang-Hoon's priorities when North Korea is finally established is to bring in physical torture for everyone and make it a legal requirement. Sang-Hoon was now beginning to make his speech:

"My fellow Korean Communists, we are all gathered here to assert our authority in creating North Korea. Now there has been rumors that we could be having outside interference. It is very likely that the USA who are doing this which would be the CIA. However, even though we are going to face outside interference I want to press ahead in establishing North Korea no matter what! We are all far too smart to let anyone stand in our way...especially the USA!"

Everyone in the room cheered Sang-Hoon's speech and clapped their hands loudly to applaud him. The rest of the Korean Communists were completely convinced that North Korea can easily be created without any drawbacks! The general attitude of the Korean Communists was that they are totally invincible!

Later on in the day Sang-Hoon was talking to some of the senior members about the possible outside interference from the CIA. His Second-in-Command Bon-Hwa Yoo was present in the small meeting. "Sir, I don't think it's the CIA who are trying to interfere with our plans." explained Bon-Hwa; Sang-Hoon's face went perplexed. "What makes you think it's not the USA?" pondered Sang-Hoon, "Well, we did extensive research & the evidence suggests that the USA are not the ones who are attempting to stop us. It is very likely someone else." explained Bon-Hwa, "You could be correct that it's not the CIA. However, it could be a rouse that the Americans are using against us. Don't forget that the Americans always want to dictate to everyone around the world. They like to control everything." explained Sang-Hoon; considering all of the evidence presented about the interference not being from the USA Sang-Hoon had decided to keep an open mind that it could be someone else trying to reign in on their parade! Sang-Hoon Gwan was not going to let anyone stand in his way!

Chapter 54:
No time to lose!

Guillaume was in Générale Lévesque's office with four other DGSE (Q) Agents who are also assigned to the same upcoming mission. The four DGSE (Q) Agents whom Guillaume will work with are: Commandant Antoine Du Bois of the French Navy, Commissaire Colonel Jean Gautier, Général Alain Fontaine & Général Timéo Guérin all of the French Army. "OK, Agents as you all have been instructed that North Korea must not be established or the whole world will descend into chaos. It has been strongly ordered that we must terminate every member of the Korean-Communists including it's leader Sang-Hoon Gwan and his 2nd in Command Bon-Hwa Yoo. They are all far too dangerous to remain alive!" explained Générale Lévesque; Guillaume and the other DGSE (Q) Agents all gazed at each other with concerned looks. They all realized how serious the mission is! "Madame! Do the Americans know about any of this?" questioned Guillaume, "No they don't Commandant Moreau. Besides it is better that way that the Americans not know about our mission. They will interfere & try to stop us." replied Générale Lévesque, "Understood Madame. I can see your logic in this." responded Guillaume. "By the way, I had to assign Commandant Moreau especially for this mission as he knows Korea very well. He had studied a lot of Martial Arts in Korea for a long while. Moreau will know all of the places in that country. I'll let you all go on your mission now...we have NO TIME TO LOSE!" explained Générale Lévesque; the five DGSE (Q) Agents all disbanded for their upcoming mission to Korea!

Guillaume and the other DGSE (Q) Agents had to first take the plane from Montréal to Paris, France as they all had to report to DGSE HQ to get further briefings. When they arrived at DGSE HQ Stéphane Bastien gave the five Agents a list of all of the names who are members of the Korean-Communists. There were quite a number of names but, even though only five Agents were assigned to the mission DGSE believed that it was enough to terminate the whole group. The DGSE (Q) Agents were strongly ordered to do the mission very discretely without anyone knowing so they don't get any repercussions! All of the DGSE (Q) Agents agreed to the request.

Later on in the day the five French Secret Agents took a plane from Paris, France to Hanoi, Vietnam to receive further information from DGSE there. After all of the further briefings was completed the DGSE (Q) Agents were now on their way to Korea for their BIG mission; they realized the importance of it all!

Chapter 55:
Arrival to Korea

Once the five DGSE (Q) Agents arrived in Seoul, Korea Guillaume began to look around; it reminded him of the good times he had spent there when he was a young boy studying Taekkyon, Taekwondo & Hapkido Martial Arts once a week. Even though the Korean Martial Arts wasn't as powerful as the Chinese ones Guillaume became fully aware of how important it still is. Guillaume's memories of the good times in Korea made him smile; but he had to quickly put it out of his mind and get on with the mission at hand.

When the DGSE (Q) Agents got through the border-control they all began to discuss on how to go about the mission. "So Moreau, where shall we start?" pondered Antoine, "Well, we need to look for the Korean separatists but, we don't know where to exactly start looking for them." replied Guillaume; the DGSE (Q) Agents realized that the first part of the mission was going to be the most difficult. "Well Moreau, we have a big dilemma. The Korean-Communists could be anywhere!" explained Jean, "Yes, you are correct in assuming this. The best thing to do is that we need to go somewhere private and let me explain more about the country of Korea; then we will all split up afterwards." explained Guillaume; the four DGSE (Q)

Agents all agreed and they all went to find a small café to discuss the mission at hand.

The five DGSE (Q) Agents had managed to find a small café in the town of Seoul so they could discuss in detail on how to complete the mission. The French Secret Agents all ordered their food & drinks, then they went to sit at a small table away from everyone else. Guillaume had the map of Korea with him and showed his colleagues of all of the places in Korea. Guillaume even showed them the part in which will be North Korea if it ever establishes as a country. The four DGSE (Q) Agents listened on with intent to Guillaume. When the discussions was completed the five DGSE (Q) Agents finished off their food & drinks; afterwards all five French Secret Agents then split up and went to look for any Korean separatist members.

Chapter 56: Located!

Guillaume was looking around on the outskirts of Seoul and noticed two of the Korean separatists; Kwang-Sun Lee & Binna Kim. Guillaume went to follow the two of them very discretely; as he was in a fairly crowded place Guillaume didn't wanted to risk using his paranormal powers. Guillaume just continued to follow the two Korean Separatists and then wait for the right moment to strike; he had to keep his distance so as not to arouse any suspicions.

Guillaume had spent forty minutes following Kwang-Sun Lee and Binna Kim until they made their way to a very quiet and secluded area. Guillaume then realized that this would be the right moment to strike; he follows on behind them. His Daemon then speaks: "Guillaume, you can kill them now. It is secluded so no-one will know!" Guillaume then decides to get closer to Kwang-Sun Lee and Binna Kim! The two Koreans then realized that Guillaume had been following them for the last forty minutes. "Hey! Why are you following us?" asked Kwang-Sun Lee angrily; Guillaume decided to play dumb for a bit! "Hey! Are you CIA?" asked Binna Kim; Guillaume then gazed directly at Binna! "No, I am not the CIA. I am DGSE, the French Secret Service!" replied Guillaume; both Kwang-Sun & Binna then gazed at each other with bemused looks. All of a sudden Guillaume did Martial Arts moves on both Kwang-Sun & Binna; they tried to fight back but, they were no match for Guillaume. When Guillaume was able to weaken both of them he then killed the two Korean-Separatists by snapping both of their necks!

Later on in the evening all five DGSE (Q) Agents met up discretely to give feedback on what happened. All five French Secret Agents had stated that they found some of the Korean-Separatists and killed them very discretely. Luckily no-one will suspect that DGSE (Q) Agents are killing the Korean-Separatists. The mission has so far gone well for the DGSE (Q) Agents but, they are aware that they still had a long way to go!

Chapter 57:
More killed!

After the progress that the DGSE (Q) Agents made with some of the killings of the Korean-Separatists they all split up again so they could do some more killings. The DGSE (Q) Agents had managed to locate more of the Korean-Separatists beforehand and then they went on their way to complete the big mission. However, they are all unsure on the location of the main-base!

Guillaume was in a different town of Korea called Kaesong and he was tracking two more Korean-Separatists. Their names are Ha-Kun Jin & Ga-Ram Hak; like he did with the other two separatists Guillaume followed both of them very discretely so as not to arouse any suspicions. It was difficult for Guillaume as Kaesong itself was a bit more crowded than Seoul; it was making him feel frustrated! A few minutes later Guillaume had lost sight of Ha-Kun & Ga-Ram in the crowd. Guillaume now didn't know what to do; then all of a sudden his Daemon spoke to him again: "Guillaume, there's a small alleyway a few minutes from where you are. Go in there and use remote-viewing to find Ha-Kun Jin & Ga-Ram Hak; then you can teleport very discretely to them. Don't worry it's OK to teleport from the alleyway no-one will notice!" Guillaume then spotted the small alleyway and went in there; as soon as he got there

Guillaume immediately began to remote-view. Whilst remote-viewing Guillaume could just about see the images of Ha-Kun & Ga-Ram; however he was unclear on exactly where they are. Guillaume continued to remote-view the two Korean-Separatists; he was still unsure on where they are located.

Guillaume had remote-viewed for quite some time still observing Ha-Kun Jin & Ga-Ram Hak; but, now the images were starting to get clearer. He could then see the Korean-Separatists go into a secluded area; Guillaume's Daemon then says to him: "Go now & kill them; it's the right time!" Immediately Guillaume teleported to the secluded area to where the two Korean-Separatists are. When Guillaume teleported to the two of them both Ha-Kun & Ga-Ram went into complete shock. "How the hell did you do that?" asked Ga-Ram; Guillaume just stood there in utter silence! "Who are you?" asked Ha-Kun; Guillaume then smiled a little at Ha-Kun! "I am Commandant Guillaume Moreau of the French Secret Service, DGSE!" replied Guillaume; at the same time the two Koreans then said: "What?" Immediately Guillaume did Martial Arts kicks & punches on Ha-Kun & Ga-Ram knocking them both down with considerable ease. Then all of a sudden Guillaume kills both of the Korean-Separatists by snapping both of their necks! As Guillaume looked down at the two dead-bodies his Daemon then says: "Guillaume! In Ha-Kun's right trouser-pocket is his wallet. Inside his wallet is the address of the Korean-Separatists main-base." Guillaume obeyed his own Daemon and went to get Ha-Kun's wallet from his right trouser-pocket. After opening his wallet Guillaume then finds a piece of paper with an address written on it; he realized that it is the address of the Korean-Separatists main-base! However, when Guillaume looked at the address he realized that it is all the way in the North of Korea to where they want to establish the country of North Korea; the town itself is called Taegwan. Luckily, Guillaume knew exactly where the town of Taegwan is located!

Later on Guillaume met up with the four other DGSE (Q) Agents; they all mentioned that they were able to kill more Korean-Separatists with considerable ease. The mission is going well for them from their point-of-view. All they had to do now is to make their way to the main-base in the North of Korea and terminate the rest of the separatists once and for all! Guillaume showed his colleagues the address and told them where it is located. After the briefing they all went together to make their way to the town of Taegwan; they are planning to kill all of the Korean-Separatists together!

The Korean Authorities were investigating the murders of the Korean-Separatists unaware on who they really were. There were no clues whatsoever which could tie all of the murders. The Korean Authorities were left completely baffled! In the Korean-Separatists base in Taegwan, Sang-Hoon was hearing from the media that so many of his group were being murdered. He was now beginning to wonder how he is getting found out; also Sang-Hoon was now getting very worried. Sang-Hoon is completely unaware that it is DGSE (Q) who are after him. Sang-Hoon and his collaborators just didn't know what to do!

Chapter 58:

Evening killings!

The DGSE (Q) Agents had arrived in the town of Taegwan located in the very north of Korea; it is evening and very dark. That would make it easier for the French Agents so as not to be seen due to the darkness. They arrived at the actual place to where the Korean-Separatists main-base is. The place itself is a huge building on the outskirts from the Taegwan town-center. "I can see why they picked a place such as this!" said Alain; the other French Agents agreed with him. "So what shall we do next?" asked Timéo, "Well, I can see everyone is in the building; there is only one option. To go all in & kill every single of the separatists!" replied Guillaume; the DGSE (Q) Agents went to get their guns ready! When the French Agents were properly armed they made their way discretely to enter the building!

When the DGSE (Q) Agents entered inside the building there was no-one to be seen; but, they all heard some voices. Very discretely the French Agents went to seek out to see where the voices are coming from; then all of a sudden they find a room with the light shining through the bottom of the door. Guillaume crouched down to peek underneath the door and he could see the remaining separatists with Sang-Hoon altogether. Guillaume then signaled to his colleagues about what he saw; then he signaled to the other Agents to go in for the kill. The DGSE (Q) Agents acknowledged his command; all of the French Agents then went to get ready to go in for the kill...there was no going back! All of a sudden Guillaume then signals to his colleagues to go in and kill all of them. The DGSE (Q) Agents suddenly burst in through the door and immediately they began shooting at all of the Korean-Separatists; everyone was screaming in the room running around trying to get away but, they had no chance! The DGSE (Q) Agents were able to kill a lot of them; Sang-Hoon witnesses all of the chaos occurring in front of his eyes. He realized that he was in a losing battle and decides to make a run for it! At a distance Guillaume could see Bon-Hwa and immediately he shoots Bon-Hwa in the head....Bon-Hwa was now dead!

All of the Korean-Separatists were killed but Sang-Hoon Gwan was nowhere to be seen! "Where is Sang-Hoon Gwan?" pondered Timéo; all of the DGSE (Q) Agents looked around to find Sang-Hoon but, he was nowhere to be seen among all of the dead-bodies. "Monsieur's! Let me go & find Sang-Hoon. The rest of you go around the building & check to see if there are anymore Korean-Separatists. You know what you've got to do!" ordered Guillaume; the other French Agents nodded at Guillaume and went around the building to check. When Guillaume was on his own he first immediately went into remote-viewing mode. Guillaume had managed to locate Sang-Hoon Gwan running into the forests and immediately teleports to Sang-Hoon! When Guillaume teleported and appeared to Sang-Hoon Gwan, Sang-Hoon had the look of shock all over his face! He was taken by surprise that Guillaume had an ability such as teleportation! "How did you do that?" asked Sang-Hoon frantically! "Never you mind Sang-Hoon Gwan; it is now time for you to die!" replied Guillaume; immediately Guillaume went into Martial Arts mode and so did Sang-Hoon. Both Guillaume & Sang-Hoon were doing Korean Martial Arts on each other....no-one was winning! But, then Guillaume began using the other Martial Arts of China & Japan to thwart Sang-Hoon. It completely took Sang-Hoon by surprise; he was now at a big disadvantage! Using the three countries Martial Arts Guillaume was able to wear out Sang-Hoon, he was now on the ground struggling to get up! "Who are you?" asked Sang-Hoon, "I am Commandant Guillaume Moreau of the French Secret Service!" replied Guillaume; all of a sudden he snapped Sang-Hoon's neck to kill him! The mission had been completed; North Korea will not be established!

The DGSE (Q) Agents gathered all of the dead-bodies together including Sang-Hoon's; next they poured petrol all over the building and then lit a match to set the building alight. Outside the DGSE (Q) Agents watched the building go up in flames then every one of the French Agents threw a hand-grenade each into the building and then they made a run for it as far away as possible! The building exploded into many, many pieces; the explosion could be heard in many parts of Korea! It was now time for the DGSE (Q) Agents to return to Quebec....mission accomplished!

Chapter 59:
Return to Quebec

Guillaume and the four DGSE (Q) Agents returned to Quebec, Canada safe & sound; Guillaume had felt a huge sense of relief considering he had three missions to do back-to-back. He was hoping that there won't be other missions anytime soon; he felt completely exhausted both physically and emotionally.

The five DGSE (Q) Agents went to report to Générale Lévesque's office to brief her on what happened when they were in Korea. She felt very pleased & relieved that the mission was a complete success and that North Korea will not be established at all. "Well done Agents! I applaud you on your great success. I know how difficult it was for you five but, you never gave up and kept on going for the safety & security of all of North America. Leave it with us, we will do the rest. Commandant Moreau, may I have a word with you in private, please." requested Générale Lévesque; Guillaume acknowledged Générale Lévesque and remained in her office. The other four DGSE (Q) Agents left immediately. "Générale, is everything OK?" asked a bemused Guillaume, "Yes, all is good Commandant Moreau. What it is you had 3 grueling missions in a very short space of time. I'm sorry that you had to go through all of this especially with the London Inferno mission. I am ordering you to take some time off so you can recuperate fully. You didn't get the chance to have a proper rest." explained Générale Lévesque; Guillaume then breathed a sigh of relief! "Merci Madame! I admit that I have been feeling very rough as of late." said Guillaume, "You're welcome! We only have small missions in the USA; we have enough DGSE (Q) Agents to deal with these...they are going to be easy ones!" explained Générale Lévesque; when they finished their private conversation Guillaume left her office immediately to return home. As Guillaume was walking along making his way out of the DGSE (Q) building he suddenly gets a message from his Daemon: "Gullaume! I strongly suggest that you go to Baffin Island and spend some time there on your holidays. There's a big reason why you must go to that province but, I am not going to tell you. I'll let you work it out but you must go to Baffin Island as I said!" When Guillaume heard the message he suddenly stopped walking. He felt very puzzled at the message from his Daemon; however he decided to take the advice of his Daemon and go to Baffin Island.

In Korea the Authorities there were investigating the explosion at the Korean-Separatists building including all of the dead-bodies found. It really baffled them a lot but, what was extraordinary was the amount of killings committed in a short space of time. They wondered if all of them were linked; they had noticed that the dead-bodies had bullets in them so it was concluded that they were murdered before the building was set alight. Now that the Korean Authorities fully know that it was done deliberately, the only question on their minds was who had done this?

Chapter 60:
Korea finds out!

Générale Lévesque had gathered all of the reports about the Korean-Separatists and produced a full account of the report. Générale Lévesque also asked her staff to print out multiple copies of her report and to put them into A4-size envelopes. She then ordered to have the reports sent to all media outlets in both the USA & Canada so people can find out about what really happened! Very discretely Générale Lévesque had also ordered the copies of the report to be sent to all media outlets in Korea. Générale Lévesque realized that everyone had a right to know!

The Korean media outlets anonymously received the A4-size report about the separatists attempting to establish North Korea. What shocked the Korean media was how dangerous it would have been on a global stage if North Korea had been established. The Korean media decided it would be appropriate to print it to press to let the Korean public aware. When it went to press the Korean public were horrified at the report; there was also great anger at this! No-one in Korea including the Korean Government ever knew about the Korean-Separatists. It was also reported on Korean television; it was headline news for all of them. However, in the end the Korean public were extremely relieved that Korea did not split into two separate countries;

they all just want to live in peace. The Korean Government had decided that the country itself will be properly monitored so something like this will never happen again; they all realized the seriousness of it all!

In both Canada & the USA the media found out about the attempted separation of Korea and how dangerous it would've been. It really shocked a lot of people all over North America; no-one knew what had gone on. However, the big question was who had managed to thwart the attempted separation? The US Government were reading about the attempted separation of Korea into two different countries; it really horrified them at what happened and they also pondered on who had prevented this from happening! Even the CIA were baffled at how & who prevented the Korean separation; they even wondered whether it was Canadian Intelligence who had done this. When the CIA looked deeper into this hypothesis they hit a brick-wall! There was not any shred of evidence that Canadian Intelligence was even remotely involved; so the big question the CIA had to ask themselves was who prevented this?

EPILOGUE

Guillaume had managed to find a place to stay at Baffin Island; he planned to stay there for five weeks. It was Générale Lévesque who ordered Guillaume to take the five weeks holiday so could recuperate properly. Guillaume was looking so forward to his big respite at Baffin Island; all he desired at this time was peace & quiet.

During his stay at Baffin Island Guillaume did his Martial Arts exercises on his own and on top of this he did a lot of meditation. It was doing him a lot of good all round; he felt more relaxed in himself. Guillaume went around Baffin Island to see what the place is like; it gave him a lot of bliss at the beauty of Baffin Island especially the mountains. Guillaume had always loved mountains; he was so fascinated by them! Overall, it had been good for Guillaume to go there for his respite as it gave him the peace of mind he required. Whilst he was walking around Guillaume suddenly receives a message from his Daemon: "Guillaume, you have a big connection to this island!" Guillaume all of a sudden had a shock; he wondered what his Daemon meant by this! He decided to just let it go for the time being.

Guillaume was into his third week of his stay at Baffin Island; he was checking out an area which attracted him and meets a Baffin Island native; his name was David. "Oh hello there! Are you lost?" asked David, "No, I am fine thank you. I'm on holiday here; I'm just checking this place out." replied

Guillaume, "Oh! You're on holiday?" queried David, "Yes, I'm here for 5 weeks. I am originally from Quebec & my boss ordered me to take time off to recuperate." explained Guillaume, "Why here in Baffin Island?" pondered David; Guillaume then paused for a bit and pondered on whether he should reveal the truth. "Well...actually it was my Higher-Self who told me to come here." replied Guillaume; David then had a surprised look on his face. "Wow! You can hear your Higher-Self?" asked David, "Yes! It is something I learned when I was in China." responded Guillaume; they carried on conversing for quite some time. After the long conversation David then invited Guillaume to meet other Baffin Island natives and Guillaume therefore accepted the invitation.

Further down the island David introduced Guillaume to his friends and family; they all gave him a warm welcome. Guillaume had felt a sense of joy in his heart; he also felt a nice tingling sensation all over his body. Guillaume had spent considerable time with the other Baffin Island natives. All of a sudden one of the other Baffin Island natives then posed a question to Guillaume: "So what do you do for a living?" Guillaume then began to feel a little tensed; he wondered on whether he should tell the truth that he is a French-Secret Agent based in Quebec! His Daemon then says to him: "Just tell them the truth!" Guillaume then took a deep-breath! "I am a French-Secret Agent based in Quebec. That is my occupation." replied Guillaume; everyone was shocked at what Guillaume had just said! Guillaume then went on to explain more about himself and his whole life-story. When Guillaume finished telling his life-story he asked the natives of Baffin Island if they could keep it all a secret and they all complied.

A couple of days later David then took Guillaume to show him other parts of Baffin Island and he met other Baffin Island natives as well. Guillaume was easily able to make friends with them and they all took well to him. Guillaume had noticed that something is wrong with Baffin Island; their homes are not in good condition and it was always cold inside every single one of them. "Guillaume, we are all very impoverish here on this island plus we have socioeconomic problems all round. We cannot get any help whatsoever; but, even though we have these big problems to deal with, we all try to stay happy no matter what." explained David; Guillaume looked around at everyone's homes. He was shocked to see how they live; he realized that their lives are extremely uncomfortable. Guillaume also found some homes that have been abandoned for some time. "So, what happened to the previous owners?" pondered Guillaume, "Well they died. The extreme cold & poor living conditions made them very sick & there was nothing we could do to help them." replied David, "You are all going to need to completely renovate your homes and install proper heating systems too. Also, all of the homes will need to have a proper hallway built in each one so you can place your shoes & jackets there. I notice that most of the homes have front-doors that go straight into the living-room area." explained Guillaume; David then looked at Guillaume and nodded at him in agreement. "They only problem is who is going to help us?" asked David; Guillaume then turned to look straight at him. "I will help you & your people. I don't know how but, it is a promise that I am willing to keep. Give it time!" replied Guillaume, "Are you serious?" asked David with a surprised look on his face; Guillaume then nodded a YES response to him.

Guillaume's time in Baffin Island had ended and it was time for him to return to Quebec. Guillaume thanked the Baffin Island natives for their warm welcome & hospitality towards him; he was going to miss them greatly! Whilst on the ferry from Baffin Island to Quebec, Guillaume suddenly had a light-bulb moment! He realized why his own Daemon had told him to go to Baffin Island; he was going to be the one who will help the people of Baffin Island! The ferry eventually arrived in Quebec and Guillaume was now on his way home; he felt determined more than ever to help the people of Baffin Island...nothing was going to stop him!

THE END.

Don't miss out!

Visit the website below and you can sign up to receive emails whenever Triple F publishes a new book. There's no charge and no obligation.

https://books2read.com/r/B-A-MVKY-GSFJC

BOOKS 2 READ

Connecting independent readers to independent writers.

Milton Keynes UK
Ingram Content Group UK Ltd.
UKHW012246050124
435526UK00004B/198